A

Tai Le Grice was born in B
New Zealand in 1973 and l
she has three now-adult children, numerous informally 'adopted'
children and two grandchildren.

Tai writes her characters from experience, if not necessarily her own
then from the many, many people she has encountered through the
course of a complex and nomadic life. Tai moved regularly
throughout her childhood and experienced the traumas of always
being 'the new kid'. She has been in a huge variety of jobs and
careers since striking out on her own, from a brief incursion into the
Army, through to owning and operating an equestrian centre, farm-
work, tourism, security work as a Corrections Officer (in the prison
service) and, finally, as a solo-parent, not only to her own children
but to all their friends as well.

Today, Tai finds herself living in a small West Coast New Zealand
town where she moved with the sole intent of seeing whether her
life-time passion for writing could become a new career.

And then there were complications, namely: more children - and
guinea-pigs!

Children and guinea-pigs? Tai is now raising her two grandchildren
and a current population of around eighty guinea pigs (not to
mention two dogs, six cats, two miniature ponies, and a horse!).
Writing tends to have to squeeze in where it can.

In summary, life is never still, always chaotic, never dull but Tai says she wouldn't have it any other way (even if she does sometimes wish there was a little more time for, well, *writing*).

For Colt and all my 'other' sons (you know who you are), whose stories, experiences, and unfailing love and trust inspired this story.

You guys are all amazing.

SMOKE AND WATER

TAI LE GRICE

CRANTHORPE
MILLNER
PUBLISHERS

A CIP catalogue record for this title is available from the British Library.

ISBN 978-1-912964-02-4 (Paperback)

www.cranthorpemillner.com

Cranthorpe Millner Publishers
18 Soho Square
London
W1D 3QL

Acknowledgements

Thank you to Jack, Maria, Tania, Raj, Liam, Eiain and all those who read the raw version of this book before its final cut and polish, gave me so much positive feedback and who, although in many cases admitting the subject matter was WAY out of their comfort zone, read it through to the end because they couldn't put it down despite themselves. You gave me courage and faith and drowned out the voice that said, 'I couldn't'.

Thank you to Vicki who, despite coming in after the first draft was written, supported the process that came after and regularly smacked me upside the head (metaphorically speaking) every time I wanted to quit.

And, perhaps most importantly of all, thank you to Kirsty who gave me a second chance to prove myself and put up with all my insecurities, my crankiness and my ignorance, and was as much a mentor and a friend as an editor. Bless you.

Prologue

They said it started in the basement; an overloaded plug, a frayed wire, a mouse chewing on a cable...

It's irrelevant now.

I'd been at swim training, as I always was 'til late on a Thursday night, and afterwards I'd stopped at Siwon's to pick up hoddeok for my mother, as I also always did, lingering to watch Min Jun in the kitchen and catch up on the latest gossip. I wasn't in any particular hurry and I didn't feel any particular need to be as there wasn't ever any significant change in the routine. By now, my much younger brother and sister would have been long in bed and Mom and Dad would be up in bed, too. Dad would most likely be on his laptop, catching up on business e-mails or an overdue report, or checking out the markets, or whatever it was he did on his laptop before going to bed, and Mom would be reading her latest romance novel. Chances were they might even be asleep by the time I got home and Mom would take the hoddeok to work with her in the morning. I'd forgotten that my older brother was home on study leave, sleeping in the downstairs den and, if I'd remembered, perhaps I'd have gone home sooner.

That's also irrelevant.

I heard the sirens as I turned the last corner into our street, not that I paid a whole lot of attention. For one, sirens were not an uncommon occurrence in our neighbourhood and for two, I'd already seen the chaos; people milling helplessly in the street while smoke billowed in great shadowy waves through the incredible brightness that was now our house, engulfed in flames.

I don't recall much beyond that.

By all accounts I'd pedalled like a mad creature, screaming for my parents, my little brother, my little sister and, before anybody could stop me, I'd thrown my bike to the curb and launched myself at the front door. It was hopeless, of course. They said afterwards that what I thought I'd heard, the screaming, was only the house collapsing in on itself, that realistically my entire family were already dead, but I was on a mission and nobody was going to stop me. Nobody did. The house did. The front door frame collapsed even as I stormed into it with my shoulder and several of the neighbours risked their own lives and limbs to drag me clear of the burning debris.

I spent the next eight weeks in hospital and another six months in rehabilitation.

Chapter One

I walked onto my college campus well into the first semester and a year behind most of my peers, in a new town, a new State, and on my own. My grandfather had offered to come with me but he'd already accompanied me for the late registration process and all the requisite paperwork and I'd rather, as I'd said to my naturally concerned grandparents, do this on my own. Bad enough to walk in alone, knowing full well the reaction I was likely to receive, without the added awkwardness of walking in accompanied by my grandparents.

The reaction, even amongst what I would've hoped were semi-mature college students, was much as I'd anticipated: girls stared and giggled and whispered behind less than discreetly raised hands and boys simply stared. Nobody spoke to me. I liked to assume this was mainly because of my exotic appearance and not because of the secret I did my very best to keep buried deep, deep inside but, you can never really be sure, can you?

My mother is, correction, *was*, Korean. My father was of Finnish/German ancestry. I have my father's height and broad shoulders, his athletic physique, and his love and, I guess, talent for swimming. I inherited my mother's distinctly Korean features and jet-black hair, though with the exception of a single lock of pure white which insists on growing in my forelock, and her coffee and milk complexion. Where the jade green colour of my eyes came from is anybody's guess but, as might well be imagined, the combination tends to make me stand out, and not necessarily in a good way. For me, at least.

Additionally, there was the tattoo.

Most of the scars resulting from the fire that claimed the lives of my family and very nearly claimed mine were on my back and shoulders, and therefore easily covered. But there was the one running up the right side of my neck, under my ear, and up into my hair line. It was a network of white lines and a single heavy raised thread where shards of glass and timber had embedded themselves in my neck and it was Grandmother's suggestion, quickly embraced by my grandfather, to get it tattooed, to take the edge off the stares and questions and perhaps divert some of the inevitable curiosity to the tattoo rather than the scar. They even personally introduced me to a tattooist, an old family friend, and then helped me pick the tattoo. I now had a beautiful Korean dragon embracing my neck rather than the hateful reminder of the deadly flames.

I loved my dragon. I still struggled, as I always had, with the stares.

"Hey, you're the new guy, aren't you? Transfer? Late admission?"

I was between lectures and I was sitting, by myself, out in the Meditation Park at the east end of the campus, completely absorbed both in my lecture notes and my own thoughts. Startled, I looked up, my breath immediately catching in my throat and my heart beating erratically behind my ribs.

The speaker was tall, conceivably even taller than me, with the same broad-shouldered physique I personally always associate with swimmers, and there was something impossibly electrifying about him. *Magnetic*. He was standing with three others but, to be honest, I could only find eyes for him. He raised an eyebrow above Paul Newman-blue eyes and tipped his head.

"Do you speak English?" he asked. "Are you a foreign exchange student?"

I blinked and lowered my head, my white forelock covering my eyes and face.

"I, uh, I… you caught me by surprise," I mumbled.

"Sorry about that," he continued, extending a hand towards me. "I didn't mean to intrude. I'm Damon."

I lifted my head and took his proffered hand. His grip was strong and firm and elicited a sharp electric tingle clean up my arm, and I barely resisted pulling back my hand, the warmth of an unexpected blush threatening at my collar. Damon nodded at his three companions.

"Ed, Brett, and Ox," he informed me. "Welcome to Seven Oaks."

"Eike," I replied, not knowing quite how to respond. "Uh, thank you."

Damon released my hand and I involuntarily found myself rubbing it as if I'd been shocked, which I pretty much felt I had been. Fortunately, Damon seemed oblivious and merely grinned, showing perfect white teeth.

"I've been reliably informed that you swim," he said. "You planning to try-out?"

"Swim?" I asked, blind-sided by the question as much as by Damon.

Damon's grin expanded. "Yeah, you know, get in the water and move your arms and legs as quickly as possible to get to the other side of the pool?"

His friends chuckled amongst themselves and colour immediately rose from my collar and into my cheeks.

"I, uh, I don't know yet," I managed to respond. "I only just got here."

Damon's eyebrow rose again. "Sure. Of course. Well, when you decide, pool's in that big building at the south end of campus and practice runs most mornings at six and every afternoon, four till six. Might see you there, then."

I muttered something that could've been interpreted as semi-affirmative and this must have satisfied him because he straightened and nodded at me. Then, his posse in tow, he turned and walked away. I stared after him with the heat only slowly receding from my face.

Truth be told, I'd not been in the water since *that* night, not even as part of my rehabilitation, though there'd been no lack of attempts by my therapists to encourage me otherwise. I couldn't face it, couldn't face the water, couldn't face the memories. *Survivor's guilt*, the post-trauma counsellor said. Misplaced, of course. It would've changed nothing if I'd not been swimming that night, except I'd undoubtedly have died in the fire too. Not that this would've been a bad thing, in my opinion. I was swimming while my family were burning. I was counting laps. I was happy. And meanwhile, they were dying. How could I go back?

I sat there for some time after Damon and his friends had left, thinking not only of the past but of the inexplicable response I'd had to Damon's presence and, as a result, I was late to my next class.

"Mr. Nylund, I presume?" the lecturer inquired of me as I walked into class.

I bowed my head. "Yes, sir. My apologies for the disturbance to your class, sir."

The lecturer smiled magnanimously at me. "I imagine you got lost. Never mind. Perhaps you could take a seat next to Mr. Taylor over there."

He pointed at a seat near the rear, next to a lanky youth with glasses and a profusion of acne, and I did my best not to make eye-contact with anyone as I headed that way. *Mr. Taylor* didn't seem in the least displeased at the seat allocation and instead grinned broadly at me as I took my seat next to him.

"Parker," he whispered out of the corner of his mouth, offering me his hand. "But you can call me Spex."

"Eike," I murmured back, taking his surprisingly dry hand and correspondingly firm shake (somehow, I'd expected damp and limp).

"You're the new guy," he observed. "I'd heard you were coming."

He had? What was with all these people having advance notice of my arrival? It wasn't as if I was a celebrity or anything. Probably more of a freak. I shot *Spex* a suspicious glance but he gave no sign of noticing as I nodded at his observation. "Yeah," I admitted casually. "I guess I am."

By the end of class, we were friends.

"You in dorms?" Spex asked as we walked out of our last mutual lecture together.

I shook my head.

"My grandparents live not far from here. I live with them."

"Oh? Whereabouts? I live near here, too."

"Ferndale," I replied. "My grandparents run the Korean mini-mart."

"True?" Spex asked, eyebrows rising above the rims of his glasses. "My parents run the bakery on the corner. Quincy's. You know it?"

"Yeah," I agreed. "I do. Grandfather sends me to get him cheese scrolls from there every other Sunday. He swears they're the best ever."

Spex laughed.

"That's awesome. You biking? Bike home with me and I'll get you some cheese scrolls for your grandfather."

I nodded.

"Yeah, I am and sure, I'd like that."

Spex and I were virtually inseparable after that. He never asked after my tattoo or my scars or my past. It wasn't that he wasn't interested, I could often see the curiosity in his eyes, but that he knew what was appropriate and when. He was also simply happy to have a friend who, like himself, didn't judge. He was smart and when I struggled with notes and assignments, especially because I was still in the process of trying to catch up, he was more than happy to help out. And I, for my part, took him out biking and hiking and taught him how to shoot hoops. His skin cleared up and he developed a healthy tan, probably for the first time in his life, and I had someone to take my mind out of myself.

That whole first semester of our friendship passed surprisingly quickly and easily. Sure, there were still murmured comments and giggles behind raised hands as I passed and there were some brief resentments in relation to my reluctance to participate in any of the athletic endeavours on campus but, eventually, the novelty of my presence died down and life developed a kind of casual, easy rhythm. It wasn't as if the past had gone, how could it? But life, as it does, simply went on.

Only life doesn't ever *just go on*, does it?

Chapter Two

I was in my room, sprawled on my bed and listening to NCT, one of my current favourite K-pop groups, on my iPod and struggling with an Ethics assignment. At high school and in my previous life, I'd got into college primarily on a swim scholarship and I was now learning the alternative was hard work. I was struggling a little.

There was a knock on my door.

"Eike?"

"Yes, Grandmother?"

"Have you got a moment to come downstairs and talk with Grandfather and I?"

I took my earplugs from my ears and pulled my study books into a pile.

"Sure. Just a moment."

I ambled downstairs, completely innocent as to the purpose and gravity of my grandparents' request, and stopped on the bottom tread. There was somebody in the parlour, I could hear the deep baritone of a stranger's voice. A guest? Not Korean, that was for certain. I shrugged and straightened out the rumples of having been sprawling.

"Grandfather, Grandmother," I said, bowing respectfully as my mother had always taught me to do in the presence of my grandparents.

"Eike," Grandfather acknowledged.

I straightened and my heart dropped like a stone. The 'stranger' in my grandparent's parlour was the head coach for the Seven Oaks State College swim team though I only knew this due to Spex having pointed him out to me.

What was he doing here?

Coach Harmon stood up and extended a hand to me. "Eike," he said, smiling pleasantly. "I'd rather hoped we might have met before now but I figured if the mountain will not come to Muhammed..."

Colour rose into my cheeks.

"Sir," I murmured, shaking his hand.

"Sit down, Eike," Grandfather instructed. "Mother, perhaps some tea?"

Grandmother bustled off to fetch the tea-tray and I, more than a little apprehensively, took a seat as far away as I could from Coach Harmon without seeming rude. I said nothing but it didn't take any great stretch of imagination to know what was coming.

"I've read your application and resumé," Coach Harmon began, "so I know your swim record and also that you received several scholarship offers. I also know about what happened and, for what it's worth, I'm truly sorry."

"Thank you, sir," I acknowledged, staring at my feet and struggling to keep from wringing my hands.

The scars on my back burned and the dragon around my neck tightened its inky grip, restricting my breathing.

Coach Harmon coughed self-consciously. "Your grandparents and I have been discussing the possibility of your returning to the pool."

The words fell like a rock dropped from a great height into a water barrel and the coach was suddenly flustered, the resultant strained silence only interrupted by Grandmother's return with the tea. It was Grandfather's turn to clear his throat as Grandmother poured.

"We know it's been difficult for you, Eike," Grandfather said, "and we can fully appreciate why you haven't been back."

I still said nothing and clung to the cup of tea Grandmother offered as if it were a flickering torch in a lightless abyss. My head rang with white noise, almost drowning out Grandfather's continuing words.

"Your parents were very proud of your achievements, Eike, as were, *are,* Grandmother and I. We think it would be a terrible shame, a great loss, if you didn't at least try to go back and carry on."

My vision blurred and my face burned in sympathy with my scars.

"Coach Harmon has a suggestion, if you'd at least be willing to hear what he has to say," Grandfather concluded apologetically.

I nodded, but any words refused to budge from my throat.

"I understand you've not been back in a pool since, well, since the fire?" Coach Harmon ventured.

Again, all I could do was nod.

"I thought that maybe, instead of coming along to an official practice, which might understandably be more than a little overwhelming," Coach Harmon continued, "you might consider coming to a private session, get back into the water without an audience, as it were."

He paused, glancing at Grandfather for reassurance before continuing.

"I have a volunteer, one of our senior swim team, who would be more than happy to be your training partner and personally help you get back into it. Whenever suits you, of course. You just let me know and I'll arrange a time."

Coach Harmon took a deep breath, seemingly glad to have got his thoughts out uninterrupted, and I tried to breathe at all. Get back into it? Go back into the water? Go back to swimming? I felt as if all the air had been sucked out of me, as if I'd suddenly been plunged into an icy bath. How could they ask this of me?

"Just think about it, ok?" Coach Harmon asked, rising to his feet. He nodded at my grandparents and reached into a pocket for keys. "I think perhaps it's best if I go now," he said. "Perhaps you should talk this over without me."

You think? I thought. *And this couldn't have been discussed with me before you came?*

I bit my lip and struggled not to vent my sudden anger in words I might later regret.

"Thank you for your hospitality and for your time," Coach Harmon continued as Grandfather escorted him out.

I sat in a vacuum.

"Please don't be angry with us, Eike," Grandmother said, sitting beside me and gently placing a hand on my shoulder. "We only want what is best for you and for you to not later regret opportunities lost."

My face burned anew but this time with shame. How could I ever be angry with my grandparents? Of course they only had my best interests at heart. I knew this. I had no doubts. At all. And yet, still. Swimming? They knew, didn't they, how I felt about it?

"I know you feel guilty, Eike," Grandmother said, snatching the thought straight from my mind, "but you oughtn't to. Your mother," Grandmother's voice caught and more guilt exploded in my heart. "Your mother was so very, very proud of you. She'd be heartbroken you'd given it up, especially if she were to think it was in any way because of her."

I'd not thought of it quite like that before, how my mother might feel if she were able to look down on me. Tears threatened to overflow from my burning eyes and I tipped back my head and clenched my teeth to keep them at bay.

"We don't want to force you to do something you really don't want to," Grandmother continued, "but we just want to give you the best possible opportunity to go back to something you love. Because we love you. Do you understand?"

I couldn't help it; a hot tear escaped to roll down my cheek. "Yes, Grandmother," I whispered, my voice hoarse. "I understand."

"Then will you at least give it a try?" Grandmother asked, putting her arms around me.

How could I say no? How could I refuse my grandparents' request? They'd taken me in when I had no other place to go, they loved me unconditionally, and I was the last living legacy of their only child, their beloved daughter. How could I not do this one thing they asked of me? If not for my own sake, then at the very least for theirs?

"Yes, Grandmother," I managed to say. I blinked back the rest of my tears and hugged her back. "Can I think about it for just a little while? Prepare myself?"

Grandfather had by now come back into the parlour and I could sense he and Grandmother exchanging glances.

"Of course, Eike," Grandmother said. "But don't wait too much longer, all right? It's already been so long."

"Yes, Grandmother," I agreed. "I promise, I'll do this. Just, well, just give me 'til after the weekend?"

"Promise?" Grandfather asked. "After the weekend you'll go and see Coach Harmon and let him make a time with your new training partner?"

"Yes," I agreed. "I promise."

Chapter Three

"Seriously? So, what're you going to do?"

I was at Spex's house, lying on my back on his bed, my hands clasped behind my head as I stared at his bedroom ceiling. There was a poster of Troye Sivan directly above my head and I was thinking, *Why?* Mind you, I was thinking *Why?* in relation to the poster and not in relation to the subject of Spex's question.

"Huh?"

Spex sighed.

"I asked you what you're going to do, about this whole swimming thing," he repeated. "Weren't you listening?"

I rolled onto my side and looked at my friend, who was at his desk re-arranging some kind of in-depth study notes.

"I'm going to go, of course," I said. "They're my grandparents. It would be disrespectful not to."

"Oh," Spex said, scribbling in the margins of the notes. "And you're ok with that?"

I shrugged and sat up, running my fingers through my hair and absently wondering if it was now standing up on end.

"It isn't," Spex commented randomly, not lifting his head from what he was doing.

"What?"

"If you're wondering if you've made your hair stand on end," Spex elaborated, taking a moment to glance at me, "you haven't. It's fine. So, are you? Ok?"

I frowned at Spex and shrugged again, smiling. "You are so weird sometimes, you know that?"

"Yes," Spex agreed. "I am and I do."

"And I'm ok," I said in reply to his question. "I guess."

Spex put down his pen and took off his glasses, pinching the bridge of his nose with two fingers and rubbing his eyes. "You want me to come with you? When you go to the pool?" he asked, replacing his glasses and returning to his work.

I thought about this as I lay back down on his bed. "No, that's ok. I think this is probably something I have to do on my own."

"You know that if you change your mind..." Spex volunteered.

"Yeah, I know. Just ask." I closed my eyes.

"Yeah," Spex agreed, his voice suddenly a good deal closer than it had been.

I opened my eyes to discover him staring down at me, his brown eyes large and wide behind his glasses.

"Spex?"

Startled, he blinked rapidly and backed up the three or four steps to sit back down at his desk.

"Sorry," he stammered. "It's just..." He cleared his throat self-consciously and stared at his notes.

Awkward much. What was that all about, then? I sat up again.

"So, are you ready to get started?" I asked, hoping to distract him from whatever had just happened.

"Uh, yeah, sure. You?"

"Better now than later," I agreed. "Mid-terms are next week and I'm still struggling with section three... and four... and five..."

I gave Spex a crooked grin and he laughed and the awkward spell was broken.

"And that's why you have me," he pointed out. "And just as well, right?"

"Right!"

I breathed a quiet sigh of relief.

True to my word to my grandparents, I went to see Coach Harmon first thing after my last class on the Monday with a further promise to Spex that I'd go to his house to study with him straight afterwards. Coach Harmon seemed more than a little surprised to see me though simultaneously very pleased.

"Eike, what a pleasant surprise."

"Good afternoon, sir. Thank you for seeing me."

The coach waved a hand at me and indicated I take a seat as he dropped onto the edge of his desk.

"We don't stand much on ceremony here, Eike. Coach will suffice. You've thought about my proposition?"

I breathed deeply and did my best to remain calm. "Yes, sir, uh, *Coach*. If you can make a time for me, then I'll make sure to be there."

Coach Harmon nodded encouragingly. "Excellent, Eike. Very good. How does tomorrow night suit, then? Say nine? That's after the pool is officially closed so there's guaranteed to be just the three of us."

"Three?"

Coach raised his eyebrows. "You and me and your partner. Is that all right? Of course, you can ask your grandparents or another support person to be there if you want to. Whatever makes you comfortable, it's entirely up to you."

I shook my head. What would make me comfortable would be forgetting about it altogether but...

"No, that's all right, Coach. Three… three is fine."

As fine as it could be.

Coach smiled. "I'll be there *just in case*," he reassured me. "Not that I'm anticipating there'll be any difficulties. After all, ducks, fish, water. Right?"

I wasn't so sure and though I tried to smile I think it probably came across as more of a grimace because Coach Harmon gave me an extremely odd look in response. "Yes, well," he said. "Was there anything else?"

I stood up and gave him a short formal bow before I realised what I was doing. Coach looked a little taken aback.

"No, thank you, Coach. Tomorrow night. Nine. I'll see you then."

I turned and bolted from the coach's office, went looking for the nearest Men's Room, and promptly threw up.

I'd recovered somewhat by the time I got to Spex's place but I must still have been looking fairly green.

"Are you all right?" he asked as I came in. "You look ill."

"I've been to see Coach Harmon," I said by way of explanation. "It's all go tomorrow night at nine."

"No wonder you look ill," Spex said sympathetically. "Come on, I'll make you a coffee or something."

"Coffee sounds great."

I followed Spex through to his kitchen and took a seat at the breakfast bar while he made us coffee.

"Can I ask you something?" Spex asked as he put my coffee in front of me. "Something personal?"

I blew on my coffee and tried not to allow my mind to wander through the possibilities. "Sure," I said. "You can always ask but I won't guarantee an answer."

"Fair enough," Spex agreed.

"So?" I asked, keeping my focus on my coffee.

"I was just wondering if you've ever had a girlfriend," Spex said. "You don't seem to've shown any interest in the girls at Seven Oaks, and there's certainly plenty of them interested in *you*, and I just wondered if, I don't know, you'd maybe left one behind, like, you know, from before."

He took a deep breath, as if he'd run out trying to get his thoughts out all in one go, and I almost spluttered coffee out my nose, instead swallowing coffee far too hot for my internal health.

"Is that an actual question?" I asked while I regained my composure. "Where'd that come from?"

Spex shrugged self-consciously.

"I was just wondering, that's all."

I blinked back the tears resulting from scalding my throat and wiped my face with the back of a hand.

"No," I admitted. "On both counts. No girlfriend and no girl I left behind."

"Why?" Spex pressed. "You're a really good-looking guy, Eike, and all the girls seem to really like you. Why no girlfriend?"

I put down my cup and swivelled to stare at my friend. Did he know? Or was he simply fishing? "Why the sudden interest?" I asked him. "Tired of my company already? Or looking for a double date?"

Spex had the good grace to blush. "Sorry, dude. I…" He looked away and shifted uncomfortably. "It's just…"

"Oh, for fuck's sake, Spex!" I snapped, suddenly irritated with him. "Just spit it out already!"

He looked as if he might actually be about to cry. "I've never had a date," he mumbled, still looking anywhere but at me. "I thought you might, I don't know, have some tips, some advice for me."

I stared at him, open-mouthed, and then, realising my mouth was open, closed it and took another sip of coffee while I gathered my thoughts.

"Dating advice? From me? What on earth makes you think I'd have any dating tips for you? Where have I ever suggested I'm so great at dating myself?" I stared at him a little more intensely and he finally deigned to meet me eye to eye. My eyes narrowed suspiciously. "You have somebody in mind, Spex?" I asked quietly.

Spex blushed. Deeply.

"You do!" I said, straightening to study him with a smirk. "Who, Spex? Who is she?"

"It's nothing," Spex muttered. "Leave it, forget it. I shouldn't have asked."

"Seriously? Who, Spex? Do I know her? Have I seen her? Does she go to Seven Oaks?"

"I said forget it!" Spex practically snarled, stalking out of the kitchen and heading towards his room. "Come the fuck on. We've got exams starting in two days, haven't we? And you're nowhere near ready."

I got nothing more out of him on the subject. At all.

Grandmother had packed my swim bag for me and I found it waiting for me on the kitchen table when I got home after my study session with Spex, along with a meal and a note written in traditional Korean hangul.

'Eike, Grandfather and I have gone out for dinner. Make sure you eat. Xxx Grandmother and Grandfather.'

I picked up the plated meal and transferred it to the microwave, overcome by a wave of gratitude for my grandparents and sorrow for the loss of my family, and sat at the table and stared at the bag.

The last time I'd seen this bag had been *that* night, the night of the fire, and I couldn't imagine where it had been in the meantime or how it had come to be here. I closed my eyes and gripped the edge of the table and tried not to let my mind go back. It was a lost cause, really. For a mind-reeling moment the room spun and all I could smell was smoke and something sickly-sweet... The memory of my own burning flesh? I ground my teeth and forced myself back into reality just as the microwave pinged. Barbeque pork. Fantastic. I raced to the bathroom just in time to once again throw up. Dinner, needless to say, was carefully wrapped in an old newspaper and then in a plastic bag (so Grandmother wouldn't know) and disposed of in the garbage. I had a glass of water and took myself to bed.

Chapter Four

Classes went far too quickly the following day and I was, apparently, even quieter than usual.

"You want to come 'round to mine?" Spex asked as we walked out of our last class.

"Can't," I said, shrugging apologetically. "I told Grandfather I'd help out in the store today. He's stock-taking."

Spex nodded though it was clear he was disappointed.

"You still going tonight?"

"Yeah," I said. "As if I couldn't, right?"

"I guess so," Spex conceded. "You going to call me after?"

"It'll be late," I warned, "but sure. Besides, if I don't, you'll be spamming my phone all night, right?"

Spex grinned. "Yeah, pretty much."

We biked home together but I continued on alone after we reached his driveway.

If classes had gone far too quickly, helping Grandfather in the store went even more quickly and before I knew it, Grandfather was calling for me to stop.

"Time to go and get ready," he said quietly, indicating his watch. "Are you sure you don't want me to go with you?"

I smiled gratefully at him but shook my head, even though my blood was already running cold in my body. "No, thank you, Grandfather. I'll be fine, I promise."

He nodded, patting my shoulder. "Be brave," he said. "It will be good, yes? You'll be pleased you did, won't you?"

"Yes, Grandfather. I'll see you at home later."

"Good boy," he said and, as he turned away, I swear I saw tears in his eyes.

Damn.

It was already well into summer twilight by the time I pedalled up to the building housing the campus pool, but I could see there were lights on inside. My stomach churned as I locked up my bike and I wondered if I was going to have to literally spill my guts into one of the big concrete garden boxes before I entered the building. Something, or someone, made a noise behind me and I spun around.

"Whoa! Dude! Sorry, did I give you a scare?"

I couldn't see a face, just a blank shadow, but something about the voice was vaguely familiar, as were the electric goose-bumps which rose simultaneously on my skin. "No. Well, yes actually. Hello?"

The shadow came closer and I recognised the broad physique of the swimmer who'd approached me right back on my first day on campus. Damon. So, this was my training partner, my swim buddy? I felt heat rise into my face and was immediately grateful for the lack of light. Seriously, what was with me in his presence?

"You ready?" Damon asked, striding alongside me and indicating the steps up into the pool building with an expansive sweep of his arm.

Ready? Hell no. Not even. Did I have a choice? Also, hell no. I plucked my swim bag from my bike and steadied myself with thoughts of my grandparents. *For you*, I thought. *And for Mother*.

I followed Damon less than enthusiastically up the steps and into the building where Coach Harmon was waiting for us by the pool.

"You're early," he said with a welcoming smile. "That's always a good start in my book. Go on and get changed and we'll begin, shall we?"

I tried not to drag my feet as Damon directed me to the change rooms.

"You shy?" Damon asked bluntly as we walked in and he threw his swim bag onto one of the benches.

"What?"

"I asked if you were shy?" Damon repeated. "It's just, I know some guys are. And you're Korean, right? I just thought you might prefer to use one of the stalls. It's ok if you do. I won't judge."

"What's that got to do with being Korean?" I asked, confused. "And besides, I'm only half Korean, and I was born in Canada."

Damon scratched his nose but didn't look in the least abashed. He shrugged and stripped off his sweatshirt, his tee-shirt quickly following suit.

"No offence meant, dude. Just saying."

He'd already kicked off his sneakers and was hauling off his track-pants and all I could do was stare. Had I ever seen a physique quite like his? I'd been around swimmers, and athletes in general, the better part of my life and I'd seen some pretty impressive bodies, but Damon? Damon was something else.

Suddenly aware I was staring and that I as yet hadn't moved, I mumbled something about using a stall after all and scampered inside one, shutting the door and leaning my forehead against the cool tiles of the wall to catch my breath. What the hell?

"I'll wait for you," Damon informed me calmly from the other side of the door.

"Great," I muttered under my breath. "Of course, you will."

"What was that?" Damon asked. "You all right?"

"Yeah, sorry. Just a mo." I stared at my swim bag sitting innocently on the wooden bench and wiped cold sweat from my face.

For fuck's sake! I swore at myself. *Pull yourself together and just do it already.* I unzipped the bag and pulled out my swimsuit.

If it had been since the fire since I'd been in a pool, it had been since at least mid-way through my rehabilitation that I'd exposed my scars to anybody, and at no time had I ever done so willingly. Obviously, I'd had no choice when I'd been seeing the doctors and specialists, but this? This was entirely different. I gritted my teeth and got out of my clothes and almost cried with relief when I saw Grandmother had packed me not only a towel and my goggles but also a brand-new towelling robe. I slipped on the robe and finally opened the stall door.

"Ready?" Damon asked, making no comment about the robe though he himself stood there in only his suit, a towel slung casually over one well-muscled shoulder.

I felt the overwhelming urge to heave again but swallowed it down and offered Damon the barest of nods.

"Right," Damon said, far too cheerfully. "Let's go."

Coach Harmon stood up from where he'd been seated by the pool as we approached. "So," he said, almost as over-enthusiastically as Damon had. "Ready then?"

So not even. But I nodded anyway.

"You intend swimming in that?" Coach Harmon asked, raising an eyebrow at me still hiding, because that's what I was doing, in my robe.

Very reluctantly, I dropped the robe… and waited.

"Holy shit!" Damon exclaimed.

And there it was.

"That is freaking awesome!" Damon continued.

Wait. What?

"How come I didn't see that before?" Damon asked, moving up to me in two quick, long strides and grasping my right shoulder. "That is fantastic!"

The tattoo! He was talking about my dragon, not the scars.

Coach Harmon was not as easily distracted as he too moved closer and turned me by the left shoulder so he could get a better look at my back.

"These bother you?" he asked. "Restrict movement? Slow you down? Cause you pain?"

Damon stepped back and I felt a disconcerting sense of regret as his hand slipped from my shoulder.

Focus!

"The scars?" I asked. "No, they're pretty good now. At least, I don't know about swimming, of course, but they don't bother me too much doing anything else. They burn a bit sometimes, when it's maybe too hot or too cold, but the specialist said I should be good."

"Ok, good, good," Coach Harmon said, letting me go and returning to his seat by the pool. "So, how about we just focus on getting you into the water and take it from there. No rush and let me know if at any time you're uncomfortable. Ok?"

Like now? I restrained a sigh and nodded. "Here?" I asked, looking out over the glimmering expanse of the pool stretching out from the edge.

"Sure, if that's where you want to begin," Coach Harmon agreed. "Like I said, whatever makes you comfortable."

What would make me comfortable would be getting dressed and going home.

"Me first then," Damon grinned, and in a single lithe arc he was diving into the pool, his body carving into the water with barely so much as a splash. He surfaced a short distance out and flicked water from his hair. "Come on then, dude," he grinned, effortlessly treading water. "Let's go."

I stood on the edge of the pool and curved my toes over the textured concrete. Right. Let's go.

Chapter Five

Your body doesn't forget. It's an instinct, and it never leaves you. My body arced out over the water as if the water were a magnet and I the steel. It was freedom. It was flying. The water beckoned like silk to skin and I closed my eyes at the sheer rush shooting through me like a drug.

And then the water closed over me.

It wasn't water, it was smoke. It wasn't the cool, clear embrace of liquid bliss, it was pain. It was agony. It was terror. All I could hear was the roaring of the flames, the crash of falling timber, the shattering explosion of glass and steel and the house collapsing in on me like a raging scarlet beast. I screamed and the screaming didn't stop until the darkness overwhelmed me.

I came to on the cold, wet edge of the pool and my first conscious thought was, *Whose lips are those?* My eyes shot open and I found myself staring directly into eyes as deep and blue as a Caribbean ocean. I promptly rolled over and vomited a torrent of water.

"Dude! Jesus, you scared the living shit out of me! What the hell was that?"

My chest ached and my back burned and my throat felt as if I'd drunk a half gallon of bleach. I coughed and spluttered and threw up more water and somebody put strong, warm hands on my shoulders and steadied me as I did so.

Damon.

"We should get you to the hospital," Coach Harmon said. "Can you stand?"

"No," I mumbled, half-leaning into Damon's neighbouring strength for support.

I was light-headed but I wasn't yet able to decide if this was because I'd clearly almost drowned or because of the unnerving effect Damon's proximity had on me. I made an attempt to sit up by myself.

"You can't stand?" Coach Harmon continued. "Damon, pick him up."

"No, no, it's ok," I argued. "Give me a minute. I can stand, I just don't want to go to the hospital."

I struggled to get my hands behind me so I could sit up and found Damon's arm unexpectedly wrapped around me. Shit. I struggled for breath and my heart hammered painfully in my chest, neither of which, I'm fairly certain, had anything to do with my recent abrupt intake of water and plenty to do with Damon.

"Here, let me help you," Damon breathed in my ear. "That was really close, bro. Coach is right, we really ought to take you to get checked out."

"No," I said, more firmly, forcing myself to regain some semblance of control. "I'm ok. I just want to get up."

Damon lifted me upright and I found myself leaning on him far more than I felt was really appropriate. Then again, my legs were unsteady and I ached as if I'd been wrestling monsters from the deep even if I did think I was probably going to be all right.

"I'll live," I said.

"If you say so," Damon replied, sounding far from reassured.

"You're bleeding," Coach Harmon observed with a frown.

"I am?"

"Your back," Coach Harmon said, standing alongside Damon to inspect my scars.

I forced down the heat rising into my cheeks, feeling exposed and self-conscious. My back, however, was numb. I couldn't feel a thing.

"I'm sure it's nothing to worry about," I mumbled. I began to shake.

"Get him in the shower," Coach Harmon instructed Damon, "and dressed. Then we'll get him to the hospital."

There didn't seem much to be gained in arguing any further at this point and I allowed Damon to help me back to the changing room, but once the door had swung closed behind us, I pushed him away.

"I'm ok," I said, my voice hoarse.

"Dude, you just threw up half the damn pool!"

"It was only about a half a bath-tub's worth," I argued, still shaking. "It wouldn't be the first time."

Damon was staring at me but he held his own counsel and said nothing. I looked around for a towel.

"Here," Damon said, tossing me a towel. "Use my spare. Yours is still by the pool, and it's wet anyway."

I barely caught the towel through my shaking and couldn't help but groan. I could feel it now, my back, and it really did hurt. I heard water running.

"You're shaking," Damon observed bluntly, "and your back's still bleeding. Get in the shower and I'll check it out for you."

I wanted to argue but, to be honest, I really wasn't feeling too good. I put down Damon's towel and I did as I was told and stepped under the water. Damon followed me. Shit. Again. I closed my eyes and focused on the water, just the water, only the water, as Damon rinsed my back.

"It doesn't look too bad," he acknowledged after a short while. "Probably just scraped it when I dragged you out of the pool. I don't think it needs anything special but I've got some antiseptic in my bag that I'll put on for you before you get dressed."

He moved away from me and stepped out of the shower.

"Damon?"

"Hmm?"

"Thanks. For saving my life."

"No problem, bro. After all, that's what I'm here for, right?"

I leaned my head against the wall and focused on the water running over my body. What exactly had I gotten myself into?

I managed to convince Coach Harmon and Damon I didn't need to go to hospital.

"It will freak my grandparents right out," I added as an extra incentive. "And then they might not want me to come back."

Coach Harmon's face creased in a concerned frown.

"You actually *want* to come back? After what just happened?"

"Yes, sir," I said. "That is, if you're still willing to help me."

Damon grinned at me and wriggled his eyebrows. "You want me to play hero for you again, I'm game. Right, Coach?"

Coach didn't look quite so sure but, after a moment, he shrugged. "Ok, for now. But this happens again, any *hint* of this happens again, and it's straight to the hospital. No arguments. Agreed?"

"Yes, Coach."

"And I want you to see the campus nurse first thing in the morning. No note from the nurse, dated and timed tomorrow morning, no swimming. Understood?"

"Yes, Coach."

Coach Harmon still seemed far from convinced but Damon got straight to the point.

"When?"

"Huh?"

"When are we going to try this again? You probably need at least a couple of days to recover and we've got a Tri-Campus swim carnival on Friday night so, Coach? Saturday morning? Early?"

Coach Harmon took a deep breath and scratched his head. "Eike?"

"How early?" I asked. "It's only that I help Grandfather in the store in the mornings and I don't want to take too much time off."

Damon gave me a look suggesting he was surprised, as if he hadn't anticipated I'd work, perhaps. I got that sometimes, though I don't know why. I wouldn't have thought I came across as privileged. I shrugged.

"My swim scholarships are obsolete and it helps me earn my keep," I explained. "Grandfather and I open the store every morning at six. I don't work weekdays because he'd rather I study but I work weekends till midday."

"You didn't have to explain yourself," Damon said. "But that's cool. I have a part-time job too and I imagine most students on campus do. Will your grandfather mind if you're here at five on Saturday? We'll have to be out by six-thirty for the early training squad anyway, unless you care to join them?"

I gave him what I hoped he'd interpret as a 'not bloody likely' look and he grinned.

"No to joining the early squad, then?" he acknowledged. "What about five?"

"What about Coach Harmon?" I asked in response. "He hasn't agreed yet."

Coach Harmon grunted. "As if I have a choice. Damon's the Captain. I tend to simply just follow suit."

"Oh."

"So?" Damon prompted.

"What? Oh, right, five. Yeah, sure, I guess. I can't imagine Grandfather will mind too much seeing as he's the one pushing for this to begin with."

"So that's settled then," Coach Harmon agreed. "Now, how about I give you a lift home."

Statement, not question.

"My bike," I argued.

"Don't worry about that," Damon said. "I'll take that home for you. You live just up in Ferndale, don't you? I'm in Parkmoor, not too far past that. I'll drop by a bit later on and bring your bike then."

It wasn't as if I had any leverage to argue so I gave him my address and let Coach Harmon take me home.

Coach dropped me at the end of the drive after I practically begged him not to risk a scene with my grandparents over what had happened. "But you go and see the nurse first thing tomorrow, right?" he reiterated. "Or I'll be here to speak to your grandparents personally!"

With a threat like that, the nurse was going to be seeing me super-early!

"Yes, Coach."

"Ok, well, take it easy and we'll see you on Saturday."

My grandparents were waiting for me when I walked in but, though they were clearly happy to see me, they were discreet enough not to badger me with questions. Grandmother hugged me and told me she'd bring supper to my room and Grandfather nodded and patted me on the shoulder before retreating to his study for a very late evening pipe and wine. I managed to get up the stairs to my room both without stumbling and without feeling the need to cough up any more of the pool but I wasn't feeling anywhere near as well as I'd led Coach Harmon and Damon to believe.

My phone was lying in the middle of my bed. Damn, I hadn't even realised I'd not had it with me. I flipped it over and shook my head, and immediately wished I hadn't because my head was really thumping. I sat unsteadily on my bed. **Six** missed calls, all from Spex. And an accompanying even dozen texts. Geez, Spex!

I called him.

"Eike?!"

"Of course it is. Who else would it be? Expecting a call from the Governor, maybe? I just got in."

"Really? What time is it?"

I checked my bedside clock. "Just gone ten-thirty."

"Isn't that kinda late?"

"What are you suddenly? My chaperone? It wasn't like I was out on a date, it was swimming, and that shit isn't exactly a stroll in the park, you know..."

For some reason I found myself hesitating about telling Spex all the details of my first swim session though whether this was because I'd nearly drowned or because it was Damon who'd saved me or maybe because of Spex's own very peculiar behaviour recently, I couldn't say.

"You going again tomorrow?" Spex asked, interrupting my thoughts.

"Hm? Oh, no, Saturday morning, early," I said. "That's the next time Coach Harmon and my partner are free." This wasn't necessarily entirely true but neither was it a lie so I didn't feel too guilty putting it that way.

"Don't forget there's a test tomorrow afternoon," Spex reminded me.

Actually, I *had* forgotten and I immediately felt sick again. My throat burned and there were several hot spots on my back where

Damon had applied the antiseptic. Despite the fact I was all by myself in my room, I blushed.

"True. Thanks, Spex," I managed to reply.

"Ok, well, you want to tell me about it tomorrow? About the swimming, that is?"

No, not really. But…

"Yeah, sure, ok. I'm just going to have something to eat and then I'm going to bed. See you tomorrow."

"K. See you tomorrow then. Night, Eike."

"Night, Spex."

I told Grandfather a partial truth, too, that Coach Harmon wanted me to see the campus nurse to check everything was all right for me to continue and so I arrived early after telling Spex I'd meet him there. Coach Harmon had already been to see the nurse and told her to expect me.

"You really ought to have gone to the hospital, you know," she said as I took off my shirt and tee.

"Yeah, maybe," I acknowledged.

She looked at my back.

"Those are some pretty nasty scars," she observed quietly.

She ran a cool hand down the worst of them, the one running crossways in a heavy raised ribbon from left shoulder to right hip. "They bother you much?"

I shrugged absently. "Not so much anymore. Just sometimes, when I get really hot or I'm really cold or when I've been working too hard."

She hummed and hawed a while, checking everything from my pulse to my blood pressure, and finally stepped back and studied me appraisingly.

"Well," she said at last, "you seem ok. How are you feeling? Honestly."

I gave another shrug. "I'm ok. Honestly. Am I good to go?"

She gave me a curious look and finally gave me a reluctant nod. "I don't see anything to immediately concern me but, if it happens again…"

"Yeah, yeah, I know," I sighed. "Go to the hospital."

She smiled at me. "Yes, the hospital. Immediately."

"Yes, ma'am."

It wasn't Coach Harmon or Spex waiting for me when I came out of the infirmary, it was Damon and the same three friends he'd had with him the first time we'd met. I dipped my head as the heat insisted on returning to my face and focused on the pavement at my feet. What was it about Damon that did this to me?

"Hey," he said as I walked out.

"Hey," I mumbled.

"How you feeling today? You all right?"

"Yeah, thanks, I'm ok. Um, thanks."

"No problem."

I shuffled my feet self-consciously and looked past Damon and his friends to see if I could spot Spex.

"He's in the north quad," Damon said.

"Huh?"

"Your friend, Parker Taylor? Spex? That's who you're looking for, right? He's in the north quad, probably waiting for you."

"Uh, yes, right, best I get going then."

"Wait a minute."

I paused mid-stride and looked back at Damon.

"Want to hang out with us later? We're heading to the courts to shoot some hoops but Ox here is bailing out on us. You could make up our two pair."

Damon's friends grinned encouragingly.

"Uhh?"

"Bring Parker if you want to. He can score for us."

My heart hammered in my chest, my pulse thumped in my ears, and I could *feel* the heat threatening to rise back into my face. I bit the inside of my cheek to ground myself.

"Um, all right, I guess. Ok."

"Sweet, see you round four. Lincoln Courts.'

And just like that, he was leaving.

I stood there for a bit, watching him go and wondering what had just happened, which was where Spex found me a short time later.

"You ok?" he asked, hitching his satchel up his shoulder and his glasses up his nose. "You look like a stunned salmon."

I dragged myself back into the real world and stared at him. "A what?"

"A stunned salmon. You're standing there looking like a stunned salmon."

"I don't know where you got that from but I think you mean a mullet," I informed him.

"A what?"

"A mullet," I repeated. "I think you mean I look like a stunned mullet, not a salmon."

Spex looked confused, not actually uncommon for him.

"Ok, whatever," I said to him. "Come on. I'm fine and we're going to be late."

I aced the test and I knew it. And it was pretty much all due to Spex, which is what I told him when I followed him out of class.

"It was nothing, dude," he mumbled, clearly uncomfortable with the praise. "You're a whole lot smarter than you give yourself credit for, you know."

I shrugged. "I still wouldn't have been able to do it without you," I repeated. "Thanks."

Spex grew even more uncomfortable and highlights of bright colour rose into his cheeks. "Yeah, well, whatever. So, what are you doing after next class? Want to come over to mine for a bit? We could pick up a movie and a pizza or something."

Which reminded me. "Actually, we've been invited down to Lincoln Courts to play hoops with my swim partner, Damon, and some of his friends."

Spex stopped dead in his tracks to turn and stare at me and I nearly ran into him as a result.

"Damon? Damon King?"

"I don't know," I said, back-stepping so I wasn't quite so close to him. "Just *Damon, my swim partner*. He never gave me his last name but he gave me the distinct impression he knew you so, yeah, maybe?"

Spex blinked. "You didn't tell me."

"I only found out myself last night and I didn't think it was particularly important," I replied, feeling uncomfortably put on the spot. "Why are you acting so weird all of a sudden?"

Spex scowled at me and his glasses slid down his nose. He shoved them back up with a gesture of clear irritation. "You really don't know?"

"Seriously, does it look like I know?" I asked in reply. "What the hell, Spex?"

Spex sighed, looking decidedly queasy.

"What's our next class again?"

"Are you all right?" I asked by way of reply. "You don't look so good."

"Let's ditch," Spex said, still looking green.

"Ditch? Spex, I've never ditched a class in my life."

"Neither have I," Spex admitted. "Seems to me we're overdue, don't you think?"

"Maybe I should take you to see the nurse first," I said. "At least you'd get a Pass. And you really don't look all that great."

Spex shrugged. "Ok."

I escorted him to the infirmary and the same nurse who'd seen me that morning was still on duty.

"Eike," she said when she saw me. "Not good?"

"Not me," I informed the nurse. "It's my friend here. He doesn't seem to be doing so good."

The nurse turned her attention to Spex. "Mr. Taylor isn't it?" she asked. "I remember you from what happened last year. It was a terrible tragedy and I'm so sorry."

I raised an eyebrow but didn't ask.

"Yeah, thanks," Spex murmured. "I was wondering if you might be able to spot me an exemption for my last class. I'd quite like to go home but I don't want a 'Failed to Attend' on my record, you know?"

The nurse nodded sympathetically. "Bad patch?"

"Something like that," Spex agreed sombrely.

"Do you need me to arrange a taxi or a ride home for you, or will Eike accompany you?" the nurse asked.

"I'll take him," I said.

The nurse wrote us both Medical Exemptions and just like that I was taking Spex home.

"That was all way too easy," I said as we biked slowly to his house. "What was all that about?"

"Damon," Spex said.

Damon? Really? Damon had something to do with last year's terrible tragedy? And Damon was the reason Spex had wanted to bail class in the first place. My curiosity was burning. But we didn't speak any further until we got to Spex's house.

"I'll make the coffee," I said as we walked into the kitchen. "Are your folks likely to be home?"

"Working till six," Spex said. "Put plenty of sugar in mine."

I made the coffee and put his mug in front of him.

"So, are you going to tell me what all of this is about?"

"Yeah," Spex said. "I am."

It took Spex the better part of an hour to tell me the whole story, in between three consecutive cups of coffee and several trips to the bathroom, supposedly for toilet breaks but, going by his red-rimmed eyes, more likely to cry and when he'd finished I understood only too well why the nurse had mentioned both a tragedy and a 'bad patch'…

Damon King, a year older than Spex and therefore the same age as me, is without any doubt the most popular guy at Seven Oaks, never mind the town of Oakridge itself. I guess I'd only missed this because I personally fail to pay any attention whatsoever to the social status of those around me and am blissfully oblivious to the popularity rankings. He's a born and bred local and the only son (he has two much younger half-sisters) of the biggest property developer in at very least the County and quite likely the State and is touted to be his father's eventual successor to the company after he graduates with a double degree in Business and Finance. He's the Captain of the swim team (this much I already knew) and is also a more than respectable football and basketball player, to the extent there were fights between the respective coaches over who would have him. And, up until the beginning of the previous year, he'd been dating Spex's twin sister, Harper.

Why didn't I know Spex even had a twin sister? Because, at the beginning of the previous year and after dating for nearly three years, Damon suddenly broke up with her, apparently without any real explanation. Admittedly, he hadn't been seen to be dating anybody since so it couldn't be said he'd ditched her for somebody else, despite his popularity and the absolutely no shortage of more than willing replacements, but Harper was by all accounts inconsolable. After persistent attempts to win Damon back, all without success, she eventually gave in to a spiral of deep depression and committed suicide by overdose four months later.

I actually had no response to make to this revelation and all I could think was: *Holy shit.*

Chapter Six

Needless to say, we didn't go to the courts to play pairs with Damon and his friends. Not having any contact details for him, I couldn't even let him know and, despite the story Spex had told me, this still made me feel a little guilty. After all, as awful as it was, it wasn't fair to blame Damon for Harper's death. Someone can't force you to be in a relationship just because they say they're going to hurt themselves if you don't. Damon might not even have known she was considering it in the first place. It was a tragedy, but I personally believe that every person's choice ends up being their own and maybe the greater tragedy lay in Harper not having received the help she clearly needed *before* she made the irrevocable choice she did.

Not to mention that I wanted to see Damon again purely for my own selfish desire to once again experience that heady rush I seemed to have only in his presence.

Not that I said any of this to Spex.

I stayed until his parents got home but I declined the invitation to stay for dinner with the excuse that my grandparents would be expecting me. I found Harper's story far too close to home for comfort and, although he was aware of my own past, I'd never discussed it openly with him. For me, the scars, in all respects, were still far too raw and the smoke rose only too readily to my mind and I was in no way ready to discuss my past as he'd been only too willing to share his. Perhaps, and I'm not proud of this thought, I found it difficult to relate to the concept of someone choosing to take their own life, especially on account of something as fickle as love, when my own family had been given no choice. To be honest, I couldn't get out of his house fast enough and I was shaking as I rode my bike home.

I excused myself as soon as I'd done the dishes after dinner and retreated to my room. My phone was ringing from the pocket of my backpack which I'd flung in a corner when I'd come home and it took me a few moments to retrieve it although I immediately wished I hadn't bothered even if the thought simultaneously made me feel guilty. It was Spex.

"Eike?"

"You called me," I sighed. "Who else would it be?"

Spex ignored me.

"You busy?"

I sincerely wished I could say I was. "No, not really. Why?"

"What're you doing?"

"Oh, I don't know. Talking to you? I haven't had time to start anything else yet. I've just come up from dinner."

"Oh."

What the fuck was up with him now? I took a deep breath. "What's up?"

"Nothing."

Translation: *Something, but I don't want to talk about it right now, even if really, I do.* Seriously? I could sense Spex's despondent shrug.

"I don't suppose you want to come over for some Minecraft?" he continued.

"I can't really, Spex. You know I have to get up early to help Grandfather in the store."

There was such a prolonged silence I almost hung up thinking we'd been cut off.

"Yeah, I guess." More silence. "Ok, well, see you tomorrow then."

"Yeah, ok."

"Eike?"

"Yes, Spex?"

"Sleep well."

And he was gone.

I stared at the phone in my hand and wondered what that had all been about but I was too exhausted to worry about it. I put the phone on my bedside cabinet and threw myself on my bed. Only a half-minute later, the phone rang again. I groaned. Seriously, Spex? I contemplated ignoring it but, when it all came down to it, Spex was my friend. I sighed and picked up the phone only to see an unfamiliar number.

"Hello?"

"Is this Eike?"

"Yes?"

"It's Damon. You didn't meet us at the courts today and I wondered if you were all right, you know, after yesterday."

Damon? My scalp tingled and heat rose once more into my face. What the fuck? How did he get my number? I sat up and ran fingers through my hair.

"Uh, yeah, sorry about that. I'm fine, it's just, well, Spex …" I paused, flustered. "I didn't have your number," I added lamely.

"I figured as much," Damon said. "I got your number from Coach."

"Coach gave you my number?"

"Well, not exactly," Damon admitted, an element of smugness in his voice. "I said I got it from him, not that he gave it to me. It was in his office, in your file."

Damon took my number from my file in Coach's office?

"Oh."

"So, I guess Parker told you? He doesn't like me much," Damon continued.

How to respond to that? "Yes, he did and no, he doesn't." I've always found the truth generally works best.

"Did he tell you to stay away from me?" Damon asked quietly.

"Not in so many words," I admitted, "but the strong suggestion was definitely there." There was one of those long empty silences where I was once again wondering if the phone had cut out. I waited.

"Want to hang out anyway?"

"What?" That was unexpected.

"There's a place at the Junction. Meg's. You know it?"

I'd heard of it though I'd never been there.

"Yeah," I admitted. "I know it."

"We're going to hang out and have a couple of games of pool. Care to join us?"

"Uh…"

"I'll pick you up from your place. Ten minutes?"

I don't know what the hell came over me but I suddenly felt the need to give in to the moment, to give in to the irresistible draw of Damon. "Yeah, sure. Ok. I'll see you in ten."

I put down the phone and rolled over on my bed to stare at the ceiling. I was *going out* with Damon, and his friends presumably. My stomach rolled and sweat beaded on my forehead.

Stop it! It wasn't like it was a *date* or something. He was my swim partner and, despite the fact I was a year behind him, we were the same age. He was being nice, trying to get to know me like somebody with mutual interests might logically want to do. Do **not** let your thoughts run away with you!

I rolled off the bed and rummaged in my wardrobe in an attempt to find something clean and appropriate to wear. Why was it most of my clothes seemed to be either workwear or sportswear? Five minutes later, I was downstairs.

"Going somewhere, Eike?" Grandmother asked, looking me curiously up and down.

"If that's all right, Grandmother," I said. "It's Damon, the guy Coach Harmon asked to help me back into swimming. He's picking me up and introducing me to some of his friends."

Grandmother smiled fondly at me. "It's about time you made some more friends," she said. "Don't be too late though, will you? You've got classes tomorrow and you're helping Grandfather, yes?"

I bowed respectfully. "I promise I won't be too late, Grandmother."

I waited nervously at the end of my drive and less than a minute later a big black four by four was pulling up beside me. Damon. He emerged from the driver's side, standing half in and half out to lean over the top of the vehicle and grin at me.

"You're ready. Excellent."

He was different not dressed for classes or swim practice and even more impossibly breath-taking. I swallowed, hard, and forced down the heat which threatened to consume me.

"Nice ride," I observed as calmly as I could manage.

"Get in," Damon said.

I was ten and already even much older girls were beginning to pay attention to me, and my brother, Xia, was fourteen.

"You need to be careful, Eike," he said to me one day as we were biking to school together.

"Careful, Xia? Why? What for?"

"You're pretty. You have to be careful."

"Pretty? Xia, pretty? Pretty is for girls. I'm not pretty!"

"Yes, you are, Eike. And that's why you have to be careful. Boys shouldn't be pretty and boys shouldn't like boys."

I'd been thoroughly confused.

"Why, Xia? Why shouldn't boys like boys?"

Xia had shrugged and looked flustered, keeping his head down and not looking at me as we pedalled side by side.

"They just shouldn't, that's all. And boys who like boys get themselves in trouble."

"What kind of trouble?"

"They just do, ok. Don't let anyone know you like boys, even if you do."

I was even more confused. I had friends and most of my friends were boys. Stood to reason. I was ten.

"So, who should I like then?"

"Like who you want, but just don't let anyone know if you like boys."

"Eike. Eike!"

What?

"You coming or what?"

Oh. Right.

I got into the truck.

"You all right?" Damon asked, sliding back into the driver's seat and slipping the vehicle in gear. "You were a million miles away."

"Yeah, sorry. I was thinking about my brother."

Damon glanced over at me, his profile, caught for a moment in the backlight of the streetlights, giving him the appearance of a character from a Japanese manga. I blinked and looked away.

"Your brother, he's dead, isn't he?" Damon asked candidly, though not unkindly.

Merely an observation.

"Yeah."

"You were close?"

I shrugged. "I guess so. He was older than me and he'd been away studying for a while. He was going to be a doctor."

"You must really miss him."

I blinked back the sudden sting of tears and gazed out the window at the passing streets. "Yeah. I do."

Meg's is a bit of an anomaly; part diner, part road-house, part pool-hall, which is why it's such a popular venue for students and locals alike. I followed Damon inside, keeping my head high and my eyes focused on his back and, not surprisingly, there was an immediate response to our entry.

The place was pretty packed for a weeknight; men, women, couples, a fairly broad spectrum of ages, occupations, and ethnic origins. I got the distinct impression Damon was well-known but there was a momentary lull in conversation when I walked in after him. Like I've said previously, I'm fairly exotic and I'm tall and reasonably well-built and, as my brother once said, I guess I'm *pretty*.

Not that I play up to this intentionally. If anything, especially given that long-ago conversation with my brother, I've done my best to be discreet and to not let the *pretty* side dominate. I took up swimming and Hapkido (a Korean martial art) and even tried, unsuccessfully, to dye the lock of white hair in my forelock. But people tend nevertheless to notice me. It's hard not to, I guess.

And they definitely noticed me at Meg's.

Damon ignored everything and everyone and instead grabbed my arm and dragged me to a table right on the dividing line between diner and bar and next to a row of several pool tables. The same three friends I'd met twice previously were there waiting for us, as well as two girls I'd not seen before.

"Eike," Damon said, unceremoniously pushing me forward. "You've met Ed, Brett, and Ox."

Ed nodded, Brett smiled, and Ox offered me a hand the size of a reasonable slab of beef. We shook and I resisted the temptation to flex my hand to check for its operational capacity after he'd released me from his grip.

"It's Amos," he said, fixing me with a determined stare, "in case you were wondering, but you ever call me that and, well…"

Looking down at my hand and at the sheer bulk of him, I didn't need too much by way of imagination to guess what 'well' meant. I smiled and offered a half formal bow. Habit. He either didn't notice or didn't mind.

"I guess I can see why they call you Ox," I said to him.

"That's right," he grinned, "and don't you forget it."

Damon indicated the two girls.

"Ox's sister and Brett's girlfriend, Amy. And Ed's sister and Amy's friend, Cara."

They were both staring at me but when I acknowledged them, they smiled warmly at me.

"Ed was right," Amy said. "You really do look like some kind of model."

I shifted my feet and cleared my throat self-consciously, not knowing quite where to look.

"Knock it off, Amy," Ox growled. "You're embarrassing him. And us."

"Sorry," Amy said, sounding far from it. "Just saying."

"Well don't," Ox added.

Damon pushed me into a seat. "Drink?" he asked. "Beer?"

"I don't drink," I said, looking directly at him and hoping he wasn't the type to push. "A soda and lime or an iced water. No straw."

Damon smiled.

"Sure thing. What about everybody else? Another round?"

I reached for my wallet but he dropped a determined hand to my shoulder and shook his head. "Don't sweat it," he said. "One of the perks of being the owner's son."

"Your dad owns this?"

"Yeah, and about half the rest of the town. Lucky me."

He didn't sound particularly proud of this confession and I let it lie. Withdrawing his hand, he turned and left, returning a short time later with a loaded tray and distributing drinks to the table.

"Soda and lime," he said, putting my glass in front of me. "No straw."

I looked up at him and for a brief moment our eyes locked, before he turned away and sat down. I bit my cheek and stared at my hands knotted nervously in my lap.

"Ever play pool?" Ox asked, interrupting my thoughts.

"Some," I said, shifting my attention to him. "My brother used to play. He'd kinda force me to practice with him."

"Excellent," Ox grinned. "Then I take dibs on you as my partner."

I glanced back at Damon but he made no objection and I couldn't help but feel more than a small measure of disappointment.

It turned out I was better at pool than I'd given myself credit for and between Ox and I we made short and easy work of the respective pairs of Brett and Amy, and Damon and Ed, Cara apparently having no interest in playing. Ox was ecstatic.

"You can be my partner anytime," he grinned at me as we were getting up to leave. "That's the first time I've ever come away with an overall win."

"No way!" Amy objected. "Fair's fair. I get him next!"

"Not even!" Brett chimed in. "I've got him!"

"People, people," Damon interrupted, raising a hand for silence. "I found him. I brought him. And I'm claiming him. So, next time? He's all mine."

I was well aware he was referring to me playing pairs pool with him but for some reason my heart lurched all the same and I stared at the floor, completely flustered.

"See what you've done now?" Cara said. "You've embarrassed him. Again."

Damon put what I chose to interpret as a brotherly arm around my shoulders and I straightened and forced a smile. "Nonsense," Damon said. "He's merely somewhat overwhelmed by our enthusiasm. Isn't that right, Eike?"

I managed to respond with something in the affirmative, maybe, and Damon marched me back to his truck.

"I'm sorry," he said as we got in and he turned the key in the ignition. "I never thought to ask how you're doing, you know, after yesterday?"

To be honest, I'd not given it any thought myself but at mention of it the spots on my back where he'd applied the antiseptic suddenly became very warm. I shifted self-consciously in my seat. "Uh, I'm fine, I guess. Good as new."

I could feel his eyes on me but he made no further comment and instead turned his attention back to the road and put the truck in gear.

"Best I get you home," he said. "Early start, right?"

"Yeah," I agreed.

He stopped in the drive and as I opened the door, he put a hand on my arm, a conspicuous tingle following his touch up my arm and out into other places. I held my breath.

"I'm glad you came," he said, his voice low and tinged with something I didn't dare interpret.

"So am I," I admitted.

He released my arm and I got out of the truck and he was gone. I stood there, rubbing my arm where his hand had lain, and watched the red taillights of his truck vanish before turning to go inside.

I didn't see him the following day, or the one after that either, and I said nothing to Spex about my evening at Meg's. Friday evening after late tutorials, Spex and I were biking home.

"You want to come over later?" Spex asked. "Grab a couple pizzas and a movie? Or maybe check out my new version of Far Cry?"

There had been no mention of either Damon or Harper since Spex's revelation and, for the most part, things seemed to be back to normal though I admit Damon was only too often in my thoughts.

"Sure," I agreed. "But just remember I've got a real early start tomorrow so I can't stay too late. Maybe just a movie?"

"Right," Spex nodded. "The store. Me, too."

"No, stupid," I corrected him, shaking my head in mild exasperation. "Swimming."

"Oh. Right," Spex said, looking away.

"You forgot?" I asked.

Spex shrugged. "No, I mean, I guess not. I guess I just thought…" He faded into silence as we stopped at the top of his drive.

"You thought what?" I asked.

Spex rolled his shoulders and shifted his glasses up his nose. "I don't know. Just, you know, after what I told you…"

Again he faded into silence. I frowned and stared at him, stunned.

"You want me to stop swimming again?" I asked, struggling to keep my voice steady. "After you know what it took for me to get back in the water in the first place?"

"Well, no, of course not. I just, well, you could ask for another swim partner, couldn't you? At least?"

I gaped at him, slack-jawed in disbelief. "You're kidding, right?" I managed at last. "Why, why would I do that?"

Spex turned around and glared at me, his cheeks glowing angry red. "Because Damon's a prick, that's why!" he snapped. "And **I'm** supposed to be your friend!"

Wow. Ok, I hadn't seen that one coming and I was genuinely lost for words.

"Maybe I should just go home," I said after Spex had nothing further to add.

"Yeah, maybe you should," Spex agreed.

I rode off and didn't look back.

Grandmother was in the kitchen when I stalked moodily in through the back door and she made me come to the table for a cup of traditional green tea.

"A bad day?" she asked me. "There's a storm cloud hovering over your head."

I sighed deeply as I pulled out a chair and draped myself over it, running a hand through my already unruly hair. "Spex is angry with me," I admitted, "and I kind of feel it's not really my fault."

"Oh?" Grandmother prompted. "Did you two have a fight?"

"Not exactly," I said. "In fact, I don't really know what I've done wrong. Or maybe I do but I don't want to feel guilty about it. Oh, I don't know."

I dropped my head onto my folded arms and groaned and Grandmother put her hand on my head and tousled my hair, something I've always associated peculiarly with her and which always makes me feel like a child again. In a good way.

"Love is complicated," she observed sagely.

Love? Who mentioned anything about love? I looked up at her with a frown.

"Grandmother?"

"Love comes in many shapes," she said, "and has many wings with which to fly. And love," she added, bending down to look me in the eyes, "always requires patience."

"I ...." I had no idea how to respond to that, especially given I didn't actually know what she was talking about.

"Give him time," Grandmother advised. "He'll work this out and he'll be back."

All right, so that much at least made sense. "Thank you, Grandmother."

She ruffled my hair some more and smiled fondly at me and I fought back a sudden desire to cry. *Stop it*, I admonished myself.

"You're a good boy, Eike. The heavens will smile on you, I promise."

Not helping. I blinked rapidly and took a deep breath. I didn't completely know what she was talking about, but somehow, I felt better.

Chapter Seven

Spex didn't call me back that Friday night and I went to bed early.

I didn't sleep well. I tossed and I turned and I tangled myself in my bedding and my dreams were filled with random visions, past mixed with present.

"Boys aren't pretty, and boys don't like boys."

Xia, biking beside me, and then his face bursting into flames.

"Are you shy?"

Damon, his Caribbean-blue eyes, the warmth of his lips lingering on mine…

"I was just wondering if you've ever had a girlfriend."

Spex, unwilling to meet my gaze, his brown eyes huge behind his glasses.

Smoke and flame and water and pain all swirling in one chaotic kaleidoscopic jumble and me caught in it like a leaf in a maelstrom.

I woke up well before my alarm and got out of bed.

Grandfather was also already awake and sitting at the kitchen table with his pot of tea when I shambled downstairs. He looked at me but said nothing and merely found me a cup and poured me tea. My swim bag was sitting on the counter waiting for me.

I fell into a chair and sat with my elbows propped on the table and my head in my hands, staring into the swirling depths of my tea, or maybe my memories. I felt completely wrecked and certainly not in the least inspired by the thought of once again facing the demons of the pool even knowing, or perhaps *because of* knowing, Damon would be there.

Grandfather sipped his tea and continued his silence.

Eventually, I roused myself sufficiently to drink my tea and force myself to my feet. It was time to go. I grabbed my swim bag reluctantly from the counter.

"Eike?" Grandfather said as I reached the door.

"Yes, Grandfather?"

"The right path is the one that brings us joy," Grandfather said, "not the one we believe others think we should take."

What was with my grandparents lately? I didn't know which I found more disconcerting: Spex's odd behaviour or my grandparents' sudden penchant for profound and obscure observations.

"Thank you, Grandfather."

I walked out into the barest hint of pre-dawn, got on my bike, and headed for the pool.

Damon was waiting for me.

"I have to admit I was wondering if you'd come," he observed as I locked up my bike.

Despite the ridiculously early hour, he was looking wide awake and, once again, spectacular. His rough-cropped summer-bleached hair was tousled in a way in which it was difficult to know whether it was accidental or styled and he was wearing black track-pants with 'infinity' symbols down the legs and a black sleeveless tee-shirt with a jacket of some kind slung casually over one shoulder. I kept my eyes lowered and did my best not to stare.

"Why wouldn't I?" I asked. "I said I would."

Damon shrugged and picked up the bag at his feet. "Considering what happened last time, and given how Parker feels about me…" He left the sentence unfinished and leapt the steps into the pool building three at a time. "Come on," he called back, not giving me opportunity to respond. "Coach is already here."

"Right then," Coach Harmon said after we'd changed and were standing poolside, "let's handle this a little differently, shall we?"

I was down with that. I had no desire to experience a repeat of last time.

"So, what's the new plan, Coach?" Damon asked, dropping to the edge of the pool and swinging his long, tan legs in the water.

"I think from right about where you're at might be a wise idea," Coach Harmon said. "Let's just get into the water a little more quietly, shall we?"

Yes, I was pretty much down with that, too. I dropped down beside Damon and he slipped into the water and drifted away from the edge.

"Coming?" he asked, dipping his head and flicking water from his hair as appeared to be his habit.

I took a deep breath and allowed myself to slide into the water.

I could feel it, feel the darkness want to reach out and once again envelop me in its unrelenting embrace, and I fought back the terror as I descended into the water. Before it could fully ensnare me in its grasp, Damon's powerful arms wrapped themselves around me and I leaned back against the welcome security of his broad chest, struggling to steady my laboured breathing which came in short, sharp gasps of near panic. Allowing him to take my weight, I closed my eyes and floated and, gradually, the darkness withdrew.

"I'm letting you go now," Damon murmured quietly in my ear, "but I'm not leaving. If you need me, just reach out and touch me."

I knew the words were not meant as they came across but I tensed and, as a result, sank. Damon drew me back to the surface and I spluttered water.

"What the hell, dude! Relax already. I said I wasn't going anywhere."

But you also said I could touch you… I allowed myself to lean into him all the same and we floated some more.

"Ok," he said after we'd drifted half the length of the pool. "Let's try that one more time. Put your hand out and I'll be right here."

I focused my attention on the proximity of his body to mine as he pushed me gently clear of him so we were now floating side by side and, as he'd instructed, I reached out a hand and laid it against him, clasping his shoulder. I was instantly reassured both by his presence and by the anticipation of his intervention should the darkness again reach out to claim me. His body was slick and warm and solid beneath my fingers and alongside my own, and suddenly the water felt less like an enemy and more like an old and familiar friend. I closed my eyes and let the water hold me, let it enfold me and caress me, and Damon's body slipped from my fingers. I started, swallowed water and sank, and again Damon drew me back to the surface.

"Again," he murmured gently.

This time, he was so close to me our bodies were practically a single indistinguishable entity. Slowly, languidly, he rolled, and I instinctively followed suit. His body flexed and, like a dolphin, he swept forwards and, again, I followed. Side by side, his body linked with mine, arms outstretched, our every movement perfectly synchronised, we cut through the water and the familiar sense of freedom coursed through my veins. I slipped free of him so we were independent of each other though still in perfect harmony and, before I knew it, we hit the end of the pool, flipped in unison, and were powering back towards where we'd begun.

I was aware of him, aware of his powerful and yet supple movements matching mine but maybe halfway back, the surge hit me. It was familiar, even though it had been far too long since I'd felt it. In that moment, *everything* ceased to exist. Damon disappeared, memory disappeared, *time* disappeared. When the surge took me, there was only the water and me. I hit the end wall and broke water with an ear to ear grin and two strokes later, Damon appeared beside me.

"Holy fucking shit!" he breathed, swiping water from his face. "What the hell was that?"

Coach Harmon was standing above me and his expression mirrored Damon's exclamation of incredulity.

"Jesus, son," he said, staring at the stopwatch in his hand and then back at me. "You really *can* swim!"

Coach Harmon only allowed me a few more laps after that, with Damon as my pacesetter and the aim, Coach Harmon said, to allow me a gradual re-introduction to the rhythm of swimming.

"Not much point in blowing all the fuses on the first day, right?" Coach Harmon said. "Slow is fast.'

As I hauled myself out of the pool, every muscle in my body screaming in complaint, I realised he was right. Damon had to help me upright and I barely resisted leaning on him as we returned to the change rooms.

"That," Damon admitted as we turned on showers, "was in … credible! I don't know quite *what* that was, but I have to admit I've never seen anyone swim like that before."

"Thank you," I murmured, feeling self-conscious and as if I'd upstaged him somehow. "I, um, thanks."

"You're going to be a force to be reckoned with," Damon continued as he stepped under the water. "Guess I'm going to have to up my game some. It's on, buddy!"

"Is that a challenge?" I asked him, putting my hands against the back wall and dropping my head between my arms to let the hot water ease the knots out of my aching back.

"I guess it is," Damon agreed. "How's your back?"

I rolled my head and heard my neck click. "I'm feeling it," I admitted.

Suddenly, out of nowhere, he was behind me and running soapy hands down my shoulders. I jumped and nearly collected my head against the wall.

"Shit, Damon!"

"Calm down," he said, calmly. "Just taking some of the knots out for you. It's not like I'm hitting on you or something."

"Oh. Shit."

My heart pounded in my ears like the percussion section of a marching band and I struggled to catch my breath. Damon rolled his hands firmly down my back and, unconsciously, I groaned. I'd clearly had no idea the impact returning to the water would have on me. Damon's hands stopped moving.

"Sorry," he said. "The scars?"

"No," I reassured him, "but I'm fairly sure every muscle in my body thinks it's been assaulted with a solid, extremely heavy object."

Damon laughed and his hands resumed their efforts. "It's been a while, hasn't it?" he prompted quietly.

"Just over eighteen months," I agreed, fighting to keep the strain from my voice.

Damon whistled through his teeth. "Out of the water eighteen months, all these scars, and you can still swim like that? You must have been a freaking porpoise before… before…" He stalled and his hands once again became still. "I'm sorry," he said, pulling back and stepping out of the shower. "I didn't mean, ah, hell… I'm sorry."

I straightened and, though I sincerely regretted losing the contact of his hands, was amazed at how much better I already felt. I turned off the water.

"It's ok," I said. "It's not as if I can pretend it never happened, you know? And in a way, it'd be nice to not be avoiding it all the time, if you know what I mean. It happened, it was shit, but the bottom line is... it happened and it was shit. Sometimes, I'd like to be able to say so." I turned around and Damon handed me a towel.

"Yeah," he said with a deep sigh. "I know exactly what you mean."

"Harper," I said, before I could stop to think.

"Yeah. Harper."

And he turned away from me and began to get dressed. I bit my lip. Shit, had I touched a raw nerve and offended him?

"Let's get together for lunch," he said. "When will you get off at the store? I'll pick you up."

He arrived at the store while I was unloading cartons of canned goods from the delivery truck and he pitched in to give a hand.

"Geez," he observed as he took a carton and hoisted it onto the trolley. "No wonder you're in such good shape."

I handed him another carton.

"You work out, too?" he asked, putting down the box and wiping his forehead with the back of his hand.

"I used to do Hapkido but I haven't done that in a while, either," I replied.

"Hapkido?"

"A Korean martial art. There isn't anywhere for me to train here and I'm not ready to change disciplines yet."

"Oh."

We finished up and he followed me to the rest room so we could wash our hands and faces.

"Is that it?" he asked. "I don't mind helping out if there's more to do before we go."

"No, that's it," I told him. "Grandfather will be more than happy for me to go now."

His truck was out in front of the store and as I got in, I saw the large box in the back seat.

"Lunch," Damon informed me. "I thought we might go up to the reservoir.'

I'd not heard from Spex all day but I thought of him now with a twinge of guilt and it must have shown on my face because Damon patted me reassuringly on the shoulder.

"Don't worry about Parker," he said. "He'll come around. He'll have to. You're the only friend he's got."

"How did you know I was thinking about Spex?"

Damon gave me a sympathetic smile. "I know the look," he admitted. "And I happen to know you're not exactly overwhelmed with friends, either."

I averted my eyes self-consciously and he grinned.

"Not to worry," he reassured me. "Now you've got me, too."

I wasn't entirely sure how I should interpret this.

It was a hot day and the reservoir wasn't too much of a drive but there was nobody there when we arrived. Damon parked the truck and got out and fetched the box from the back seat.

"Come on," he said. "There's a spot just up under those trees with a really good view out over the valley."

I followed him obediently as he led the way.

He'd gone to quite some trouble with the contents of the box and there was no shortage of food as well as various cans of soda and bottles of water and juice.

"I'd have grabbed us some beers," he said as he cracked the tab on a Coke, "but I'm driving and I seem to remember you don't drink."

He turned to look at me. "Choice, or not permitted to?" he asked, eyebrows raised in curiosity.

I paused with a bottle of water halfway to my lips and looked at him. He shrugged.

"Your grandparents seem fairly traditional," he said by way of explanation.

This was true but they weren't the reason behind my personal choice.

"They wouldn't object if I chose to drink," I said. "They're fairly relaxed with me. Very relaxed even. Circumstances perhaps." I shrugged and stared out at the summer haze over the valley. "I don't know if they'd have been so easy-going if, well, you know."

Damon nodded and his gaze followed mine out into the distance. "Do you think about them much?" he asked. "I mean, I know you probably do but, you know, is it consciously or is it more, like, accidental?"

I knew exactly what he meant and although nobody had ever asked me quite as directly before, I was glad he'd brought it up.

"Sometimes," I said, "as in sometimes it's by choice. Mostly, it all just comes back to me without warning. Like a repeating nightmare."

"Sometimes I can almost feel her sitting next to me," Damon said, his voice flat and distant. "As if I could reach out and touch her. But when I turn around to look for her, she isn't there anymore."

"You were really close then?" I asked, knowing he was referring to Harper and feeling an irrational stab of jealousy.

"Yeah," he admitted, his voice low and soft and heartbreakingly sad.

"So, why'd you break up then?" I asked, at the same time wondering how far this might stretch our tentative same-page relationship.

Damon sighed very deeply and bent his knees, wrapping his arms around them and resting his chin on them. "I loved her," he said, "but I wasn't *in* love with her, if you get me. And I couldn't give her what she wanted. In the end, trying to please her and not being able to very nearly broke the both of us. I didn't feel as if I really had a choice. I was trying to set her free."

"What do you mean," I asked, "that you couldn't give her what she wanted? What was it she wanted, exactly?"

He released his knees and stretched his legs, putting his arms behind him and leaning back to stare at the sky. "She wanted commitment, security, expressions of affection, comfort, contact... *things*, things I wasn't ready for, some things I was *never* going to be ready for. I don't know. No matter what I gave her or offered her to compensate for the things I *couldn't* give her, it never seemed to be enough."

I tried not to stare at him though his presence was as magnetic now as it had been on every other occasion I'd been in his company. Perhaps due to his melancholy mood, even more so.

"So, what happened?"

"She said she was going to do it," Damon admitted, so quietly I barely heard him, "but she'd said that before, so many times. She'd even made several attempts or at least made out she had, every time she thought I wasn't sufficiently committed, you know? She'd cut herself or take something or do something reckless to make me prove to her I was still there for her." He blinked and turned away "In the end, I just couldn't take it anymore and..."

His voice tapered off and his head bowed and I saw just how close he was to tears. I shuffled closer to him so our shoulders touched.

"I didn't believe her," he whispered. "When she called to say she'd done it, that she'd over-dosed, I told her, I told her…" His voice caught and I heard the sheer depth of his agony. "I told her she was a stupid, lying bitch, and then I hung up on her."

"Parker knows she called you?" I asked, shocked at his revelation but keeping my voice steady so he wouldn't know. I suspected I already knew the answer.

"That was the last phone call she ever made," Damon sighed. "The last person to ever speak to her was me and they found her phone still in her hand."

He fell silent but I could feel him shaking against me and I knew he was crying. What else could I do? I put an arm around his shoulders and he immediately turned to bury his face against me, and wept.

I don't know how long we sat there. The sun waned and shadows began to appear across the hills and still we sat. Eventually, of course, Damon's tears stopped and some while after that he released his grip on me and straightened, to stare blankly out over the valley.

"I've never told anybody that before," he said. "Not a single soul. Ever."

"Thank you," I said. "For trusting me."

"Ah, Eike," Damon sighed, half to himself, "you obviously have no idea how easy that is."

I held my thoughts in check but couldn't help but think how much I wished I could say the same. How much can I trust you, Damon? How much can I tell you? I glanced across at him and wished I had the courage to ask.

Chapter Eight

It was far later than I'd anticipated when we drove home and Grandfather and Grandmother looked genuinely concerned when we walked into the house.

"Eike!" Grandmother exclaimed. "Where have you been?"

I dropped my head and offered a low bow in remorse.

"I'm so sorry, Grandmother, we completely lost track of time. We... I should have called."

"Are you all right? You're not hurt, are you? You didn't have an accident?"

Grandfather put a soothing hand on Grandmother's shoulder.

"You can see he's all right, mother. Why don't you go and make some tea?" he said. "Eike, your grandmother was very worried. *I*, too, was worried. Where have you been?"

"I'm so terribly sorry, Grandfather. Damon and I..."

I didn't know what else to say and I looked helplessly at my grandfather. He sighed and shook his head.

"It's all right, Eike. You're home now, and you're safe. I suppose that is the most important thing."

Grandfather seemed to notice Damon for the first time, standing silently just inside the front door and shifting from foot to foot uncomfortably.

"Is this Damon?" Grandfather asked.

"Yes, Grandfather. Yes, this is Damon," I said, relieved to change the subject and perhaps break the tension. "He's the captain of the swim team and he's also my swim partner, you know, the one who's been helping me with getting back to swimming."

Grandfather offered Damon a short, courteous bow and Damon, much to my surprise, gave Grandfather a bow in response.

"It's a pleasure to meet you, sir," Damon said. "And I'm sorry if we worried you. It's all my fault. I was the driver."

Grandfather smiled and shook his head.

"Time escapes us all from time to time," he said, "especially when we're young. Please, come in, and welcome to our home."

He indicated Damon follow us through to the parlour and take a seat just as Grandmother came in with the tea tray.

"Have you eaten?" Grandmother asked. "You've been gone since midday; you must be starving."

"I'm really sorry, Grandmother," I said again. "Please don't worry about us. I can take care of it and find us something."

"Nonsense," Grandmother said, happy to have something to which to switch her attention now she'd relieved her anxiety. "Please, have some tea and I'll go and fetch something. I won't be long."

She bustled back to the kitchen and Grandfather looked appraisingly at Damon.

"I can see the swimmer in you," he observed quietly, "but there's something more, isn't there? Do you fight?"

"I'm sorry, sir, what?" Damon asked, taken aback by Grandfather's question.

Grandfather looked at me, waiting for me to put the question in the right words.

"I think he's wondering if you do martial arts or something, not whether you're a thug," I translated with a smile.

"Yes," Grandfather agreed with a nod. "Do you fight?"

"Ohh," Damon said. "Oh, right. Yes, sir. I do Taekwondo."

He did? I hadn't known and I looked at him with even greater respect although I wasn't entirely surprised. Grandfather nodded, also impressed.

"Very good, very good," he said. "And you are our Eike's new friend?"

Damon grinned. "Yes, sir. I am."

For some reason, this simple statement made me feel profoundly happy.

At that moment, the phone rang.

I could hear Grandmother answering it and then she put her head around the door and called me.

"Eike, phone. It's Parker."

Spex? Calling the house? I got up, confused, and felt my pockets. My phone. Where on earth was my phone? Still patting at myself, though it was apparent my phone wasn't on me, I walked over and took the phone from Grandmother.

"Hello?"

"Eike! Where have you been? I've been calling you all day!"

"You have? I'm sorry but I don't know what I've done with my phone. I think I might have lost it somewhere."

There was a prolonged silence and I wondered if Spex was trying to decide whether or not to believe me.

"What's up?" I asked him.

"I, uh, I wanted to say I'm sorry, you know, for yesterday," Spex said. "I was being a jerk."

"Yes," I agreed. "You were."

"No need to be harsh," Spex objected, sounding put out.

"I was only agreeing with you," I pointed out. "And you were. A jerk."

Spex laughed begrudgingly. "Yeah," he admitted. "I guess that's true. Truce?"

"Truce," I replied.

"You busy?" Spex asked.

A guilty heat rose to colour my face. "Yeah, I am a bit," I admitted, not elaborating.

"Oh. Are you going to be free later?"

At this point, I wasn't too sure. Damon hadn't said anything about any further plans but still…

"I don't know yet," I said.

"Oh, ok. Um, well, do you want to call me if you're free? I could come over and we could watch a movie, or something."

"Yeah, ok, I'll do that," I said, biting my lip as the guilt nipped at my conscience. "I'll catch you later then. Ok?"

"Yeah, ok." He paused. "Eike?"

"Yeah, Spex?"

"I really am sorry." And he hung up.

Grandmother was standing behind me as I hung the phone in its cradle.

"Everything all right?" she asked me.

"He apologised," I said.

She nodded and smiled as she patted my shoulder in that way only grandmothers seem able to do.

"I said he'd come around."

"Yes, you did," I agreed, smiling back at her.

But my eyes drifted to where Damon was sitting talking to Grandfather in the parlour. Grandmother followed my gaze.

"He's handsome," she observed softly.

I started and turned around, blushing, and she put a gentle hand on my head.

"Be honest with yourself, Eike," she said. "But trust your friends enough to be honest with them, too."

I had more than a sneaking suspicion she knew far more than her words might on the surface indicate and my blush deepened. She tousled my hair in that familiar way of hers and returned to the kitchen while I leaned with my face to the wall and tried to re-group my thoughts.

"Why don't we go up to your room for some privacy, give your grandparents some space?"

Damon. I was startled, and he was standing so close behind me that, as I turned, we ended up face to face, our noses almost touching. I stalled and held my breath and Damon smiled.

"What?" he asked softly. "This bother you?"

He leaned in even closer so it was now our mouths that were almost touching. He tipped his head and I swear his lips brushed across mine. Adrenalin coursed through me, making me giddy, and I gasped and pulled back, collecting my head against the wall. Damon didn't move but the smile spread.

"You *are* shy," he said. "Come on, show me your room."

He reached for my arm and turned with me as I indicated the stairs. Reluctantly, I followed him as I brushed a thumb across my lips. Did that really just happen? We got to the top of the stairs and Damon led me unerringly to my room, not difficult as it happened to have my name plastered across the door in bold black letters, and half dragged, half pushed me inside. Once inside, he released my arm and firmly closed the door.

"I've been wondering what your room might look like," he said, looking around him with obvious interest.

I breathed a silent sigh of relief that I'd developed a dedicated habit of keeping an orderly room and stood decidedly uneasily as he took two long strides to throw himself on my bed.

"What are you waiting for?" he asked, making himself comfortable. "Are you just going to keep on standing there?"

I remained where I was, staring at him in apprehension. He was beginning to make me nervous. "What are you doing?" I asked him.

Damon grinned. "I'd have thought that was fairly obvious," he said. "I'm making myself at home."

Yes, actually. That much *was* fairly obvious. The question was, *why*? I still made no effort to move and Damon sat up, propping pillows behind him. His brow furrowed as he studied me.

"Do I make you nervous, Eike?" he asked.

I caught my lower lip between my teeth and contemplated how best to answer him, once again opting for the truth. "I'm wondering what *exactly* you're doing," I said.

Damon's face shadowed a fraction as he considered the implications of my statement and he suddenly looked a whole lot less certain of himself.

"Don't you like me, Eike?"

The surprise must have registered on my face because he almost smiled again before his frown returned.

"Of course I do," I answered him, "but now I'm wondering what it is you mean by that…"

Damon looked into his lap and his hands knotted. Nervous? Damon? He hadn't struck me as the nervous type. I took a step closer. Perhaps the emotion from his confession earlier lingered but he looked very much as if he was once again about to cry. I didn't know. I didn't know him well enough to even begin to guess what might be going on with him.

"Damon?"

Damon sighed deeply and swung his legs off the bed. "I'm sorry. This was a mistake," he said, his voice heavy. "I think…" He paused and rose unsteadily to his feet. "I think I misunderstood."

I couldn't help it. He looked so uncertain standing there, so lost and insecure, I wanted to comfort him. I took the last steps to reach him and laid a tentative hand on his shoulder.

'I wish I knew what to say," I said softly. "I'm trying to figure you out."

He stood there, not moving, and then he pushed me gently away. "I assumed and I shouldn't have. I'm sorry, Eike. I think I should go."

My arms dropped to my sides and I stared at him. Assumed? Assumed what?

"Damon?"

But Damon was already at the door.

"I'll see you Monday night? Seven? At the pool?"

"Um, yeah, ok, sure. Is that when we're swimming again, then?"

"Yes," Damon said, "and, for what it's worth, I'm sorry. And thanks, by the way. For today. It was important to me."

Before I could respond, he was gone and I heard his urgent footsteps descending the stairs before fading as he reached the hall and then the front door. There was the click of the door and I sat on my bed and wondered what the hell had just happened.

I was thirteen when I discovered what my brother had meant when he'd said pretty boys get into trouble.

My brother had a best friend, Paul, whom he'd known since first grade. They were inseparable. They played ball and rode bikes and went hiking and swimming and did what boys generally do when they're with their friends. Of course, there were other friends too, quite a number of them because Xia in particular was very popular, but Xia and Paul were almost a couple, they spent so much time together.

It never occurred to me 'til it was too late that Paul spent so much time at our house because it was as much me as it was Xia that he wanted to see.

"Come play hoops with us, Eike", "Come riding with us, Eike", "Come camping with us, Eike", "Come to the movies with us, Eike"...

I at least worked out quickly enough that Xia wasn't half as enthusiastic about having his younger brother tagging along as Paul was and besides, I had my own friends so often I declined or I'd take a friend with me but often, too often, it would be just the three of us. Paul always seemed able to contrive to have me closest to him and he'd touch me, seemingly casually; an arm over my shoulders, a hand on my knee, close but never overtly so. I know I was oblivious at the time and I can only assume Xia was too.

One day, Paul was waiting outside the cultural centre where I attended Hapkido classes. And he was on his own.

"Eike, I'll give you a ride home," he said, opening the door to his car.

"My bike," I recall saying.

Paul had shrugged and smiled encouragingly. "I'll get it for you later. Come on, I'll treat you to a burger and shake on the way home."

I had no reason to be suspicious. This was my older brother's best and oldest friend and I'd known him practically my whole life. I got in the car.

He didn't drive me home. He drove me out of town and stopped in a layby.

"What are we doing?" I asked, still not really knowing what was going on but beginning to get nervous.

Paul had unbuckled his seat belt and put his hand on my knee as he leaned towards me.

"Come on, Eike. You know what we're doing, don't you?" he breathed into my ear, his grip on my knee tightening.

"No, no I don't. I want to go home now, Paul."

Paul grabbed my shoulders and, before I could even comprehend what he was doing, he was kissing me. I whipped my head back and pushed at him as hard as I could, spitting the taste of him from my mouth, but I was thirteen and he was seventeen and practically a grown man. He put an arm across my chest and held me down and put a hand in my crotch and grabbed me. Hard. It hurt!

"Come on, Eike." He was breathing hard now and his breath was hot and wet on my face. "You know you want it. You've always wanted it, haven't you? Let me be the first."

His grip on my crotch tightened and he pushed himself onto me, forcing his mouth onto mine. With his other hand he squeezed my cheeks so that he could push his tongue between my lips and into my mouth. My arms were trapped between his much larger body and mine and my face was caught in his grip and so I did the only thing I could think of; I gave in. I gave a groan and sort of sagged into him and he relaxed, just for a moment, a moment long enough to release my cheeks and push his tongue even deeper into my mouth.

I bit him.

He yelped and flung himself backwards, leaving me with the metallic taste of blood in my mouth, and then he hit me, his open hand catching me a solid blow directly up one side of my face. My head smacked into the side window and perhaps I even blacked out for a moment. The next thing I knew he was fully on top of me and his jeans were open.

And that was when I began to fight.

Even in a confined space and still buckled in, I knew my Hapkido, and I got enough of an advantage to break free and get out of the car.

I began to run, though my head was swimming and my body ached, not least in my groin where he'd been grabbing me, and the last I heard was him screaming after me, "You little fuck! You tell anyone and I'll kill you!"

I never did tell anyone, especially not Xia. But it wasn't because of Paul's threats, it was because of what Xia had said. *'Pretty boys get into trouble.'* And I simply didn't want to confirm that maybe that was what I was, a *pretty boy*. Paul stopped coming over and though I'd never told anyone, and I can't imagine Paul ever did, sometimes I would catch my brother looking at me and I wondered if he'd guessed. When I finally made it home that night, with a black eye and a multitude of bruises, I said I'd fallen off my bike, but I always wondered if he knew.

But we never talked about it.

Sitting on my bed now, in the wake of Damon's sudden departure, I couldn't help but think of Paul. The touches, the contact, the hints I'd missed of where his mind had been at. Paul wasn't gay, in fact, he was probably one of the biggest homophobes I'd ever met. He'd only been infatuated with me. He'd wanted to try it with me, just me, that was all. I knew this now and since Paul, I'd seen the signs again on several uncomfortable occasions. *Pretty boys get into trouble.*

I felt sick.

Damon putting antiseptic on my back. Damon rubbing my back with soapy hands. Damon leaning over me, his lips brushing mine. Damon, *'I'm sorry. I misunderstood.'*

I immediately wanted nothing more than to run.

I got up and changed into running gear and grabbed my iPod and earplugs and as I was about to leave my room, Grandmother knocked at my door.

"Eike, dinner's ready."

I opened the door and Grandmother's face fell when she looked at me.

"Eike?"

"I'm sorry, Grandmother, I… I have to go out."

"And your friend?" Grandmother asked, looking past me into my room.

She'd obviously neither seen nor heard him leave.

"He had to go home," I said. "Is it all right if I have dinner later?"

I could see the questions she wanted to ask but she nodded and stepped aside. I walked down the stairs with quivering legs, let myself out into the pale shadows of a warm summer night, and as soon as I got out of the drive… I began to run.

Running is a lot like swimming except you can do it pretty much anytime and anywhere. When you're running, time stops. When you're running, there are no questions, only answers, because there's only you and the road you're running on. Running is one of the ultimate freedoms. Nobody questions you when you're running. If they judge you, you won't know. The encroaching twilight was a friend hiding me from enemy eyes and shielding me from bias and prejudice. Running gave me power. I ran and ran and ran.

I don't know for how long I ran or how much distance I ended up covering and I definitely don't think I consciously had a destination in mind but eventually, at around the time I'd about run myself out, I found myself at the reservoir where I'd been with Damon earlier in the day. Fortunately for me, though I admit this surprised me, there was still nobody there. I guess I'd expected, given the relative isolation and the spectacular view, that it might be a popular lover's lane, that there'd be cars parked up and couples steaming up the windows or, at the very least, groups of college students gathered around make-shift bonfires, drinking. But there weren't and I was glad. I jogged slowly to the trees under which we'd had lunch and under which Damon had also confided in me his history with Harper and threw myself on my back on the grass to stare at the sky. My favourite K-pop playlist kept me company as I lay there, my legs aching and my breath still hitching in my chest and my heart pounding behind my ribs and maybe, for a while, I dozed off.

I don't know how long he'd been standing there staring down at me while I lay with my eyes closed, oblivious to him.

Damon.

Somehow, his presence didn't really surprise me. Perhaps I'd even known he would come here. Maybe that was how I'd come to be here myself, like some kind of psychic magnetism.

"Hello again," he said. "Can I sit with you?"

"Free parking," I said, waving a hand at the grass and not bothering to move.

He dropped gracefully to the ground beside me and lay down and put his arms behind his head.

"What're you listening to?" he asked.

"Nothing now," I said, holding the iPod over him and indicating the blank screen. "But, if you must know, it was K-pop."

"K-pop?" he asked.

I shrugged, not that he could see me. "Korean pop music. B.A.P., NCT, Noir, Stray Kids..."

"Oh," he said, his tone indicating he had absolutely no idea who or what I was talking about.

We lay in silence.

"I'm sorry," he said after a while. "About earlier."

"So you said," I acknowledged.

"It's just, I think I like you, Eike," he continued, like he didn't want to but couldn't stop himself. "I think I like you probably a good deal more than is good for either of us."

Chapter Nine

The words hit me with all the force of a wrecking ball against glass.

I think I like you, Eike. I think I like you probably a good deal more than is good for either of us…

Xia's words echoed in my head and inwardly, I cringed.

Pretty boys get in trouble.

Paul.

You know you want it.

And now Damon.

I think I like you probably a good deal more than is good for either of us.

Did he even know what he meant? Did I? My head spun and I felt sick. In truth, I wanted to hear exactly what he'd said, *I like you*, but now the moment was here, I didn't know what to do with it.

I'm sorry. I misunderstood.

I stared at Damon and tried to organise the thoughts racing through my head. What was it he thought he'd misunderstood? What was he trying to tell me and was it really what I thought it might be? What do I do now?

Love comes in many shapes and has many wings with which to fly.

Grandmother.

The right path is the one which brings us joy, not the one we believe others think we should take.

Grandfather.

There was only one way to find out what I wanted to know. I leant over Damon, closed my eyes, and kissed him.

I'd never kissed a boy. I'd never kissed a girl. I'd never kissed anyone at all. Paul had kissed *me* but that had been a different thing altogether, and now, here I was, kissing Damon.

Somehow, my lips knew exactly where they were meant to be and somehow, it felt perfectly right. And the response was instantaneous and completely unexpected.

Damon sighed and his mouth opened to mine and his arms came up and enfolded me and drew me down to him. His lips were softer than I'd anticipated and his mouth was hot and smoky and eager. If I knew nothing about kisses, it was clear Damon knew enough for both of us and, though I know how clichéd it must sound, I honestly could have drowned inside that kiss. We finally came up for air but only for Damon to pull breathlessly at my tee-shirt.

"Take it off," he muttered, his voice hoarse with emotion. "Take it off and get over here."

I hesitated for a moment but then I was stripping it off even as he threw aside his own and then his hands were on my body, his fingers tracing my scars, his mouth tasting my skin, his breath hot and rapid and matching my own. He went no further and though the ache, the actual physical pain, was unlike anything I'd ever experienced, I understood this was as far as it would go. And I was grateful, though it was easy to tell his pain must surely equal mine.

We eventually ended up with me on my back, Damon straddling me, hands either side of my shoulders, looking down on me, and if I'd been slick with sweat when I'd finished running, it was as nothing in comparison to the state I was now in. My lips felt swollen and bruised but it was a sweet pain and they ached for more, and I reached up a hand to him. He pulled back and evaded me.

"Just a moment," he whispered. "I just want to look."

I sank back and allowed him his moment, just as content to have my own.

"Where did you come from?" he asked, more of himself than of me.

I said nothing, the question not intended for an answer, and watched him. He was gentler the next time he lowered his mouth to mine, tracing my face with his mouth, kissing my eyelids, my forehead, my cheeks, my throat.

If I'd never kissed anybody before, I'd certainly never touched anybody before and most definitely not the way I touched him. I'd never before been able to appreciate the true beauty of skin over muscle when it flows beneath your fingertips or the form and shape of a body not your own and to explore Damon was like a fantasy, a surreal experience of pure visceral joy of which I couldn't get enough.

We explored mutually and, though there was a limit to our wanderings, it was enough, even if only barely. Eventually, however, we rolled apart to lie side by side, our breathing finally returning to some semblance of normality and the immediate adrenalin of the moment subsiding. Damon arranged himself in such a way that he could pull me into the crook of one arm, the other meanwhile languidly stroking my bare upper body.

"Hey," I murmured half-heartedly, flexing beneath his electric touch. "You want this to start all over again?"

He chuckled, his amusement vibrating in my ear. "Maybe," he admitted, but he stopped anyway, to draw me more tightly against him.

I shifted to my side and threw an arm across his chest and a leg over his and there was a conspicuous pressure against my thigh, matched by an ache of my own, which we both continued to ignore.

"We should probably get back," I observed, wanting to do nothing of the kind.

"Probably," Damon agreed, brushing his fingers up my side and raising instant gooseflesh on my skin. "Your grandparents will definitely be worrying about you and, once again, it appears to be my fault."

"Hmm," I sighed, in no hurry to move.

Damon slid out from under me and kissed me, very lightly. "Come on," he said, levering himself upright. "I'll take you home."

I rose reluctantly to my feet.

"Hey," Damon said as I raised my arms to put my tee-shirt back on. "You're bleeding."

"Huh? How can you even tell?" I asked, trying to turn my head to look, unsuccessfully, at my own back.

It was dark and all we had was moonlight, even if it was from an almost full moon.

"Trust me," he said, his fingers tracing my back, the electric tingle I associated peculiarly with him, following his touch. "I can tell."

Trust you? My thoughts flashed back to my earlier unasked question of him and I smiled to myself. Trust you, Damon? Yes, perhaps I do.

"Oh," I said, my skin shivering in the wake of his fingertips. "Hardly surprising. Don't worry about it."

He dropped his head and kissed my back.

"Jesus, Damon! Did you just kiss my blood?"

Damon laughed and grabbed me around the waist to run his tongue up my back. "Yes," he admitted. "I think I just did."

And then he darted away from me before I could respond any further. *Christ!*

"Come on," he called. "Truck's over here."

I spent the drive back to my house with a maelstrom of overwhelming emotion swirling through my head. Damon laid his hand on my thigh as he drove and I allowed myself to lay my own hand over it, entwining my fingers with his. Was this real? My body, *everything*, ached with a kind of detached euphoria, like a surreal out-of-body delirium.

"What are you thinking about?" Damon asked, glancing across at me even as he used his knees to steady the wheel while somehow managing to cross an arm over to change gears. Like everything about Damon: impressive.

"You," I said honestly.

"You're grinning," Damon observed. "Like the Cheshire cat."

"I should think I should be," I agreed.

"I've not seen you smile like that before," Damon said. "It suits you."

Like who you want, but just don't let anyone know if you like boys.

My smile slipped.

"Hey," Damon said, his hand flexing on my thigh. "What'd you do that for? Why'd you stop smiling?"

I looked out the window and suddenly I was neither quite so happy nor quite so sure of myself.

"What will people say?" I whispered, turning to look at our intertwined fingers and fighting the urge to pull free. "What happens next?"

I was afraid, very afraid. I was afraid of what people might say but I was even more afraid this might be it, that Damon might have had his fun and by tomorrow he might wish to pretend it had never happened at all. I dared not look at him and my heart sat like a stone in my chest.

Damon laughed and it was strong and powerful and carefree and full of pure, honest joy. I stared at him.

"Who gives a fuck?" he said. "I don't give a sodding damn what anybody thinks."

My heart soared.

Damon pulled up at my house and I unbuckled my seat belt. Damon reached out and put a hand on my arm.

"Wait," he said. "Going without a goodbye?"

I grinned. Hell no, I wasn't.

I leaned towards him and we put our hands behind each other's necks, drawing each other closer, claiming each other with our kiss as if for each of us it was less a kiss than a brand of ownership. My lips burned and my mouth ached as we withdrew from each other.

"I'll call you tomorrow," he said.

"Promise?"

"I promise."

I got out of the truck and watched him pull out of the driveway, the taillights fading far too quickly into the darkness. Putting my hand to my mouth, I walked to the door.

"Hey."

I must have leapt a good couple of feet into the air and I nearly drop-kicked him where he sat.

"Jesus, Spex! What are you doing here?"

He stood up from the retaining wall he'd been sitting on.

"Was that Damon?" he asked, not answering my question but indicating the road down which the truck had only recently disappeared with a tilt of his head.

Shit! Had he seen us? I thought about Damon's truck and, in particular, about the windows. Tinted. And it was dark. Hopefully…

Go with the truth.

"Yes," I admitted. "I went running and ended up at the reservoir. Damon happened to be there so he brought me home."

And that was true, I simply had no intention of filling out any added detail. Need to know and all that and Spex definitely didn't need to know.

"Oh," Spex said.

"So… what are you doing here again?"

"What? Oh, I called and your grandmother said you'd gone out. She said you were running so I thought I'd come and wait for you.'

"Why didn't you go in then?" I asked. "It's not as if you haven't met my grandparents plenty of times already and they wouldn't have minded."

Spex shrugged.

"I didn't want to disturb your grandparents," he replied. "Besides, I guess I wanted to talk to you, privately, first."

I almost sighed but managed to keep it to myself. Now what? "Well, I'm cold and I need a shower," I told him instead. "Coming in or staying here?"

Spex stood up.

I led the way and I sincerely hoped what I'd just been up to didn't show too obviously. My lips felt swollen and bruised and I also wondered if I'd bled through my tee-shirt, though at least it was black and had a logo on the back. I called out to my grandparents as I walked in to let them know I was home, and went straight upstairs to my room, Spex in tow. I grabbed my towel off the back of my chair.

"I'm just going to take that shower," I informed Spex, already manoeuvring out of my room. "Make yourself at home."

I only realised just how physical my day had truly been after I got into the shower. My legs ached, my back ached, my shoulders ached and, going by the burning sensation from shoulder blades to hips, I was fairly scraped and scratched, though how much of this was due to Damon's enthusiasm and how much to wrestling bare-skinned on raw earth was impossible to tell. For a short while, the water ran red. Crap. Seriously?

I dried myself very cautiously and wished Damon were here to apply something to my back, this thought eliciting a response requiring me to turn the shower to cold and get back in. Spex was waiting for me in my room and the last thing I needed was any more evidence of my recent encounter with Damon or of where my thoughts might be at. Shivering, I wrapped my towel around my waist and wished I'd had the foresight to take my robe into the bathroom. I could only hope Spex wouldn't notice anything.

Naturally, he did.

"What happened to your back?"

I focused on my recent cold shower and forced the colour down from my face.

"My back?" I asked innocently.

"Yeah, it's all scraped up."

"Oh, right. I, uh, it must have been when I got up to the reservoir. I was pretty done in when I got there and I took my shirt off."

"Your shirt off? Was that before or after Damon got there?"

"What? What the fuck, Spex?!"

Spex looked suitably contrite. "Sorry, that was inappropriate."

"You think?"

Even if he was pretty much on point. I hurried to put on clean jeans and tee.

"You want me to put something on that for you?"

No. Hell no. "Thanks, but I'm all right. I really don't feel a thing."

"Are you sure because…"

"Seriously, Spex. I'm fine!"

"Oh. Ok."

Spex was sitting on my bed and I noticed he had a rucksack at his feet.

"What's with the bag?" I asked.

Spex looked down and colour touched his cheeks. "I was kinda hoping you might let me stay the night."

My eyebrows rose and my mouth (my *bruised* mouth) fell open. "What?"

Spex shifted uneasily. "I already let my folks know I was. Staying, that is. I … I just have to get out of my house for a bit and I was kinda counting on staying here. I haven't got anywhere else to go."

Shit.

"It's ok if you'd rather I didn't," he said, getting more than a little reluctantly to his feet. "I know I've been, well, I'd understand."

I took a deep breath and let it out through my teeth in a long sigh of resignation.

"Ah, what the hell, Spex. Stay already. After all, that's what friends are for, right?"

Spex grinned at me as if he'd won the damn lottery as he fell back onto my bed.

"Yeah," he agreed. "Thanks, Eike."

"Whatever," I said with a shrug.

We shared my bed because there was nowhere else for him, and neither of us slept very well.

For my part, my thoughts were, quite understandably I should think, full of Damon. If I'd been on my own I'd have found a way to relieve some of the pressure, but I wasn't and trying to keep the evidence of the emotions I'd discovered in Damon's presence from Spex was a challenge I hadn't anticipated. It wasn't as if I could just keep running to the shower for a *time out*. Spex moved a lot and he managed to get uncomfortably close on more occasions than I care to count and, at some point, I woke to find Spex pressed hard against my raw back. I groaned, rather loudly I thought, because it damn well hurt, and tried to push him back, only to discover that Spex was suffering frustrations of his own.

I stiffened, as in my *body* stiffened and tried, unsuccessfully, to get even closer to the wall. Spex had a leg over mine and an arm flung across my shoulders and his face was pressed to the back of my neck.

And that wasn't the only thing pressed uncomfortably close.

"Spex!" I rasped, only half under my breath. "Spex! Move the fuck over!"

Spex moaned in his sleep and pressed even closer. *Jesus!* I tried to get a leg clear far enough to kick him.

"Spex!"

Spex's grip around my shoulder's tightened and his hand slipped down my tee-shirt and onto bare skin. I did the only thing that came to mind as an option. I head-butted him. I didn't have a lot of room, the wall being in the way, but I took what space I could make and I flicked my head backwards and felt the back of my head connect with the top of his. Spex woke up.

"What the fuck? Oh, oh shit! Oh, sorry, man!"

Spex rolled violently backwards, almost rolled off the bed, and reached out to grab me to save himself. We rolled together and I ended up lying half across him. Even worse. I untangled myself and sat up and so did Spex.

"Dude! Seriously!" I clutched at what was now my torn tee-shirt.

Spex blinked, looking even more vulnerable than usual without his glasses, and his face burned with embarrassment.

"I am so, so sorry. I … I didn't mean to. I swear."

I ran an agitated hand through my hair, knowing it really was an unruly mess now, and tried, carefully, to scramble over the top of him with minimal further contact. This was less successful than I'd hoped, my usual agility hampered by my abrupt awakening, my aching back, my torn tee, and my equal embarrassment at our predicament, and my leg dragged over... well, it dragged over the main point of our predicament. Spex yelped and grabbed for his groin and then, realising the full extent of his dilemma, burst instantly into tears. Which at least eliminated the cause of the problem as it pretty much took all the wind out of his sails.

"It's ok," I said, even though it was far from. "It happens."

Spex hugged himself and hung his head in shame. "I shouldn't have come," he said. "I should've known this would happen."

"Known what would happen?" I asked. "That? Happens to all of us so don't worry about it." I pulled off my tee and scrambled around for a new one, meanwhile wishing I'd gotten Grandmother to put something on my back because it burned.

"Want a hot chocolate or something?" I asked. "Now that we're awake anyway?"

"You're not mad with me?"

"Nah," I reassured him. "Ok, so don't go making a habit of it or anything but no, I'm not mad. You were asleep, right? It's not as if you were doing it on purpose or anything."

Spex blushed even harder, if that were possible. "Yeah, yeah, I was asleep, definitely asleep!"

"So, ok then. Let's just forget about it and not make a big deal out of it, ok? You want that hot drink or not?"

"Yeah, ok. Coffee, sugar, lots of sugar. And Eike?"

"What?"

"Thanks, thanks for not being mad."

I shrugged. I wasn't mad but I sure as hell wasn't comfortable. I put a hoodie on over my tee and went to make coffees.

"How is Parker?" Grandfather asked later that morning. Spex had gone back to bed but I was wide awake and still aching. "He seemed somewhat troubled last night."

"Spex? Sleeping," I said. "I don't know but I think maybe he's had trouble at home or something. He didn't sleep well."

Grandfather nodded sagely. "He is fortunate to have such a friend as you," he observed. "You are a special person and a good friend. But be careful, Eike. Sometimes, what *we* see as one thing, others see as something else."

I wanted to ask him what he meant but his words far too closely echoed Xia's which still resonated in my mind and I decided that perhaps I didn't really want to know.

"I'll just go let him know we're off to the store," I said.

"I'll wait outside for you," Grandfather said.

The store was close enough to walk to and he would wait for me in the driveway. I jogged back up the stairs.

Spex was still asleep and lying sprawled on his back now that he had the bed all to himself. Unfortunately, he was also still quite clearly in the throes of whatever fantasy he'd been in through the night and I turned my back on him in case he woke up and thought I'd been staring.

"Shit, Spex. You *really* need a girlfriend," I muttered under my breath.

Spex groaned and rolled over. "Eike?"

"I'm off to the store," I told him, "and I should be back about midday. Stay in bed as long as you like and Grandmother will look after you when you decide to get up. There's a clean towel on my desk if you want to take a shower."

"Uh, ok. Thanks. You don't want me to come with?" Spex asked, his voice muffled with residual sleep.

"No, that's ok. Grandfather and I pretty much have our own system and to be honest, you'd probably just end up getting in the way. I'll see you later, ok?"

"Yeah, ok. If you say so."

I opened the door.

"Hey, Eike?"

"Yeah?"

"Thanks, you know, for letting me stay and for, well, for everything."

"It's nothing. Really. I gotta go, ok? Later."

And I bolted back down the stairs. Suddenly, life appeared to be getting remarkably complicated.

Chapter Ten

Damon turned up at the store just before ten.

"You were going to call," I said, surprised, and pleased, to see him.

"I did," Damon informed me. "Your cell-phone's dead and your grandmother told me you were here so I figured I might as well just come over and see whether, if I gave you a hand, you might get off early."

My cell-phone. That's right, I still didn't know what had happened to it. Maybe not entirely a bad thing if it meant Damon had taken it upon himself to simply turn up.

"I don't know about getting off early," I said. "It's been pretty busy today and I actually thought I might end up working late. Why? Did you have something specific in mind?"

"I do actually," Damon admitted, looking just a little uncertain, "but I'd rather not tell just yet. Let's go and see your grandfather first."

Grandfather shook his head at me.

"Forgetful boy," he admonished me. "It's Sunday and we close at noon. Go, go. I'm not that old yet that I can't handle my own store."

"Thank you, Grandfather," I grinned at him, giving him a respectful bow and moved when Damon did likewise.

"Thank you, Grandfather," Damon said. Grandfather smiled at him, clearly pleased.

I followed Damon out to where he'd parked his truck in front of the store but stopped before I got to the kerb. Noticing, Damon turned back to me.

"What's up? Forget something?"

Not exactly, more like remember something. Xia, back to haunt me yet again.

Boys aren't pretty and boys don't like boys.

I shook my head and forced Xia's voice from my mind to smile at Damon.

"It's nothing," I said. "I didn't sleep too well."

And wasn't that the truth. I got into the truck and Damon slid in behind the wheel.

There was an immediate silence, not exactly uncomfortable but as if, now that we were here alone, neither of us knew quite what to do next.

"I missed you last night," Damon said, just as I'd begun to think the silence had gone too long to be broken. "I was alone and lonely and all I could do was think of you."

I looked down, profoundly relieved. Even though Damon had turned up to see me and even though he appeared no different, I guess I'd still had the underlying expectation he might have regretted last night, his good humour no more than a façade to cover his preference it all be forgotten, never to be mentioned again.

You little fuck! You tell anyone and I'll kill you!

I rubbed my eyes and took a halting breath.

"Eike?"

Damon, sounding extremely insecure. Was he thinking the same thing about me? That I might have regrets and was wishing he hadn't brought it up? I rubbed the back of my neck and turned to him with a hesitant smile.

"I was thinking about you, too," I told him. "You kind of pitched me a curve-ball, you know, and I'm still working things out."

He nodded, not looking up from the steering wheel and his hands tightening. "Is there a but?" he asked.

"Not exactly," I admitted. "More of a confession."

Aside from thoughts of Xia and Paul, I was feeling unreasonably guilty about Spex's unexpected sleep-over, even though absolutely *nothing* untoward had happened between us, or not intentionally at least.

"What?" Damon asked, his voice strained. "You're not ready? You want to think things over? You're already seeing somebody?"

"None of the above," I tried to reassure him. "It's Spex. Parker. He stayed at my house last night and, in all likelihood, he's still there."

Damon's grip on the wheel tightened sufficiently to turn his knuckles white. "Oh?"

"It's not like that, if that's what you're thinking!" I said, horrified. "Christ, if you hadn't worked out as much already, I ... I've never! You're the first!"

Damon's features softened and his hands eased their grip on the wheel. Just as well. I'd begun to think it might buckle under the pressure.

"Really? I'm flattered."

"You ought to be," I agreed. "But that doesn't change the fact that Spex is at my house, and he still isn't overly thrilled about you."

"Does he know?" Damon asked. "About last night?"

"No," I reassured him. "Nobody knows."

"Oh," Damon murmured dubiously. "So, what do you want to do?"

I had to think about this before I could make a response. I'd never had a plan to begin with but if I'd had one, this wouldn't have been it. Or not exactly.

"What was *your* plan?" I asked, throwing the question back at him.

"I was planning to take you shopping," Damon replied, turning to look at me directly for the first time since we'd gotten into the truck.

"Excuse me? You what? What for?"

Damon shrugged and waved a hand at me. "Look at you," he said. "No offense but you're hiding something pretty spectacular under all that ridiculously baggy clothing. I thought you might be ready for a change of image." He paused and took a deep breath as if mentally steeling himself. "How am I supposed to appreciate what I have if I can't see it?"

My mouth fell open and I stared at him. What he had? Me? I didn't even know where to begin interpreting this unexpected statement though I had to admit that, in regard to my wardrobe at least, he had a point. It had all been part of the camouflage, *pretty boys get into trouble*, even if it clearly hadn't worked quite as I'd intended.

"Um," I said, not knowing what else to say.

Damon reached out and cautiously stroked my cheek before running his thumb over my lips and, for some inexplicable reason, I moved as quick as a striking snake and caught it in my mouth. Damon looked understandably startled and instinctively tried to withdraw his hand but I closed my teeth on his thumb and rolled my tongue over it.

"Stop it," Damon said, not sounding particularly convincing. "You have no idea what you're doing."

Oh, I thought I had a pretty fair idea. I released his thumb but I did it slowly and he kind of groaned as he withdrew.

"Jesus, Eike. How am I supposed to drive like this?"

I had no need to look to know what he meant.

"Are you quite certain that ridiculously baggy clothing is all that ridiculous?" I asked innocently.

Damon sighed and rearranged himself uncomfortably in his seat.

"You have a point," he conceded, "but I still want to take you shopping."

"In that case," I said, "I still need to go home first. I have to talk to Spex and I'm going to have to get changed. Overalls probably aren't particularly practical for a shopping trip."

"True," Damon agreed. "On both counts. Even if," he murmured, turning his head away, "you do look rather delicious just as you are.'

I coughed self-consciously. "Drive already," I ordered him.

Damon obeyed.

Spex was no longer at my house when I returned and, still not knowing the whereabouts of my cell phone, I called him from the house phone. He took a while to answer and when he did, he didn't sound well.

"You home alone?" I asked.

"My folks have gone out," he said. "I don't actually know where but I'm glad really. I'm not feeling so good."

"Flu?" I asked, thinking it was more than likely the after-effects of a disturbed and *disturbing* sleep-over.

"I don't know," he mumbled, sounding pitiful and only succeeding in making me want to sigh in frustration. "I just want to go back to bed."

I bit back the response I wanted to make, which was something along the lines of *harden the fuck up* given I'd been up since dawn working while he'd been able to sleep it off, and made myself smile sympathetically, even though he couldn't see it.

"Can I come over and talk to you?" I asked. "It's kind of important."

There was silence followed by a tired sigh. "Can it wait?" he asked. "I'm sorry but I really just want to be on my own for a while."

I closed my eyes and resisted the urge to grind my teeth. "I guess so," I said, "but look, I really do need to come over and talk with you later. Ok?"

"Yeah, all right. Give me a call tonight or something."

"Ok, well, feel better. And, um, get some sleep or something."

He mumbled something I couldn't hear, and thought maybe I didn't want to, and hung up and I was left staring at the phone thinking that hadn't gone anywhere as I'd anticipated.

I found Damon in the kitchen having tea with Grandmother.

"I could get used to this," Damon said, indicating Grandmother's Korean tea service. "It's kinda nice, soothing, you know?"

"Good to know," I murmured, a bit taken aback by him.

Grandmother patted me affectionately and followed by ruffling my hair. Damon raised a curious eyebrow and grinned at me but I didn't care. Grandmother was always going to be welcome to ruffle my hair, although if Damon wanted to mess it up some too…

I bit the inside of my cheek and turned my gaze away and I heard him stifle a snort and knew he'd probably guessed exactly what I'd been thinking.

"Damon tells me he's taking you shopping," Grandmother said. "I think that is a splendid idea."

I raised my eyebrows and looked at her, wide-eyed in surprise. "You do?" I asked.

Grandmother smiled and tousled Damon's hair too and, although he ducked his head and blushed, I got the impression he was pleased.

"I'm going to have a shower and get changed," I informed nobody in particular.

Damon stood up. "Then I might as well wait for you in your room," he stated casually, and followed me up the stairs.

He caught me just inside the door, closed it behind us, and pushed me towards the bed.

"Damon?"

"Quiet a minute," he said, pressing me down onto the bed.

I sat and he stood over me, straddling my knees, his eyes fixed on mine.

"Last night," he said, his voice strained. "You and me, what was that?"

"I don't know," I admitted, not backing down from his gaze. "I was wondering the same thing myself."

"Do you regret it?" he whispered huskily, leaning closer. "Do you wish we hadn't, that it hadn't happened?"

"No," I said. "Not now. Not ever."

Damon heaved a sigh which sounded very much like profound relief. "Good," he murmured, and he dropped his weight onto my knees, pushed me backwards and followed me to plaster his mouth over mine. I have to admit I didn't offer much resistance but I did protest just a little as he came up for air.

"Damon, Grandmother!" I managed to remind him.

"She's downstairs," he pointed out, "and besides, it's not as if I intend to go anywhere near as far as I'd like to."

Without giving me time to respond, he once again smothered my mouth with his. I admit I was relieved to know he intended some measure of restraint and yet, at the same time, a part of me wished he didn't need to.

"Is it," he breathed, raising himself only enough to look down on me, my hands pinned above my head by his, "as if suddenly everything makes more sense? Why is it that I can't get enough? I swear I can't help myself, Eike. You're like a drug I've only just discovered and never before realised how much I needed."

He ran his open mouth down my cheek and down my throat and back up before taking my lower lip between his teeth. *Jesus!*

"Am I going too fast for you?" he sighed, not making any effort to stop what he was doing. "I feel like an avalanche, as if I'm somehow going to smother you and ruin it all."

I *tried* to take a deep breath, difficult given not only that he was sitting astride me but also what he was doing to me, and tried to put my thoughts in order. Despite his seemingly having become suddenly unstoppable, I understood pretty clearly what he meant. All those years bottling up how I felt and hiding who I really was, just in case somebody figured it out.

Like who you want, but just don't let anybody know if you like boys.

My mantra for life. And now, finally, the floodgates had opened and the mask had been torn away and he'd said it exactly right; it was like an avalanche. And unstoppable.

I didn't know how to put into words how I felt and, unconsciously, tears began to build.

"Ah shit, Eike. I have. I'm ruining this. I'm screwing it all up."

He released my hands and leaned back, about to get off and leave, and I grabbed him. I managed to lift myself sufficiently upright to wrap both arms around his neck and I dragged him back down with me, plastering my mouth over his. He resisted, pulling away from me, his body tightening in denial, and then he was groaning deeply and clasping my face.

His mouth left mine and he pressed me back and leaned away, gasping for breath.

"Stop! Stop now," he demanded, his face flushed and his chest heaving. "You keep doing this and I don't know if I'll be able to control myself anymore. Stop!"

I didn't want to but, once again, I knew exactly what he meant. The pain was almost unbearable and I don't know which of us needed a shower more. Damon disengaged himself and stood up, his breath coming in short, rapid gasps.

"I take it that's your answer, then?" he asked after a bit.

"You take it right," I agreed. "Can I have that shower now?"

Damon straightened, cracked a kink from his neck, and stared at me, his blue eyes sparking.

"Jerk," he said mildly. "After what you just did? Me first."

"After what I just did? You started it!"

"And finished it. I'm in the shower."

He stood up and grabbed *my* towel off the chair.

"What do you plan to wear then?" I asked, not bothering to move from where I lay. "Or do you plan to get back into the same clothes?"

"You and I aren't so different," he observed, only barely pausing with his hand on the bedroom door. "I intend to raid your wardrobe, of course."

Of course.

He walked calmly out the door in pursuit of the shower and I clasped my hands behind my head and grinned like I'd gone crazy.

Admittedly, perhaps I had.

Damon intended to pay. I'd made an attempt to take my wallet, had done some rough calculations in my head while I'd showered and figured I'd be ok as long as he didn't intend to get too extravagant.

But he wouldn't hear of it.

"Look here," he said, pulling his wallet from the back pocket of his discarded jeans with the intent of putting it into his borrowed baggy ones. Mine. He flourished a black card under my nose.

"See this? Limitless," he said. "The singular advantage of having an old man who's positively loaded. And I never use it."

He stuck the card back in his wallet, the wallet in his pocket, and laughed.

"Oh, dear god," he chortled. "If he had any idea what I intend using it for!"

"I take it your dad isn't going to be too happy when he finds out then?" I asked, pulling on boots and lacing them up. "Is he going to?"

"Eventually he'll find out," Damon sighed, staring off into space before shrugging absently. "But let's just say I'm not in any kind of hurry for that to happen because, when it does," his voice tapered off and he laughed self-deprecatingly. "When it does..." he continued, his face suddenly etched with pain, "all hell will break loose."

I paused in my lacing and frowned at him. "Damon...?"

"Don't," he said. "Don't even. This isn't your problem, it's mine, and no way in hell is my old man going to ruin this for me."

He bent over and lifted my chin to once again claim my mouth with his before straightening and laughing at the expression I must've had on my face. I sucked my lower lip into my mouth and half-glared at him. He ignored me.

"Come on, boyfriend. Let's move."

Boyfriend? I didn't know I qualified as such but I was hardly going to get into a debate over semantics with him at this point. I followed him.

Chapter Eleven

Damon parked the truck at the huge Centreville Mall and I found myself hesitating. He came around to my side of the truck and opened the door for me with an exaggerated flourish.

"This what you were waiting for?" he grinned.

I paused before swinging my legs reluctantly to the ground and closing the door so he could lock the truck.

"Not exactly," I admitted, running a hand through my hair and spiking it into an erratic tangle to match my thoughts.

"Suits you," Damon observed, indicating my Sonic-style hair. "What's up?"

I kicked at the ground and sighed, and Damon laughed.

"Don't tell me a tough, swims like a dolphin, fights like a shark, guy like you is afraid of a little bit of shopping?"

"Umm…"

"You'd rather be here with your grandparents?" Damon asked, feigning horror. "I'm offended."

I didn't know what it was exactly, or how to put it into words. Damon was intending to go shopping with me or, more accurately, to shop *for me*, and he'd referred to me as his *boyfriend*. What did that make him? My *sugar daddy*? And what did that make me? His *toy-boy*, his *pet*?

My thoughts must have been obvious to him because, before I could anticipate him, he'd swatted me. Hard.

"Fuck you," he said. "Come on and stop making such a dick of yourself."

He grabbed hold of my arm and began dragging me towards the mall entrance. What could I do? I gave in and followed him.

As it turned out, despite my misgivings, shopping with Damon was more of a comedy than a tragedy. He was an irrepressible and irresistible force and it seemed no matter where we went, no one could refuse him nor spare him any service. We sailed in and out of every conceivable menswear, sportswear, and accessory store the mall had to offer and, everywhere, we were surrounded by good humour, courtesy, laughter, and unlimited offers of assistance. By the time I begged him to stop so we could at very least catch a coffee and a breather, my sides ached from laughing and my head was spinning. Not to mention I was burdened like a mule with bags and boxes and packages of all shapes and sizes.

"One more stop," he said, pushing me mercilessly in front of him.

"Seriously?" I groaned. "What could we possibly not already have?"

"A cell phone," he said. "If you think I'm going to go traipsing all over the countryside every time I want to talk to you, you're seriously mistaken. And I happen to want to be able to talk to you *any* time."

My mouth curled as I considered the implications of this. I wasn't sure if *any* time was necessarily going to work for me.

"You can always turn the damn thing off," he laughed, reading my thoughts and clipping me across one ear, presumably to emphasize his point.

"Trust me, I will," I muttered.

He clipped me across the other ear and it wasn't as if I could do a whole lot about it given the load I was burdened with. I swore indignantly.

"Serves you right," he snorted.

"You'll keep," I grumbled, but quietly.

Despite my objections, he did what it appeared he did very well, ignored me, and bought the latest in communications technology.

"I'll need a bloody pilot's licence for that thing," I grizzled as he marched me towards the centre-court coffee shop he insisted was his favourite.

"Quit your whining," he said. "You can always ask Parker to help you navigate it. He's good at that sort of thing."

This might've been true but this was also not the point.

"Sit," he commanded, directing me to a table far too public for my liking.

"What am I now? Your pet Pekingese?"

"They're Chinese, not Korean," Damon informed me with a straight face. "Now sit, and stay."

I did. Damon went to order coffees.

I arranged the bags and various parcels around my feet and stretched the knots from my back and shoulders.

"Hey! Eike, isn't it?"

I looked around in surprise. Amy and Cara, from the pool games at Meg's.

"Hey," I said. "Amy and Cara, right?"

Amy grinned and grabbed Cara's hand to take seats at my (*our*) table.

"What are you doing here?" Amy asked.

I indicated the array of packages around me. "Shopping," I said.

"Awesome. On your own?"

"Uh?"

Well, this could get awkward. What do I say?

Before I could think up an appropriate response, Cara was leaping back to her feet, her chair almost tumbling over in the process.

"Damon!" she shrieked, piercingly enough for me to wish I'd had sufficient advance warning to clamp my hands to my ears. "You're here, too? This is great!"

She launched herself at him and if he hadn't been carrying a tray of coffees she might well have wrapped herself around him like a python around a tree. I raised an eyebrow. So that was how it was.

Managing to avoid her determined insistence on clinging to him, he put the tray down and, very deliberately, took my face in his hands and … kissed me! Right there in public! I can categorically say I don't know who was more surprised, me or those two girls.

"Miss me?" he whispered in my ear, nipping my earlobe for good measure.

Amy squealed and I thought Cara might be about to cry and then I glanced over Damon's shoulder and saw … Spex!

Oh … holy … shit.

What was he doing here? He'd said he was staying home, going to bed, needing time to himself. His gaze met mine, and I froze.

"Eike?" Damon shook me and his brow furrowed. "What's up?"

Spex was striding our way, his expression unreadable. And then he was at our table and slamming a box down in front of me so violently the tray jumped and coffee spilt. Before I could say a word, he'd turned on his heels and was leaving.

"Spex!"

He didn't stop, didn't even pause, and before I had a hope of getting to my feet and past Damon, tangled as I was in all the shopping, he'd vanished back into the crowd and was gone.

"What the hell was all that about?" Damon asked, looking equally as stunned as I felt.

Amy and Cara were speechless, caught between the unexpected events of Damon's kissing me and Spex's whirlwind arrival and departure. I looked at the box he'd put in front of me and my heart sank. It was a cell phone. The exact same model Damon had only just purchased for me. *Oh shit!* That's what Spex had been doing. He'd been out buying me a new cell phone. I stared out across the centre court and wondered what the hell I was supposed to do now.

"I'm sorry," Damon said when we'd returned to the truck and before he'd started the engine.

"What for?" I asked him, running a hand over my face and turning to stare out the side window at the parking lot. "It isn't as if it's your fault."

"I know, but maybe if I hadn't been such an arse and kissed you…"

I switched my attention back to him and raised an eyebrow. "You regret that?"

Damon scowled. "No, I don't. Not kissing you but…" He let a heavy sigh hiss through his teeth and looked away, his hands tightening on the wheel.

"It was presumptuous of me. I was being, I don't know, possessive, I guess. I just wanted people to know, I wanted those girls to know, that you're mine and I'm yours."

My heart thumped far too heavily behind my ribs and I struggled to find breath. *Mine? Yours?* Possession, or something else?

"Am I?" I asked, the words sticking in my throat. "Yours?"

Damon immediately threw the question right back at me. "Aren't you? Don't you want to be?"

My jaw tightened. Was I? Did I? Was love really that simple? Could it be? Damon sighed again and shifted his hand to the ignition switch, perhaps assuming there'd be no answer, and I reached out to place a hand on his arm. That thought, *was love really that simple?*, was the first time I'd ever in my life allowed that word to appear in my mind in its current context. Love. Was that what this was? Was that, or a version of it, what I was feeling? Damon paused, studying me warily, and I thought about it some more, analysing how safe I felt in Damon's company, how *free*. I leaned towards him and pressed my lips to his cheek.

"I think I'm falling in love with you," I murmured in his ear.

Damon started. "What? What did you just say?"

Shit. Too fast? Had I miscalculated and inadvertently blown it? My heart raced and I felt more than a little sick but, in for a penny, in for a pound and it was too late to back off now.

"I think I'm falling in love with you," I repeated, waiting for the sky to fall.

I don't know what reaction I was anticipating but Damon turning around and grabbing me, to once again claim me with his kiss, was probably not it.

"I think I fell in love with you from the moment I first laid eyes on you," he admitted breathlessly, tears brightening his eyes. "I don't know how and I don't know why but I swear, Eike, for me, I'm *already* in love with you."

All thoughts of Spex momentarily forgotten, I sat, stunned, at this completely unexpected revelation. I blinked awkwardly and managed to straighten in my seat, withdrawing from Damon's embrace as I gathered my thoughts along with my composure. If I thought I'd blind-sided him, he'd done a hell of a job of turning the tables on me.

"Just as well I'm not going anywhere then, isn't it?" I murmured, running fingers across my swollen lips where Damon had bitten them in his enthusiasm.

Damon reached out to touch me, his fingers following my own across my lips.

"What are we going to do about Parker?" he asked.

"We?"

"We," Damon affirmed, withdrawing his touch and leaving my skin aching in its absence. "This needs to be sorted. He's your friend and I can't keep having him hate me, or hating you because of me. I feel sorry for him but truly, Harper wasn't my fault and he needs to move on. This isn't good for any of us the way it is."

I had to admit I couldn't agree more.

"Let's go find him," I suggested.

Damon started the truck.

We returned to my house and while Damon unloaded the shopping from the truck, I called Spex's cell and then his house. Not unexpectedly, nobody answered. I replaced the phone to lean my head against the wall.

"He won't pick up?" Damon asked, putting his arms around me and resting his chin on my shoulder.

"No," I said, "but I guarantee he's home. Where else would he be?"

"So let's go over there."

"You think?"

Damon did nothing more than run a fingertip up my cheek but, despite thoughts of Spex, a profound heat ignited deep within me. I closed my eyes and fought to steady my breathing.

"What's up?" Damon murmured, his voice husky and stirring up even more by way of a response.

Oh, *something*, I thought with a groan I didn't dare release. Damon's hand moved down my shoulder and across my collarbone and down towards my navel.

"Stop it," I muttered without conviction.

"Stop what?" Damon asked innocently, the hand now paused on my navel tightening sufficiently to send tremors shimmying through my body.

This time there was no possible way for me to suppress my groan.

"You know perfectly well what," I growled, arching my back and still making no attempt to move his hand.

Damon shifted his hand slowly south, his fingertips edging under the waistband of my jeans, and I clenched my teeth as much in frustration as in anticipation.

"I mean it," I gasped, failing to sound very much as if I did and feeling I'd seriously lost control of the situation somewhere along the way. "Stop it!"

Damon chuckled and removed his hand while I struggled to get myself under control.

"You're a prick!" I grumbled irritably as I straightened and readjusted my clothing.

"I'd say go and get changed but we might never get out of your room," Damon smirked.

"Asshole!"

"Shall we go then?" Damon asked, his tone changing, and the mood along with it. "We might as well get this over and done with."

I squared my shoulders. "Yeah, let's do this."

We pulled up at Spex's house and Damon turned off the truck.

"How do you want to tackle this?" he asked. "Am I going in with you?"

I'd been thinking about this on the very short drive from my house to Spex's and, although I wasn't entirely sure how things might end, I knew how they had to begin.

"I'll go in first," I said. "If it goes badly, I'll come back and cry on your shoulder or something. But, if it goes well, I'll come and get you and we'll move on to phase two."

"Phase two?"

"Phase one is to get him to talk to me," I explained. "Phase two is to get him to talk to you."

"Is there a phase three?" Damon asked, his expression serious.

"Phase three is we live happily ever after," I replied with a tight smile.

"Right," Damon agreed. "Well, good luck and watch your six!"

True that. Who knew what Spex was likely to do or how he was likely to react? I got out of the truck and walked apprehensively to the front door. Spex had been my first friend upon my arrival at Seven Oaks and he was still my best friend because, whatever Damon was, he was something else entirely, and I simply couldn't imagine my life without Spex in it. I knocked on the door.

And nobody came.

I shouldn't have been but I was disappointed. What had gotten into Spex lately that he had to be so damn difficult? I knocked again. Harder. I thought I caught some faint suggestion of movement from upstairs but still nobody came and I began to get a little irritated. I tried the door handle. Locked. Ok. I stood there for a moment, thinking about it, before retreating down the path to take a loop to the back of the house. The back door was unlocked and so I just walked in.

"Spex?" I called.

Nothing.

"Spex!" I called again, louder. "Spex, you jerk! If you're here, you better get your damn arse down here or I'm coming looking for you!"

Still no sign of anybody but I definitely heard movement from up the stairs and I headed determinedly for Spex's room. I didn't bother to knock, just opened the door to find Spex sitting on his bed staring straight at me.

"What're you doing here?" he demanded, his face sullen and his eyes red as if he'd been crying.

"What the hell do you think I'm doing?" I replied. "I'm here to talk to you."

"There's nothing to talk about," Spex said. "Fuck off!"

Despite his bitter words, I could tell Spex's heart wasn't in them and I came into his room, closed the door, and dragged his desk chair over to facing him.

"What the actual fuck, Spex?" I asked. "What's up with you?"

Spex glared at me. "You're a jerk," he said.

I shrugged. "Quite probably, but could you try being a little more specific?"

"What's up with you and Damon?" he asked bluntly.

"I wanted to explain this to you this morning, but you didn't want to talk to me."

"I'm listening now," Spex said.

"Are you?"

Spex's eyes narrowed and his mouth tightened into a grim line. "Don't fuck with me, Eike. I just want to know what's going on with you and *him*."

I tried to keep my eyes fixed on him but it was difficult given the intensity of his glare. I looked away and rubbed self-consciously under an ear.

"The bottom line is that I'm probably in love with him, Spex. That's it. That's the whole of it, no more and no less. I didn't ask for it to happen, I didn't plan for it to happen, but there it is." I paused and looked up. "And you're my best friend. Forgive me for wanting it all."

The next thing I knew, I was on my back on the floor, chair and all, and Spex was on top of me, fists flailing. I raised my arms to block him but all the wind had been knocked out of me and, as I was sprawled in a heap with the chair, there wasn't a lot of room for manoeuvre.

"Spex! What the fuck, Spex?!"

I managed to get a grip on an arm and rolled with him, pinning him underneath me and bringing up my knees to hold him in place.

"Quit it!" I snapped, putting him in a lock. "Just quit it already!"

Spex struggled a bit longer but it was half-hearted. He knew he had no hope against me and after a short while he lay still, his head rolling to one side. Tears slid down his nose.

"Why?" he whispered. "Of all people, why him?"

"Can I let you go now?" I asked, leaning back and relaxing my grip.

Spex sighed and collapsed, all the fight already out of him. I got up and offered him a hand and, reluctantly, he took it. I pulled him to his feet.

"We don't choose these things, Spex. They simply happen to us."

Spex took off his glasses, which were hanging askew over one ear, wiped his face with the back of an arm, and reached down to pick up the fallen chair.

"I hate you," he said quietly.

"If that makes you feel better," I said.

Spex closed his eyes and swayed on his feet and I reached out a hand to steady him. Instead of pulling away from me, Spex threw his arms around me.

"I'm sorry, I'm sorry," he sobbed, dissolving into tears. "I don't hate you. I miss you."

I hugged him back, cautiously, not wanting to encourage anything even more awkward, and patted him reassuringly.

"I never went anywhere, you dick."

I released him carefully and pressed him onto his bed, taking the chair for myself as he regained control of his tears and once again wiped his face on his sleeve.

"Want to tell me what this is really all about?" I asked. "Is this about Harper?"

"Fuck you," he said, so softly I could barely hear him.

I said nothing and merely waited, straddling the chair backwards and resting my chin on my arms folded over its back.

"She was quiet," he said, more to himself than to me. "I couldn't hear her voice anymore, after you came, after you made everything all right again."

My heart lurched for him and tears pricked at my eyes, but I clenched my teeth and continued my silence.

"And then *he* has to come along and ruin everything," Spex continued, his voice rising into bitterness. "*He* has to come along and take you from me, just like he took her."

I took a deep breath. This had to stop. *Spex* had to stop.

"Spex."

Spex looked up at me, as if he'd only just remembered I was even there.

"It's not Damon's fault and he didn't take anything from you. Not Harper, and certainly not me. You have to move on."

Spex glared at me anew, his jaw tight and his face suffused with angry colour.

"What the fuck would you know?" he spat angrily.

I raised an eyebrow and forced myself to remain calm. "If there's one thing I can relate to, Spex, it's loss."

For a moment I thought Spex was about to launch himself at me again but instead, he deflated, folding in on himself like a punctured balloon.

"He wasn't there for her," he whispered.

"It wasn't any longer his place to be," I reminded him. I took another deep breath. This needed to be said: "Were you?"

That was it right there. That was the heart of the matter and the cold, hard, raw truth. I knew it well. The guilt. The burden of wanting things to be different, of needing to lay blame, somewhere, anywhere. And Spex had transferred his guilt squarely to Damon and then, by association, to me. He crumpled. He folded. He curled into a ball and began to sob.

I didn't touch him. I didn't move. I sat and waited for the tears to stop which, of course, they eventually did. Spex lay there, arms wrapped around his pillow, gasping for breath and, finally, he sat up.

"I'm sorry," he said, wiping his face with his now decidedly worse for wear sleeve.

"What the hell for now?" I asked.

He shrugged.

"For everything, I guess. I ... I thought ... I thought it was me. I thought I was going crazy." He paused and his face reddened. "I thought I was in love with you."

"You're not," I said.

Spex shook his head. "I just didn't want to lose you."

"Just as well you didn't then, isn't it? I'm a bit pig-headed like that. Harder to shake than fleas off a junk-yard dog."

He managed a strained smile. "Thanks for that visual."

"You're welcome."

"What now?" he asked. "What do I do now?"

I studied him critically. "Well, for a kick-off, you could go and wash your face, and change that soggy shirt," I suggested. "You're a mess. And after that, I think you'd best come and talk with Damon."

Spex started, his eyes widening and his face draining of colour. "Damon?"

"Yes, Damon. He's waiting outside in his truck."

"He's here?"

"Yes."

"Oh, shit." Spex rubbed his eyes and blew a strained breath through pursed lips. "Is he really mad with me? He must want to beat the living shit out of me."

"I imagine the thought may on occasion have occurred to him," I admitted, "but no, he doesn't want to beat the living shit out of you. He'd like to make things right. In fact, I think he'd quite like to be your friend."

"Seriously?" Spex looked genuinely surprised. "He doesn't hate me?"

"Why the hell would he hate you?" I asked. "He loved Harper, you know. In his own way. Any other complications aside, he simply didn't know how to deal with her."

Spex gave a grim laugh. "He wasn't the only one. She was always so, oh, I don't know, *emotional*. Everything was always so much more dramatic than it needed to be."

I understood the family resemblance there… but I kept that to myself.

"Ok," Spex agreed. "Let's do this already. Want to make coffee while I get cleaned up? And bring Damon in?"

"You ready for this?" I asked.

"No, not even," Spex admitted. "But if I don't do it now, I might never be."

I stood up and rested a hand on his shoulder. "Friends?" I asked.

He smiled up at me even if the smile was still somewhat strained. "Always were, you prick," he said.

I grinned at him. "Takes one to know one."

"Well?" Damon asked as I approached his side of the truck, his arm slung casually out his open window. "Do you need my shoulder or are we moving on to phase two?"

I grinned at him and made a 'follow me' motion with my head.

"I'll take that as a confirmation of phase two," he said. "I don't suppose we have five minutes?"

"Why's that?" I asked, pausing to study him curiously.

"I got lonely sitting here waiting for you," he grinned mischievously, "and I was wondering if Parker might be pummelling you or something. I figured you might like to take a few minutes so I can confirm you're all in one piece."

I laughed at him, meanwhile thinking how close he was to the mark, and backed away from the truck. "I'm fine, thank you. And I can guess only too well what your welfare check will turn into. You can wait."

"What if I can't?"

I winked at him and vaulted the bonnet of the truck, bolting towards the house before he could get out of the truck. Even so, he still managed to catch me as I got to the back door, wrapping an arm around me and slamming me into the wall of the house.

"Do you know you drive me crazy?" he muttered, biting my ear.

"You *are* crazy!" I growled at him, ducking my head out from under him and pushing him away. "Now control yourself before I have to *force* some control on you!"

"Is that a threat or a promise?" he asked with a wicked grin even as he stepped back and released me.

"Both," I assured him. "My Hapkido may be rusty but I guarantee it'll still nail your Taekwondo. You haven't a hope."

"We might have to see about that," Damon laughed. "Sounds like a challenge to me. Now, are you coming or not? Stop pissing about already!"

"Me?" I spluttered. "Me, pissing about?"

But he'd already disappeared through the back door.

"Damn it!"

I'd made coffees and Damon and I were sitting, discreetly and initially to Damon's objections, on opposite sides of the kitchen table when Spex came down the stairs looking a hundred percent better than when I'd left him. He paused nervously in the kitchen doorway.

"Hey, Damon."

Damon stood up, offering his hand. "Hey, Parker."

For the briefest moment, I thought Spex might be about to turn and bolt but he didn't and instead came forward to take Damon's hand. Damon pulled him close and clapped a brotherly arm around Spex's shoulder.

"It's been too long, buddy."

Spex tensed and then, just as he had up in his room, he relaxed and gave in. He squeezed Damon tightly in return.

"Yes," he agreed. "It has."

Chapter Twelve

"You swimming again tonight?" Spex asked me as we biked home after classes the following day.

"I am," I replied. "You ok with that now?"

"Yeah," Spex said. "I am. Now. You coming to mine first? Work on that assignment due end of next week?"

"Sure, if you don't mind me going home to get changed first."

Spex glanced over at me and grinned. "Feeling a little uncomfortable, are we?" he chuckled.

I scowled. I was, at Damon's insistence, wearing part of the new wardrobe he'd bought for me and yes, I'd been more than a little uncomfortable all day. I'd certainly attracted a whole new level of attention and not least because of Damon's added insistence of making no secret of his infatuation with me.

"Yes," I agreed with a heavy sigh. "Is it really that obvious?"

"You could say that," Spex chortled. "I can tell you for free that if you didn't look like one of those exotic male super models before…"

"Not helping," I grumbled irritably.

We stopped in his driveway and Spex swung off his bike.

"You've certainly given people something to talk about," he added.

I grunted something rude under my breath and Spex laughed.

"I think you've pissed off as many of the guys as you have the girls," Spex observed. "Or maybe I should say *disappointed*. Who knew?"

Certainly not me.

"I'll be back soon," I said, changing the subject.

"Yeah, well, be careful," Spex advised me, his tone changing abruptly.

I tensed. "What's that supposed to mean?"

Spex's expression darkened and he fixed me with concern written clearly in his eyes.

"Not everybody is equally accepting of Damon's *coming out*," he said, no hint of humour remaining in his tone. "And not everybody is as open-minded as he'd obviously like to think they are. They wouldn't dare touch him, him being who he is and all, but you? You're fair game."

"Jesus, Spex! Way to go for putting the wind up somebody."

"Just saying, is all," he said. "You just want to be careful, ok?"

Boys who like boys get themselves in trouble.

Xia again. How I wished I could stop hearing his voice.

"Right, well, it's only half a block between my house and yours so I'll try not to get myself lynched between here and there and back again."

"I'll be waiting for you," Spex informed me.

This wasn't anywhere near as comforting as it sounded.

I tried not to think of what Spex had said and tried even harder to keep Xia's voice from my mind but I have to admit my back was burning all the way home, and it had nothing to do with the scars.

Boys aren't pretty and boys don't like boys.

... if you didn't look like one of those exotic male super models before ...

Boys who like boys get themselves in trouble.

Not everybody is equally accepting ... and not everybody is as open-minded ...

You're fair game.

I'd seen it before, even if I'd managed to keep *myself* safe all this time. It had only added to my determination to keep my secret safe, seeing others who hadn't been so careful, and hearing the horror stories; the *boys who liked boys* broken and bleeding in the streets after they'd been caught by the anti-gays and bullies.

My skin crawled. It was all very well Damon making a statement on his own account, insisting on touching me or kissing me in public, but Spex was right. Damon was the son of somebody powerful and important, and he was well-known and well-liked in his own right, and thus as good as untouchable. Who was I? Nobody. And thus, *fair game.*

My heart raced and my pulse throbbed in my ears and I was suddenly very grateful for the shelter of home.

I put my bike in the garage, bolted upstairs, and stripped off what suddenly felt like clothing far too provocative for my good health. Then I stood, half-naked, in my room to gather my thoughts.

What was I doing? What was Damon doing? He'd been making no secret of his feelings for me right from the moment he'd kissed me in the mall and I chewed my lip anxiously and wondered how I was possibly supposed to rein him in.

Standing there, I realised there was no going back now. What was done was done and once the cat was out of the bag, as the saying went... Even if he did, somehow, agree to be more discreet, not something I could see happening any time soon, it was already far too late. I flexed my arms. Maybe it was equally about time to return to my Hapkido as I was currently returning to swimming. I might well need it sooner rather than later.

I biked back to Spex's just as quickly as I'd earlier biked home and feeling just as vulnerable despite my determination not to give in to my apprehensions and I arrived breathless and sweaty.

"What'd you do?" Spex asked as I threw myself on his bed. "Do a return run to the reservoir first?"

"Not exactly," I croaked, still struggling for equilibrium if not necessarily breath. "But I blame you."

"Me? Why? What'd I do?"

"Put the fear of god in me, that's what."

"Is this because of what I said on the way home?"

"What do you think?"

"Sorry, Eike. I didn't mean to freak you out or anything. I just want you to be careful, that's all."

I rolled over and hugged his pillow and then sat up and threw it at him. He ducked and the pillow bounced harmlessly against his bookshelf from which he fetched it and threw it back.

"I'm just trying to have your back," he added, "even if you can be a right jerk."

"Trust me," I said, "I have it in mind."

Damon called me on the phone Spex had bought for me. The one he'd bought, he'd kept for himself.

"No point in adding fuel to the embers," he'd said.

I was grateful for his discretion, at least in this regard.

"I'll pick you up from Spex's," he said.

"Why? I've got my bike and there's no need for you to go out of your way."

"I don't want you biking home alone in the dark," he said. "I'll pick up your bike as well but, from now on, I'll pick you up for swim practice."

"I've been biking alone in the dark the better part of my life," I informed him coolly. "What's changed?"

"Me. I'll be there at ten to."

He hung up.

"What was that all about?" Spex asked.

"Seems Damon has the same concern for my safety that you do," I replied.

"Oh," Spex said.

"Exactly."

True to his word, Damon turned up at Spex's house at ten to seven though he didn't come in, just honked the horn.

"Boyfriend's calling for you," Spex smirked.

"Jerk," I said, swatting him, but I collected my things and went out.

"I took the liberty of picking up your swim bag from home," Damon told me as I swung myself into the truck. "I also told Grandmother I'd look after you and get you fed afterwards so she wouldn't have to worry about you."

I studied him appraisingly. "You can be quite the gentleman when you want to be," I said.

"What? I'm not always?"

"Hardly."

He reached out and squeezed my thigh, far too high up for comfort.

"See," I said, punching him, not lightly, in the shoulder. "Concentrate on the bloody road!"

He laughed but removed his hand.

We beat Coach Harmon to the pool and Damon surprised me by producing a key.

"Captain of the swim team," he said by way of explanation. "Coach doesn't always feel the need to come along to the training sessions."

Most of the lights were still on but the changing rooms were dark and he hauled me through the door and pressed me to the wall without bothering to flip any switches.

"Now what?" I muttered, unable to see a thing. "Coach will be here any minute."

"He's not here yet though, is he?" Damon responded, his breath whispering against my face and his body pressing close to mine. "I quite like the concept of you and I alone in the dark."

"Do you just? And what if I don't?"

Damon's lips and tongue stroked my cheek and I groaned aloud to an all-too-familiar ache.

"Are you saying you don't?" Damon murmured, pressing even closer, one hand against the wall and the other sliding suggestively down my side, making the ache worse.

"No," I gasped, "but if there's to be any hope of me getting into my swimsuit, you need to get off me right now!"

"You are such a spoil-sport," Damon sighed, making no effort to move and instead running his tongue over my lips.

I snapped at him, missed, and he ran his hand between us and down my belly. My knees buckled.

"Dangerous," Damon observed softly. "I can see I'm going to have to watch out for you."

"Damon, please."

I didn't think it was possible but he pressed closer still until we were groin to groin and ache to ache. I closed my eyes and waited for disaster.

Finally, he moved, and I slid down the wall and put my head between my knees to catch my breath.

"You are a real jerk, you know that?" I managed to tell him.

Damon laughed. "I thought you said I was a gentleman."

"I take it back. Now help me up and turn on the damn lights."

He did both and I took it upon myself to have a shower before I got changed and by that time, Coach Harmon had arrived.

"How are you feeling today?" he asked, studying me closely and casting several glances at Damon who was already in the pool.

Did he know? It wouldn't surprise me in the slightest. News travels fast in closed communities like colleges, never mind in small ones like Seven Oaks, especially when it involves someone like Damon.

"I'm fine thanks, Coach. Ready when you are.'

"Then what are you waiting for?"

"Nothing, Coach."

Without hesitation, I moved to the edge of the pool and dove in.

This time there was no darkness, there was no smoke, there were no flames. The water enveloped me only as it should and with a single sinuous movement I was alongside Damon. I surfaced and barely refrained from touching him as I most definitely had the desire to.

"I hope you're ready," I said instead.

"Oh, I'm more than ready," he informed me, flicking water from his hair and grinning at me with an obvious challenge in his eyes. "Bring it on!"

But we were a single synchronized unit as he turned to dive beneath the surface and I followed, and we were side by side, stroke for stroke to the end of the pool, flipping, and returning. We broke water at Coach Harmon's feet.

"Coach?" Damon queried, looking up at him.

"It seems our issues are more than resolved," Coach Harmon observed, looking at me. "I have somewhere else I could be so do you two want to continue and lock up when you're done?"

"Sure, no problem," Damon agreed, and I noted he didn't bother to look to me for confirmation. "I've got this."

I raised an eyebrow and Coach Harmon turned his attention to me. "Should I take it that from hereon in you'll be happy to join our regular training sessions?" he asked.

"Yes, Coach. No problem."

"Good, good. Well, any problems, you've got my number, so I'll leave you guys to it. See you next time, Eike."

"Thank you, Coach."

And with that, he was gone.

Despite having the pool and, in fact, the entire building, to ourselves, Damon didn't lose focus as I fully expected he might. We did laps and he stopped me often to check I was doing all right.

"No pain?" he'd ask. "No cramps? No panic?"

Finally, it seemed he was ready to call it a day and this time there was no need to assist me from the water. He tossed his towel onto the bench as we walked into the change rooms, stripped off his suit, and turned on the shower.

"How're you feeling?" he asked me. "How's your back? Honestly."

"I'm fine," I said, doing my best to keep my eyes in a safe place without a lot of success. "A bit tight maybe, but nothing to be concerned about."

"Hmm," he mused. "I'll take the knots out anyway."

I couldn't help but smile.

"If you insist," I said.

"I do. Get your arse over here."

I willingly obliged and stepped under the water with him.

"Haven't you forgotten something?" Damon murmured in my ear.

"Not that I'm aware of. What?"

"Well," Damon said, his body close to mine, "there's only us here and I'm fairly sure you're not half as shy as I first thought you were."

"What?"

Damon ran a hand down my back, stopping just above my tailbone, and a tremor followed his touch. I sucked in a shocked breath.

"You think maybe you could lose the suit?"

I couldn't help it, it was pure reflex and totally out of my control. I blushed. Deeply. And Damon laughed.

"You *are* shy," he observed with intense amusement. "You need some help with that?"

"No!" I said, my face hot and my respiration rate rapidly increasing.

I slid out of my suit and tossed it out of the shower and Damon pulled me closer before turning me around to face the wall. I closed my eyes, on the verge of hyperventilating, and Damon put his hands on my shoulders.

"Just taking out the knots," he said, his voice husky and sounding as breathless as I was.

Yeah, right. Whatever.

But that was where he began.

With soapy hands he worked my shoulders and neck and after a bit I relaxed, pressed my hands to the wall, and dropped my head between my arms, just as I'd done on the previous occasion he'd done this. I had to admit he was good. With professional expertise, he worked the knots and aches out of my muscles and for a moment I completely forgot what our relationship had only recently become. Until his hands slid over my buttocks.

I immediately tensed.

"Relax," he murmured. "This is muscle too."

Sure, but I certainly wasn't accustomed to strong, soapy hands running over them. His hands moved back up, over my hips, my stomach, my ribs. My breathing once again quickened and my legs were weak. He lowered his mouth to one shoulder, moving up my neck and under my ear and I found myself turning to meet him, my mouth seeking his. His hands, meanwhile, didn't stop moving and, as our mouths locked, I followed suit, as ready to explore his body as he was already exploring mine.

"Lights on or off?" he asked, pulling back, his breath coming in short, hard gasps between his words.

"I really don't give a fuck," I managed to reply.

The ache was back, that hot, hard throbbing that seemed to have been waiting from the first time I'd laid eyes on him back on that first day of college. And going by the heat lying against my thigh, I wasn't alone.

"Are you afraid?" Damon asked, his voice unsteady.

Yes, no, I don't know.

"Of you? No."

"And this? What we're about to do? Are you afraid of that?"

I was barely standing now, my legs like jelly and my stomach a churning butterfly swarm of anticipation.

"No," I managed to whisper.

"That's just as well, Eike," Damon practically snarled in my ear, "because I don't think I could hold this much longer."

And before I could really register what was happening, he'd turned me back to face the wall.

Did we have any idea what we were doing? No. Had Damon had any previous experience? Like this? Highly unlikely. Had I? Most definitely not. We were clumsy and desperate and rough and raw. Damon was powerful and although I imagine he did his best to control himself, he was no gentle lover. He sank his teeth into my neck and his hands clasped my hips, my shoulders, as if he were clinging to the edge of a cliff he was about to fall from. I braced myself, but my legs were unsteady and I had absolutely no idea how to prepare myself for him. It was pain, it was pleasure, it was everything we could have hoped for and nothing we could have expected. It was perfect.

We stood under the water for a long time, not moving even though the ache had gone and all that remained was a profound and lingering warmth, until finally Damon roused himself and turned off the shower.

"Come on," he said. "Time to go."

I followed him reluctantly and picked up my towel. Carefully.

"I am profoundly grateful," I observed, "that I am not biking home."

Damon blushed. "Did I hurt you?" he asked. "I swear I didn't mean to, I just, it's just … you do this thing to me. It's like a drug."

"I'm not bloody fragile," I told him. "I mean, I'll be honest and say I'll be feeling you for a while but no doubt it'll get easier. And trust me," I added, "it was worth it."

"Are you sure?" Damon insisted. "Maybe next time…"

"Next time what?" I asked. "You'll go easier on me? Like hell you will. Now come on already. I'm freezing!"

He intended to take me out for dinner at Meg's but, as I pointed out to him as delicately as I could, there was no way I was going to have a hope of walking in there without every single soul present guessing exactly what had just happened between us.

"I'm sorry," he said.

"Like fuck you are. And neither am I. Are you going to react like this every time?"

"Every time?" he asked, blinking at me.

"You're not suggesting that was both the first time and the last time, are you?"

Damon grinned, discomfort instantly forgotten. "Hell, no!"

"Then get the fuck over it and let's get drive through. I'm starving."

He stopped the truck in the driveway.

"Can I walk you in?" he asked. "Should I?"

"It's possible you may have to," I suggested with a low groan.

"Really? Is it that bad? Shit, I said I was sorry."

He once again sounded genuinely concerned and I laughed at him.

"I'm kidding, all right? I'm fine. Seriously."

"I should probably still walk you in," he said.

"What the fuck, Damon? It's not as if this is the first time you've dropped me home and it's not like I'm a blushing first date or anything. Cut it out, already! Besides," I added, "the last thing I need is any more temptation."

"Temptation, is it now?" he asked, his tension easily deflected.

"Yes," I admitted. "So, I'm going to go now and I'll see you tomorrow. And if you could be a little bit less obvious, *especially* tomorrow, I'd appreciate it."

Damon chuckled. "I'll do my best, though I offer no guarantees. Do I get a goodbye?"

"I think you've had quite enough of me for one night," I informed him, and before he could respond I was out of the truck and heading for the door. It seemed to me there was a considerable delay before I heard his truck pull away.

Chapter Thirteen

There is something indescribable in giving yourself over totally and completely to trusting, never mind loving, somebody else, to letting go of all fear and doubt and simply giving in to the moment. For the first time in as long as I could recall, Xia's voice was finally silent and I understood completely what Spex had meant when he'd said, *I couldn't hear her voice any more, after you made everything all right again.* That was exactly how I felt about Damon. Damon silenced my brother's voice. Damon took the power out of Xia's warning words. So what if *boys liked boys*? Damon did nothing to hide the way he felt about me and, with him at my side, I neither cared, nor felt as if I had anything to fear.

Perhaps I'd become as foolish as he appeared to be. All caution blown to the wind, it never occurred to either one of us to consider the potential repercussions of our undisguised feelings for each other. His friends readily accepted us, far from what I admit my expectations had been, and this did nothing to lend us to discretion. I imagine, thinking on it afterwards, that his friends had always suspected in which direction Damon's inclinations had lain and thus they were able to be genuinely happy for him, and for us. In any event, they gave no indication they were in the least disturbed or offended by our very blatant relationship and, if anything, were wholly supportive.

Oddly enough, though Damon made no secret of his possession of me, nor me of him, for some reason, as far as many of the girls were concerned, this seemed to make us only the more attractive. Forbidden and unattainable fruit or something? Or something else. I don't know but if we had any intention of sailing below the radar, that opportunity very quickly passed us by.

For me, with Damon and his friends, who were now my friends as well, as my personal entourage, any fears Spex and Damon had expressed for my safety seemed unfounded. I felt bullet-proof and invulnerable. I was living in a private bubble of euphoria from which I felt I couldn't be broken. Life was perfect.

"You are happy, Eike?" Grandmother said to me at dinner one Saturday night as I checked my phone yet again for a text from Damon to say he was on his way.

"Yes, Grandmother," I said, giving her a genuine smile. "I am happy."

Grandmother nodded and looked to Grandfather, who smiled.

"Damon makes you happy?" Grandmother asked softly.

"Yes," I agreed without hesitation. "Damon makes me happy."

"Then we are happy for you too, Eike."

"Thank you, Grandmother."

If my grandparents had any doubts or reservations about my relationship with Damon, they kept silent and never once expressed any judgement. I couldn't have put into words how grateful I was to them for their support and I honestly don't know what I would've done if they'd chosen to take any other stance. I loved and respected my grandparents deeply and I would never, ever have wished to have stood against them, but Damon had become a part of my life I don't believe I could live without.

Fortunately, it was not a choice they forced me to make.

Damon arrived as I was putting away the last of the after-dinner dishes.

"You didn't text," I said as he came up behind me and put his arms around me to rest his head on my shoulder in what had become his trade-mark gesture.

"Hmm," he sighed in my ear. "I wanted to surprise you.'

He bit my ear and then my neck, his hands drifting down, drawing me close and clearly indicating where his mind was at. I reverse head-butted him, if only half-heartedly.

"Damon, respect!"

"Sorry," he murmured, sounding anything but and stopping nothing.

"I mean it," I said, shifting sideways to put the dishrack away and forcing him to side-step with me. "Where are we going anyway?"

"Meg's," he said, pulling my shirt far enough free of my jeans to place his hands against my bare skin.

I stomped on his foot.

"Ouch!" he exclaimed, pulling his foot free and releasing me. "You can be so rough."

"And you can be so disrespectful," I countered. "Can't you at least wait until we're out of the house?"

"Your grandparents don't seem to mind," he murmured, edging back into position behind me and putting his hands on my hips.

I elbowed him in the ribs. "That," I pointed out, "is because they choose not to look, because they know how to exercise discretion, something which you appear to lack. There's no need to be disrespectful in their house."

Damon sighed deeply and retreated. "You're right and I'm sorry. Forgive me?"

"I might," I said, grabbing my jacket off the back of a chair. "Are we collecting Spex on the way?"

"Yes," Damon replied. "I've already told him to be ready at the end of his drive and we wouldn't be long."

"Oh," I said, "so I see how it is. You talk to Spex but not to me?"

Damon grinned.

"Jealous?"

"Yes," I admitted, glaring at him from beneath a frown. "What do you intend to do about it?"

"Let me get you in the truck and I'll show you," Damon chuckled.

"You are shameless."

"I know."

Being Saturday night, Meg's was packed. Damon casually took my hand and shouldered his way to where his, *our,* friends sat and Spex followed us, staying close to reduce the risk of becoming separated from us in the throng. Ox and Brett gave up their seats for us and went in search of more and Damon pulled me into his lap while indicating Spex take the remaining chair.

"I could so get used to this," he said, resting his chin in my neck while locking his hands around my waist.

Although I did my best not to, I couldn't help but notice that, although those at our table seemed neither to notice nor to care, people elsewhere were definitely looking, if not directly staring.

"Damon," I muttered, shifting uncomfortably.

"What? Them? Fuck 'em," Damon laughed. "Do I look as if I care?"

"No," I admitted, "but then you never do."

"Does it bother you?" he asked, merely tightening his grip on me and blatantly running his tongue up under my ear.

"I don't know," I replied honestly, unconsciously leaning into his caress, "but sooner or later, and probably sooner at this rate, your father's going to find out and even with what little you've said, or not said, about him, that kind of bothers me."

Damon sucked a breath sharply through his teeth. "Fuck him, too," he said bitterly. "He can go to hell!"

He squeezed me, bit my ear possessively, and pushed me free so he could get to his feet. The conversation, for now at least, was over.

"Drinks," he said. "I'll be back."

"You two are just so gorgeous together," Amy said, leaning towards me across the table. "And I don't think any of us have *ever* seen Damon this happy. You're good for him."

I blinked, embarrassed, and heat rose into my face. "Um, thanks," I murmured.

Amy laughed. "And look at Cara and Spex," she added, tilting her head.

"What?"

I turned to look in the direction she'd indicated and my eyes widened in surprise. Cara was perched in Spex's lap, much as I'd a moment ago been perched in Damon's, and she had her hands locked behind his neck, whispering in his ear. Spex was grinning broadly, his arm wrapped *very* comfortably around Cara's waist. Well, knock me over with a feather! Go, Spex!

Damon returned a few minutes later and quickly noticed the new seating arrangement between Cara and Spex.

"I see somebody's moved on," he observed quietly into my ear, and I wasn't sure to which one of them he was referring.

"It does appear that way," I agreed as he placed the tray of drinks on the table. "A bit of a relief, to be honest."

"Why's that?" Damon asked, leaning over me and tilting his head.

I grabbed his hair and pulled him closer.

"I was getting tired of her mooning over you and him mooning over me," I admitted, and kissed him, fairly indiscreetly.

When we disengaged, he smirked lecherously at me. "What happened to subtlety?" he asked, stabbing at me with an accusatory finger.

I shrugged. "If it's good enough for you…" I grinned at him.

He lifted a hand as if to cuff me and at that moment Brett and Ox returned, dragging spare chairs. Damon took one to sit beside me, putting an arm around my waist and dragging me closer so he could lean into my shoulder.

"Not quite what I'd prefer," he admitted, "but does this qualify as more discreet?"

"Bit late," I pointed out, "but yes."

"Whatever you want," he murmured, attempting to consume my ear.

We played pool and, true to everybody's predictions at commencement of play, Damon and I resoundingly kicked butt.

"Absolutely no fair," Ed complained as we returned to our table after the last round. "At the very least, I think we should draw for partners or something."

"I couldn't agree more," Ox muttered, not very quietly, he and Ed having lost by the greatest margin.

"Hey!" Ed growled, kicking Ox in the shins.

"Just saying," Ox shrugged, giving Ed a friendly shove. "I won the last time we played, which is what happens if you have Eike as a partner."

Damon grinned smugly and hugged me possessively.

"Which is why there's no way this side of hell freezing over that I'm giving him up," he said.

"You're a jerk," Ed informed him.

"Yes, and what do you plan to do about it?"

Ed frowned.

"That's what I thought," Damon laughed.

He drew me towards him and kissed me.

Ed screwed up his face and everybody laughed.

"Right," Damon said, pulling me into his lap with him as he sat down. "Time to make some plans."

"Plans?" Brett asked. "What kind of plans?"

"It's my birthday next week…" Damon began casually.

"Wait! What? Why didn't you tell me?" I asked in surprise, twisting to look at him.

"I'm telling you now," Damon replied. "Now, quiet. I'm trying to talk."

"I…"

Damon put his hand over my mouth.

"Quiet or I'll be forced to *make* you quiet!"

I shut my mouth and Damon removed his hand.

"That will keep," I muttered under my breath.

"I sincerely hope so," Damon whispered in my ear, and then, "Now, as I was saying before I was so rudely interrupted, it's my birthday next week and I was thinking that, *just because*, we might have to do something special."

"A party?" Cara squealed.

"*So* last week," Damon replied with a sigh of mock disgust. "No, I was thinking we should go to Temptations and really make an event of it."

"Temptations?" Spex asked, sounding shocked. "The night club?"

"Well, yes," Damon replied. "The night club. What else would I mean?"

"Dude," Brett said, no doubt merely voicing the thoughts of all of us, "in case it had escaped your attention, most of us, maybe even all of us, can't go." He turned to look around the table. "Who of us here, except for Damon, has a Black Card?"

There was silence and Brett looked at Damon with a clear 'I told you so' expression.

Damon shrugged. "You guys overthink things too much and you have no faith. After all, perks, right?"

I twisted to look at him again. "Your father's?" I guessed.

"Yes. I may not like the bastard but it doesn't mean I can't take advantage of what's his. You guys just make sure you're free *next* Saturday night and leave the rest to me."

And so that, as far as Damon was concerned, was that.

We dropped Spex back at his house and then, instead of driving on towards my house, Damon u-turned the truck.

"Um," I queried nonchalantly, "wrong way?"

"Right way, actually," Damon responded, equally as nonchalantly.

"My house, in case you'd forgotten, happens to be back the other way," I reminded him with a suspicious frown.

"As if I didn't know that already," Damon snorted.

"So ... what are you doing?"

"I happen to have another surprise for you."

"Oh?"

"Your overnight bag is in the back-seat, which Grandmother packed for you so I'm assuming it has everything you're likely to need, and I'm taking you to the Winchester Royal Grand."

My mouth dropped open as I turned in my seat to stare incredulously at him. "The Winchester? As in the hotel? *That* Winchester?"

"Yes. I'm tired of making out with you in my truck and in the shower and at the reservoir. I want some space, and a bed. I want to actually *sleep* with you and as I can't do that at your house out of respect for your grandparents and I most definitely can't take you to *my* place, I've booked us a room. As a matter of fact," he added, as casually as if mentioning he was planning on getting us both a haircut, "I've booked us the Penthouse Suite."

"You're shitting me," I said.

"Since when have you known me to make any kind of joke in respect of you and me?" Damon asked.

He had a point.

The Winchester Royal Grand is the biggest hotel in the county and the jewel in the crown of the Kings' hotel empire and I felt decidedly out of place as Damon handed the keys of his truck to a valet and took both our bags through the vast marble-floored lobby.

"Mr. King, sir," the desk clerk said respectfully as Damon leaned against the counter.

"Good evening, Adam," Damon replied with a nod. "Penthouse, please."

"Yes, sir, it's all ready. Shall I send someone up with your bags?"

"No, thank you. I think we'll manage," Damon smiled. "But if you could send room service as per our previous arrangement?"

"Certainly, Mr. King, sir. I'll have them up shortly. Shall we say twenty minutes? To give yourself and your, uh, *friend* some time to make yourselves at home?"

Damon raised an eyebrow but offered nothing to satisfy the desk clerk's unspoken curiosity.

"Thank you, Adam," he said. "Have a good evening."

"Thank you, sir. Enjoy your stay."

Damon's lip twitched on the edge of a grin and there was a definite glint in his eye.

"I plan to, Adam."

I followed Damon towards the elevators, keeping my eyes focused on his broad shoulders, his muscular back, his breath-taking physique, not wanting to acknowledge the attention we were receiving, and Damon grabbed my arm to hurry me along. He pressed the 'Up' button and was hustling me inside even as the elevator doors were opening. Fortunately, the elevator was empty because the doors had no sooner shut before he'd driven me against the back wall and pinned me with his body.

"I very, very desperately want to do something extremely bad to you right now," he whispered huskily in my ear, his hands already demonstrating just how sincerely he meant his words, "but this damn thing has a camera in it."

"Clearly just as well," I groaned, sweat breaking on my body and my knees going weak.

"Doesn't stop me doing this, however," Damon observed, invading my mouth with his tongue.

Jesus!

I was gasping for breath when we finally reached the top floor and Damon hauled me out of the elevator. I stood awestruck at the vast expanse of the apartment beyond the elevator as he casually picked up our bags and told me to 'make myself at home'.

It was like the set of a James Bond movie and I can honestly say I'd never seen anything so opulent in my life. The space, incorporating the entire central upper floor, was beyond vast, it was ludicrous and not unlike finding a single living area built into a school gymnasium. Who could possibly ever require this much space, especially for a one-night stay? Most incredible and awe-inspiring of all were the glass walls, they could hardly be termed windows, opening out to what I assumed was some kind of exotic timber decking and a spectacular infinity pool, and beyond that the twin vistas of the night sky and the glittering kaleidoscope of the city.

Damon returned from wherever it was he'd deposited our bags and put his arms around me, burying his face in my neck.

"Will it do, do you think?" he asked.

"Will it do? Jesus, Damon!"

Damon laughed and breathed into me, pulling me closer and running his mouth absently over my skin.

"You have no idea how long I've waited to be able to find an opportunity to get you here," he murmured. "I have every intention of making it worth every moment."

I closed my eyes to lean back into his embrace and at that moment, the elevator pinged.

"Room service," Damon informed me, releasing me and turning away.

Had it been twenty minutes already? It certainly hadn't felt like it but Damon returned a moment later, followed by a uniformed valet and a well-laden trolley.

"Will there be anything else, sir?" the valet asked, keeping his eyes on Damon.

"No, thank you," Damon replied. "I think that'll be all."

The valet turned away.

"Wait!" Damon called after him.

"Sir?"

"Please inform the desk that we're not to be disturbed," Damon said. "Short of an actual impending disaster, not so much as a phone call. Understood?"

"Yes, sir. Absolutely. Do not disturb."

Damon grinned, the valet backed away, turned and left, and we were alone.

We were alone and in the Penthouse Suite of the Winchester Grand Hotel. I needed a little time to acclimatize or assimilate or whatever it was I needed to do, but Damon was in no mood to accommodate me.

"Come on," he said. "There's a pool."

Very observant of him. Yes, there was.

"No suit required," Damon added with a sly grin, dropping his jacket suggestively to the floor.

I stared at him.

"What?" he asked, pausing halfway through pulling his tee-shirt free of his jeans. His lips twitched halfway to laughing at me. "Nothing you haven't seen before."

This was entirely true but there was something vastly different between stripping in a pool change room and stripping here in this ridiculously huge and far too brightly lit suite.

"The lights bothering you?" he asked, reading my thoughts as he had a disconcerting habit of doing.

I shrugged and Damon clapped his hands. My mouth dropped open as the lights dimmed.

"What the fuck?"

Damon clapped his hands again and the lights dimmed some more. "Better?"

"I guess so," I said, still not moving.

"I always said you were shy," Damon chuckled, removing his Doc's and casually unbuttoning his jeans.

It was beginning to occur to me just where we *really* were; his father's hotel. His father's iconic number one hotel. What was Damon really doing? What was this really all about? I chewed my lip and shifted my feet apprehensively. I wasn't shy; I was nervous, maybe even more than a little afraid.

Damon strolled towards me, his unbuttoned, unzipped jeans hanging on his lean hips, his bare, sun-burnished torso gleaming in the muted lights and my breath caught as he put his hands on my shoulders, all other thoughts driven temporarily from my mind by his ever-intoxicating presence.

"There's just you and me, Eike. There's nobody to see and nobody to judge. What are you afraid of?"

Not you, I thought, my heart racing, but…

"Nothing, it's just…"

"Stop over-thinking things," he said, bunching my shirt in his hands and rolling it up my sides.

I closed my eyes, allowing him to remove it, and he tossed it aside to run a hand over my ribs, the other pulling me closer so he could put his mouth to mine. His tongue flickered between my lips and heat rushed through me like a spring tide.

"Not so hard, is it?" he murmured, running his tongue up my cheek bone and under one ear.

Depends on what you're referring to, I thought, struggling to breathe. How was it he always managed to do this to me?

His hands shifted to my hips and, with a parting kiss, he turned me around and drew me closer, his fingers moving without hesitation to undo the dome, the zip. His mouth caressed my shoulders, my neck, my scars.

"You are as intoxicating," he said, "as whiskey or Patrón. When I am with you…"

He didn't finish the sentence and instead hooked his fingers into my jeans and slid them down my hips. I was already gasping for air but I didn't move, forcing myself to remain still while he finished relieving me of my clothing until I was left naked while he remained half-dressed. I was also in what could be considered a rather vulnerable position, with Damon down on one knee, his cheek pressed to my hip.

"Interesting," he murmured.

One way of putting it and I fully expected him to take advantage of his position. Instead, he rose smoothly to his feet, drawing a finger delicately after him and nearly bringing me to my own knees. I was definitely struggling by now but he ignored me and pushed me firmly in the direction of the pool.

"Not yet," he said. "We're going swimming."

I stumbled out to the pool and Damon's hand slipped from my shoulder. A moment later he strode past me, also naked, and in a single, spectacular somersault plunged into the pool. To me, the water was like a flame to a moth: a lure I couldn't resist even without the added attraction of Damon's presence, and I was soon in the water alongside him.

For those who've never experienced it, swimming naked is exhilarating at the best of times. But to be swimming naked with someone like Damon was an experience all its own. He was free in a way even his extrovert personality couldn't fully express out of the water and his every movement was like a dance; fluid and sinuous and beautiful. I matched him, turn for turn, lap for lap, and dance for perfect dance. We never touched and we didn't have to for it to be the most sensual experience of my life.

Finally, floating side by side on our backs, staring up at a perfect star-studded night sky, Damon reached for my hand.

"Are you happy, Eike?" he asked.

"Happier than I've ever been in my life," I admitted honestly. "And you? Are you happy?"

"I want this moment to never end," he said, "but…"

He released my hand, rolled, and dove under me to surface on my opposite side and dunk me, before grinning at me as I re-surfaced, spluttering with surprise.

"…I am fucking starving! Come on, let's eat!"

He dove again and emerged poolside to swing himself gracefully from the water, while I followed somewhat regretfully in his wake.

Chapter Fourteen

Though Damon might often tease *me* about my apparent shyness, *shy* was definitely not a word which could be applied to him. Without bothering to grab so much as a towel, he swept naked into the suite and drew the trolley the valet had delivered earlier towards the cluster of white leather sofas arranged to face out over the deck.

"Come on," he called out to me. "Stop pissing about already and get over here."

Unlike Damon, I wasn't quite as comfortable inside my own skin, even in the privacy and security of the hotel suite, and I grabbed one of the plush white spa towels from inside the giant sliders and wrapped it around my waist.

"What did you have to go and do that for?" he scowled. "You're spoiling the view."

I ignored him. "What've we got?" I inquired, dropping down beside him on the sofa.

He grabbed at my towel but I'd anticipated him and jabbed at his sternum with two straight fingers. He jerked back his hand with a pained expression and a sharp exclamation.

"Shit, Eike! What was that for?"

"Dessert comes *after* the main course in my experience," I informed him blandly, indicating the trolley with a tilt of my chin. "I asked, what've we got?"

Damon rubbed at his chest. "You can be so harsh," he grumbled. "Your point?"

"I could show you," he suggested, leaning towards me.

"Did you require another reminder?"

"No," Damon sighed. He lifted the cover off the trolley.

Damon had gone all out selecting the items for the trolley and he took great pleasure in making me sample from everything, from oysters to olives and more cheeses than I knew existed, to strawberries and chocolate.

To help wash it down, he raided the Penthouse liquor cabinet, which was also extensive.

"I don't drink," I reminded him as he offered me a shot of Patrón.

"Can I ask why?" he asked, putting the shot glasses on the table as he sat to face me. "Not that I wish to push you into something you don't want to do, I'm just curious."

I shrugged, sighing as I stared into a vacant space somewhere past his left shoulder.

"My brother, Xia, I guess," I said. "It was what he said and what it meant to me and I guess I just kind of developed a fear of losing control as a result. And drinking, to me at least, equates to losing control."

To be honest, not only was it the first time I'd ever pursued the origins of my aversion to drinking but it was also the first time I'd discussed my brother, and those words of caution, with Damon or with anybody else. I dipped my head and blinked back tears and Damon, as I'd once done for him, remained silent and waited.

"*Boys don't like boys, and pretty boys get into trouble,*" I murmured, half to myself.

I looked up at Damon and it must have been obvious my tears were waiting to fall.

"Do you think I'm *pretty*?" I asked him.

Damon grinned.

"Pretty? You? Honestly?"

I nodded, my heart catching in my throat. Damon shook his head.

"No," he said. "I don't know how old you were when your brother suggested you were *pretty*, but could you be called pretty now? No, not remotely and not even. Eike, you're gorgeous, I'll grant you that, and ask *anybody* and they'll tell you the same thing. But *pretty*? No."

He leaned closer and placed an arm around my shoulders, his skin cool against my own, and very gently kissed my cheek.

"And *I'm* here now. Whatever trouble your brother anticipated, we'll face it together, ok?"

I nodded, breathing deeply. How could I not be instantly reassured by Damon's presence and his seemingly limitless confidence? Damon picked up one of the shots of Patrón, tipped it into his mouth, and kissed me.

"It's getting really, really late," he murmured as the combined fire of Patrón and his kiss coursed through me, "or very, very early depending on your perspective. Can I take you to bed now?"

"Time for dessert?" I murmured, running my tongue over my lips to savour the lingering aftertaste of his loaded kiss.

He tipped the remaining shot into his mouth and kissed me again, this time simultaneously relieving me of my towel, and I arched up against him, the combination of Patrón, his kiss, and his hands a completely new and intoxicating experience. Without further word, Damon drew away from me, took my hand, and led me to the bedroom.

Whereas the décor in the main suite was primarily white, the bedroom, in stark contrast, was furbished in far darker shades. The vast expanse of the bed, which dominated the room, was dressed entirely in black; black sheets, an abundance of huge black pillows, and a heavy black swans-down comforter. The curtains were black, whereas the walls were a soft pearl grey reminiscent of rain clouds at dawn. The plush shag-pile carpet was a swirl of varying shades of charcoal and grey and the light shades were opal shot with silver.

The overall effect was not so much one of opulence as of decadence and I stood at the bedroom door and stared, momentarily overwhelmed. Damon let go of me long enough to clap his hands to dim the lights before once again taking hold of my hand.

He pulled back the comforter and pushed me gently to the bed before positioning himself on one elbow beside me.

"Do you still hear him?" he asked, his free hand gently caressing my body, his fingertips leaving a trail of goose bumps in their wake.

I closed my eyes, floating on the blended effects of swimming, alcohol, and Damon, and managed to shake my head. "Not like I once did," I replied. "Not for a while now, but sometimes."

"Sometimes when?" Damon asked, leaning over me, biting me, and rolling his tongue in a spot that had me arching my back and groaning in response.

"Times like when you kiss me and touch me in public," I managed to respond in between struggling to breathe.

Damon shifted gradually downwards and my breathing became even more erratic.

"And now?" he continued, his exploration of my body taking nearly all my capacity for coherent thought.

"I… I…"

There was no way I could've spoken even if I could've remembered what it was I wanted to say. Damon's hands, his mouth, his body on mine, stole every remaining memory I had of Xia and I allowed myself to descend into the erotic fantasy world of Damon's making. My body moved of its own volition, seeking his, and we rolled together, our bodies interlocked into one.

If our first and subsequent encounters before our night at the Winchester Royal Grand had been clumsy and raw, driven more by primal lust than by technique and repeatedly limited by our location, this was something else entirely. The bed was more than sufficiently large to accommodate the both of us, no matter which way our passions took us, and it was deep and warm and soft. Damon demonstrated there was nothing he was unwilling to explore and, as for me, I simply surrendered to him and went along for the ride. When at last we'd exhausted both our imaginations and our energy, he pulled up the comforter and we lay curled in each other's arms and slept without dreaming.

I don't know at what time I awoke, as the heavy black drapes eliminated all light from beyond the windows and there was only darkness to greet me, but I awoke to Damon making it more than clear he was by no means done with me and that he was ready for more. It was as if awakening in a dream, an extremely sensuous and erotic dream, his mouth and hands drawing me from sleep in a manner I'd very definitely never before experienced. The result was beyond spectacular, arising from dreaming into an arc of indescribable pleasure, and when he rose up my body to cup my face in his hands and kiss me, I could taste myself in his kiss. It was surprising but not in the least disturbing and it was instead as if there was nothing left to share, as if everything that was both of us had become blended into one. He drew me in, absorbed me, fulfilled me, and it was surreal, leaving us suspended in a state completely divorced from reality.

If I'd thought I had nothing more to give, I was wrong, and it wasn't long before I was once again willing to accommodate him, his hands clasped to my shoulder, my hip, his body pressing close to mine and his heart beat resonating through my skin. I turned my head so his mouth could find mine and consigned myself to him even when he struggled to control his obvious passion.

"It's ok," I told him, when his mouth left mine. "You don't need to be gentle for my sake. Whatever you need, I can handle it."

"I can't," he groaned. "I can't! I don't want to hurt you."

I wrapped my arms around the pillows on which I lay and pressed my body against his.

"Let go, Damon. For Christ's sake, just let go."

And he did, and when it was over and he'd rolled away to lie spent and exhausted on his back beside me, I put my head to his shoulder and an arm across his chest, my body close and my heartbeat keeping time with his.

"Are you ok?" I asked him.

His eyes were closed but there was the faintest smile on his lips. "You are the most incredible thing that has ever happened to me," he whispered. "How could there be life without you?"

"Why should there be?" I replied. "I love you."

And I realised only in that very moment that I did, truly, deeply, and completely.

We got up very late in the morning and Damon called down for breakfast to be sent up. While we waited, we showered, and Damon again demonstrated his seemingly insatiable capacity for intimacy.

"Jesus, Damon," I groaned as I struggled to get dressed, "I swear it's worse than competing in an Ironman Challenge with you!"

Damon grinned as he drew on his jeans and rose smoothly to his feet to pull on a clean shirt.

"Ironman, am I now?" he asked. "You Hapkido fighters, no stamina."

"I'd rise to that bait," I said, "if I was still able to do so, but I hereby admit that I have no choice but to concede defeat. You win."

"Are you sure you don't wish to rise just one more time?" Damon teased, taking the opportunity while I balanced precariously on one leg attempting to get my own jeans on to test his query for himself.

"Yes," I assured him. "Now fuck off!"

Damon laughed and sauntered from the room to greet the valet with the breakfast trolley.

It had gone well past mid-day before Damon finally conceded it was probably time to go home.

"One more swim before we go?" he asked suggestively.

I eyed him sceptically. "Swim? Is that what we're calling it now?" I snorted. "I don't think so, buddy. I know where your so-called *swim* will lead and I, for one, am done."

He came around behind me and wrapped his arms around me, biting my ear as his hands strayed south.

"Are you quite sure you can't be tempted?" he asked softly, almost pleadingly.

I leaned back into him, sighing and closing my eyes to his caress, but I wasn't about to be swayed.

"Undoubtedly, if you were to keep this up, I would be helpless to resist," I admitted, "but I would hold you solely responsible for my inability to function for the rest of the week, and haven't we got a swim tournament on Wednesday?"

It was Damon's turn to sigh, deeply and with infinite regret, before he straightened, though not without first stealing my breath with a strongly suggestive parting squeeze.

"As you wish," he murmured in my ear, "but don't say later that you have regrets."

I re-gathered my composure and my breath, and adjusted my clothing, and barely refrained from kicking him in the shins.

"You're a jerk," I informed him.

"Agreed. Shall we go?"

"Yes," I said. "We bloody well shall."

We held hands on our way down in the elevator, Damon discreetly managing to keep from any more intimate contact, and we emerged on the ground floor to cross the lobby towards the reception desk still hand in hand. A man was standing at the desk, his back to us, and as Damon registered his presence, his steps began gradually to slow. The man turned.

I saw the resemblance immediately; the height, the breadth of shoulder and chest, the near white-blonde hair but, whereas Damon's eyes were the warm blue of Caribbean ocean, this man had eyes like slivers of ice and whereas Damon had the slighter and more graceful physique of an athlete, this man had the broader and more powerful build of a natural pugilist. He was quite clearly Damon's father, and he didn't look at all pleased.

Coming to a standstill, Damon instinctively placed himself in front of me.

"Dad," he said, the word sliding like an icicle from between his lips.

The tall man, immaculately dressed in a striking steel-grey suit and smoke silk shirt which only served to emphasize his formidable frame, said nothing but his face was hard and his mouth a grim line.

"Damon," he said at last. "Adam told me you were here but I told him he must be mistaken. And when he told me you were not alone, I fired him." His gaze raked over Damon like a blazing torch before shifting to me, still standing half-concealed behind Damon's shoulder.

"Is that *it*?" he asked, his voice as slick and deadly as Damascus steel. "Is *that* your half-breed toy?"

His tone dripped contempt and tension rose as visibly in Damon as an inexorable tide even as my blood ran cold. This was Damon's father? How was it even remotely conceivable that my pure and beautiful Damon could possibly be the son of this pitiless and dangerous man?

"He is not an *it*, Father," Damon said, his voice extraordinarily steady. "And he is most definitely *not* my *toy*. He's my boyfriend."

There was absolutely no warning and it all happened so fast there was no way we could either have anticipated it or taken any kind of evasive action. In just a few long, determined strides, Damon's father had crossed the space between us and cross-hooked his own son.

The blows were powerful and accurate, as quick and lethal as the attacks of a striking snake, and Damon was lifted clean from his feet and thrown several feet across the floor. His father followed him, to stand over him, his fists clenched, his jaw tight, and his eyes blazing with a hard light that made my blood freeze in my veins. In shock, I could only stand and stare.

"You dirty little bastard," Damon's father swore, his voice low and deadly. "I had no idea I'd raised a fucking queer but if you think I'll accept it just because you flaunt it in my face, you can think again!"

Damon raised himself on one elbow and glared at his father as he wiped blood from the corner of his mouth. His cheek and jaw were already swelling and there was a significant cut under one eye from which blood dripped steadily to the tiled floor, but he was undaunted as he rose slowly to his feet. "Fuck you," he said softly.

This time the blow was aimed directly below his sternum and he doubled over, the wind leaving him in a rush that echoed through the silent hotel lobby. He sank slowly to his knees and this time I moved, sliding across the marble to fall to my knees at his side.

"Damon!" I cried, throwing my arms around him and blocking his body from his father with my own.

I fully expected to be kicked or at the very least dragged to my feet and struck but instead, Damon's father looked down at us, his face a blank mask, before turning and walking away, and not a soul in that accursed hotel moved, not to come to our assistance nor to say a word to that singularly terrifying man in grey. I helped Damon to his feet and, despite my silent offer of support, he insisted on standing on his own account though he took my hand with a grim resolve, clinging to it as if his life depended on it.

"Come on," he said. "Let's go."

It was all too obvious he was in a great deal of pain but he walked determinedly upright alongside me to where our bags sat undisturbed in the middle of the foyer. Reaching down to take mine, he handed it to me before picking up his own. We turned and left the hotel and the last I saw of his father was as he headed indifferently towards the hotel bar.

I insisted on driving, there being no way Damon was capable of doing so.

"I'm taking you to the hospital," I told him. "You need a doctor."

"No!" Damon said, and the set of his rapidly blackening jaw and the steel in his equally blackening eyes made it clear there would be no reasoning with him. "Take me to Ox's place. His mother is a nurse."

"I take it she's seen you like this before then?" I observed, calmly I thought, given the circumstances.

Damon looked out the passenger window. "It's not the first time," he admitted.

I wanted to ask him why he didn't do something about it, why he didn't go to the Police and lay assault charges or something, but I already understood why he didn't. Not a soul had moved, not a soul had intervened or come to us even after his father had left us there in the middle of the hotel foyer. Realistically, what chance did Damon have against the abuse of his father? I thought of Damon's kindness, his loyalty, his unfailing love for his friends and their equally unfailing love of him, and was left both in awe of him and very nearly overwhelmed by an immense wave of affection for him. This was his life, his reality, his role model for behaviour, and yet he was as far removed from his father as the moon is removed from the sun.

"How?" I asked, unable to express the question any more clearly.

"My mother," Damon replied, innately understanding what I'd meant to ask. "She had the same limitless capacity for love and compassion as your grandparents do. Everything I do and everything I am, I owe to her and I do for her."

I barely dared ask but I felt he was waiting for me to, so he could tell me and relieve himself of the secret of it.

"What happened to her?"

Damon sighed and then coughed and groaned. He broke into a clammy sweat and his golden tan appeared to fade to grey before my eyes. He wrapped an arm around his middle as his jaw flexed against the pain. "They say it was an accident," he said. "That she drove too fast and lost control and left the road, up on the summit near the reservoir." He stared again out the passenger window and I saw the tension in the lines of his silhouette as I glanced sideways at him. "But I think everybody knows," he added quietly, half to himself, "though nobody is ever going to admit they even *think* it, that it was no accident and that, somehow, *he* killed her."

Sweet Jesus! His mother, and then Harper? How was he still Damon as I knew him? He turned, painfully, and laid a hand on my shoulder.

"You go on, don't you?" he said, once again reading my thoughts. "You go on and you do the best you can by their memory, because that's the way you honour them."

I thought of my family and my grandparents and of the way Grandmother had spoken of my mother when I'd been asked to return to swimming, and I understood exactly what he meant.

Ox was in his driveway tinkering with his motocross bike when we pulled up and he took one look at me behind the wheel and Damon slumped against the passenger door and knew instantly what was going on.

"Mom!" he called out. "Mom! It's Damon!"

He'd already left what he was doing and was at Damon's door before I could extricate myself from the driver's side. I reached him in time to take one side of Damon while he supported the other and between us we half-carried him into the house where Ox's mother, a capable looking woman in jeans and plaid shirt, and Amy, met us in the kitchen.

"Take him through to your room, Ox," Ox's mother instructed us, and I immediately liked her on account of not using Ox's given name in front of his friends.

I followed Ox's lead and we took Damon through the kitchen and down the hall to what was obviously Ox's room. Very carefully, we helped Damon onto Ox's bed.

"What happened?" Ox's mother asked, and I knew she was referring not to who had done this to him or even to the circumstances but to what injuries she ought to be looking for.

"Jaw, face, and stomach," I informed her. "He's been holding his middle all the way here."

Damon groaned. His face was a terribly unhealthy shade of pale and there was a sheen of sweat on his brow and cheeks. Dark rings were beginning to appear under both his eyes and the shadow that encompassed one entire side of his face was definitely not natural.

"Get the kit," Ox's mother instructed Amy. "And a bowl of warm water, a flannel, and a towel," she told Ox.

Amy and Ox left the room with an urgency born of too much practice and I stepped back to allow their mother more room to manoeuvre, though staying within Damon's line of sight.

"Damon?" she asked, pulling Ox's study chair alongside Damon's bed and taking his hand to put her fingers to his wrist and check his pulse. "Where does it hurt, honey?"

She glanced at her watch and counted off the seconds before putting his hand back alongside him, and Damon's eyes fluttered as he made an attempt to focus on her. I wondered if he was about to pass out but he placed his hands on his abdomen and Ox's mother very gently lifted his shirt. I couldn't help myself. My breath caught in a sharp intake of shock and I pressed a hand to my mouth. Oh, Damon!

Damon's belly was distended and rapidly beginning to bruise, a deep black circle just above his navel clearly indicating the shape of his father's fist. Ox's mother laid a hand over it and Damon groaned deeply, a single tear sliding down his cheek as his eyes closed.

"I know, honey, and I'm sorry but I have to know what he's done," Ox's mother said softly as she gently palpated around the bruise before shifting her attention both outwards and downwards.

Damon was struggling not to tense against her exploration and I could only imagine how much self-control he must be exercising to not cry out. He whimpered and my heart nearly broke for him.

Ox and Amy returned and I backed up even further though I wanted nothing more than to take Damon's hand in my own. Perhaps reading my thoughts or perhaps simply needing my reassurance in his misery, Damon reached out a hand to me.

Chapter Fifteen

"It isn't actually as bad as it looks," Ox's mother reassured me after she'd given Damon anti-inflammatories and something for the pain and he'd finally drifted into a fitful sleep. "Despite appearances, there's no internal injury, it's only bruising and it'll subside over the next few days."

"How often?" I asked, my voice low with emotion. "How often does this happen?"

We were sitting in their kitchen with a cup of tea and she looked at me as if really noticing me for the first time.

"You're Damon's boyfriend, aren't you?" she asked. "The one Ox and Amy have been telling me about."

"Yes," I admitted, freely and without hesitation. "I am. That's why this happened."

I turned my head to stare blankly out the kitchen window and closed my eyes. I didn't feel guilty, at least not in the sense of feeling I could've done anything to prevent what had happened, but I did sincerely wish Damon could've been just a little more discreet. What had his father said? *If you think I'll accept it just because you flaunt it in my face!* Was that what Damon had intended? Had he somehow thought that if he turned up with me, in public, at his father's biggest hotel, his father would have no choice but to at least *pretend* to accept Damon's choice? I thought of Damon's father's response and the state Damon was now in. I don't think it would be too far from the truth that if acceptance had been Damon's plan, his plan had failed spectacularly.

"This definitely isn't the first time and it happens more times than I'd care to tell," Ox's mother was saying. I forced myself back into the room and tried to focus on her words. "And it definitely isn't your fault, nor his either. Damon and his father have a curious love-hate relationship and chances are that once Damon recovers from this, his father will do something equally as impressive to the opposite side of the spectrum to make it up to him."

Thoughts of four-by-fours and credit cards crossed my mind.

"They've been doing this for years," Ox's mother continued, "ever since his mother died."

"When?" I asked. "When did he lose his mother?"

"He didn't tell you?" Ox's mother pulled her ponytail through one hand and drew her lip between her teeth. "Maybe I shouldn't be telling you any of this," she said quietly, glancing at the kitchen door as if Damon might suddenly appear.

I shrugged. "He told me she was killed in a car accident." I didn't mention Damon's suspicions. "He also told me about Harper," I continued instead, "though we try to focus more on good memories than on bad."

Ox's mother reached out and patted my hand.

"Amy said I'd like you and that you were good for Damon. I see now what she meant." She tilted her head and her expression became thoughtful. "Just tell me if I've stepped over the line but you lost your own family too, didn't you?" she probed quietly. "Ox tells me you have some terrible scars."

I rubbed my dragon self-consciously and shrugged.

"Damon and I have that in common, I guess. He was saying on the drive over here that it's memories of his mother that keep him from letting his father change him, that keeps him from letting the bitterness get to him, I guess. Which is why I wondered, you know, when?"

"Damon was twelve," Ox's mother replied. "And his father got re-married less than three months later to a pregnant bride."

What the actual fuck? No wonder there were doubts about the *accident* and perhaps no wonder Damon chose to take on the world full-on the way he did.

I wasn't exactly happy about taking my leave but, as Ox's mother pointed out, there was nothing further I could do and what Damon needed most was rest. Ox drove me home in Damon's truck.

"He'll be ok," he reassured me as I got out of the truck and grabbed my bag. "Trust me, he's tough and we've been here before. Mom will look after him and so will Amy and I. I promise he'll be all right and if there's any change, I'll call you."

I smiled at him though the smile came hard. "Thanks, Ox."

"No worries, buddy. I'll see you tomorrow."

I went straight to my room, dumped my bag, and got changed. I was angry, frightened, worried. Xia's words had returned with force to my mind and through them, overlapping them, overpowering them with their recency, were the scornful words of Damon's father. *Is this it? Is this your half-breed toy?* I saw Damon fall, saw his face as he forced himself upright, saw his pride and determination. My fists clenched in rage and I took myself to the garage where, without bothering to stop and bind my hands first, I attacked the full-length punching bag Grandfather had hung there for me on the day I'd first arrived from the rehabilitation centre. Grandfather found me there twenty minutes later, slick with sweat and my knuckles stripped and bleeding. He said nothing, merely took my shoulder and turned me away so he could bind my hands for me, and then braced the bag so I could continue.

Eventually, I wore myself out and slid to the floor to put my elbows on my knees and my head in my hands. Grandfather dropped stiffly to a crouch in front of me.

"Do you need to talk, Eike?" he asked.

"Yes," I said.

Grandfather sat beside me and put his gnarled old hand over mine and I told him everything, leaving out only the unnecessary intimate details. When I'd finished, Grandfather patted my shoulder reassuringly and gently urged me to my feet.

"Come inside, Eike. Have a shower and then come to my study. It's been a while, hasn't it, since we spent some time together?"

"Yes, Grandfather, it has."

I did as I was told.

Grandfather was waiting for me in his study and he'd poured us both a glass of wine. It was the only time I ever drank alcohol, with Grandfather, and I still clearly recalled the first time I'd done so, on my family's first death anniversary. Grandfather handed me the glass and told me to sit down, which I did, worn out both physically and emotionally. Grandfather lit his pipe and we sat there, for a while not saying anything at all.

"You know I lost both a brother and my best friend in the Gwanju uprising," Grandfather finally said, breaking the silence.

I looked at him and shook my head. No, I hadn't known. My grandparents didn't talk much about their personal lives before leaving Korea, and my mother hadn't elected to fill in any of the blanks on their behalf. Grandfather nodded sadly.

"I was not there at the time," he began. "I was in Hong Kong with your grandmother and for a very long time I carried the guilt of not having been there, though what I could have changed, I do not know."

This I understood only too well.

"We all carry our burdens of guilt, Eike," Grandfather continued, "but at the end of the day, we walk the path we choose and there is nothing to be gained in looking back over our shoulder at where we have been because then we will only miss the path that lies ahead."

I bowed my head and studied my bruised and bloodied knuckles.

"Damon's path is his to walk but if you choose to walk it alongside him, and he walks alongside you, keep in mind that all the hurdles are yours to share as much as are the straight and easy roads. Do you understand?"

Grandfather paused and drew on his pipe as he looked at me with an intensely grave expression. I shifted uneasily under his scrutiny and he lifted an eyebrow though he didn't smile.

"And the path you have chosen will have more hurdles than most."

This much I could not deny. "What should I do, Grandfather?"

"If this is what lies as true in your heart then stand by him and the path will open before you. Do not look back and do not second-guess yourself. There is no such thing as standing still, there is only moving forward or sliding back. Even when you think you are merely standing still, everything else will continue to move and it will pass you by and leave you behind."

"I'm not leaving him, Grandfather."

Grandfather's serious expression faded and he smiled around the stem of his pipe. "Sometimes it is not about leaving or staying," he observed, "it is about being brave enough to know which the right choice is to make at the time."

I had no reply to make to that.

Damon called me while I was at the store with Grandfather early the following morning.

"Eike, I was just wondering how you were, you know, after yesterday."

"Damon! What're you doing up? And I should be the one asking you that. How're you feeling? Are you all right?"

Damon sighed, though not too deeply, and I caught the shrug in his tone. "Oh, you know, I've had better days."

I laughed humourlessly. "You think? Are you still at Ox's?"

"I'll pick you up from the store and drive you to school. Want to call Spex and ask him if he'd like a ride too, or should I?"

"What? What the fuck, Damon? No! Shouldn't you be resting up or something? Aren't you in bed? You shouldn't even be up never mind even thinking about coming to school!"

A sound very much like a snarl came over the phone.

"I'll see you at the store in half an hour. Be ready."

"Damon!"

He hung up and a half hour later he was walking into the store.

He walked tall and I have to admit he hid it well but it was there all the same. The pain. His jaw was violently bruised and swollen, the varying shades of black and blue extending up one side of his face and encompassing both eyes, and it only served to make his eyes seem even brighter and more intensely blue than ever. Like chipped ice. Almost like his father's.

Although he wore a loose black shirt over equally loose-fitting black pants, there was something about his posture and the way he moved that suggested he was extensively bound around his middle and possibly up over his ribs. His expression was grim.

Grandfather laid a paternal hand on his shoulder as he walked in the door and said something to him, to which Damon responded with a short and very awkward bow. Definitely bound beneath that shirt. He managed a strained smile when he saw me.

"Morning, handsome," he said. "How're you doing?"

I shook my head as much in dismay as amazement at his presence and gave him a very careful hug, but he was having none of it and drew me close, even though he couldn't entirely stifle the accompanying groan of pain.

"Damon!"

"Do me a favour, will you?" he asked, his voice husky though I couldn't tell if this was emotion or an inability to breathe properly.

"Anything!"

"Shut the fuck up and stop worrying about me. I've got this."

"Damon ..."

"I mean it, Eike! Not one more fucking word!"

He was still holding me and when I gave him an extremely reluctant nod, he pressed his split and bruised lips to mine.

"Thank you," he murmured. "For not leaving me."

"I couldn't even if I wanted to," I told him, my voice catching in my throat, "and I definitely don't want to."

Damon stopped for us to collect Spex along the way and he gave Damon a sympathetic pat on the shoulder as he climbed into the back seat.

"I'm sorry, dude," he said. "You know, if there's anything you need, anything I can do."

I turned to look questioningly at him.

"Ox told me," he explained. "He figured you'd need all the moral support you could get, both of you, and I guess he didn't want me putting my big foot in my mouth, you know, accidentally."

"Thanks," Damon said curtly. "Now, can I ask you the same favour I asked of Eike?"

"Sure, dude. Anything."

"Shut the fuck up and don't mention it again, not to me and not to anyone else, either. Clear?"

"Yes, sir."

Despite my silent protest, because I dared say nothing out loud to him, Damon insisted I still attend swim training, even if he at least begged off. Coach took one look at him, nodded and said nothing, and sent me off to get changed. Fantastic. It seemed everybody was silent witness to Damon's ongoing ordeal while he wouldn't accept any acknowledgement even if anyone were willing to give it. I wondered if it had always been this way or whether everyone, Damon included, had just gradually realised the futility of challenging it.

After practice and after I'd showered without Damon's customary massage or even his company, he drove me home.

"Can I ask you another favour?" he said as we pulled up my drive.

"Do you even need to ask? Just tell me what you need."

Damon stared out the windscreen, his hands still on the wheel.

"Can I stay with you?" His voice was low, hesitant. "I don't really want to go home just yet and I'd just as soon not go back to Ox's, either. Not that they haven't been wonderful to me but…"

"There's no need to explain," I told him. "I get it and of course you can. Now?"

Damon nodded gratefully.

"I've still got my overnight bag from, you know. It'll do."

"It will," I agreed. "Come on in."

Although my grandparents were well aware of Damon's injuries, there being no secrets kept in our house, they treated Damon no differently than they'd ever done and had no objection to my request for him to stay. After dinner, while I was clearing the table and getting ready to do the dishes, Grandmother put on the kettle for our traditional after dinner Korean tea.

"If you would like to take a shower, Damon," Grandmother said, "I am certain Eike can help you. And I can put that binding back on for you when you are ready."

Damon blushed and offered Grandmother a formal bow, even though his movements were awkward and stiff.

"Thank you, Grandmother. I would appreciate that."

Grandmother smiled and left the kitchen to return a short time later with an ornate china jar inscribed with Korean symbols which she put on the table. "Use that on his injuries," she instructed me, indicating the jar. "You will not need a lot so be gentle."

As if I needed to be told.

"You can find him something of yours to wear, yes? And when you are ready, I will come and help you with the bandages."

I bowed deeply and respectfully and added a grateful kiss to her cheek. "Thank you, Grandmother."

She smiled at me and her eyes sparkled with tears. "You are a good son, Eike," she said. "Your mother would be proud."

I took this as the greatest compliment she could have given me, her acknowledgement of me before the memory of my mother, and I hugged her. She patted me on the back, ruffled my hair, and turned away, and I blinked back tears of my own.

I was distracted from my thoughts by Damon's sudden attempt to rise from his place at the table and I stared at him from beneath raised eyebrows.

"Where exactly do you think you're going?" I asked. "Can't you see I'm not ready to take you up for a shower just yet? I've got dishes to do, and there's tea."

"I'll help with the dishes," Damon said. "After all, I've eaten too, and I think the time I could be considered a guest has probably come and gone already."

"Not a snowball's chance," I stated firmly. "Sit down. Right now. And," I stared at him with narrowed eyes, "not one more word!"

He braced his hands on the table and for a moment it appeared he was about to ignore me until he glanced over at Grandmother who was standing with her hands on her hips staring at him. He slowly, if reluctantly, eased himself back into his seat, looking across at Grandfather, who shrugged.

"Don't look at me," Grandfather said. "I have no intention of arguing with either of them."

I did my best to help Damon up the stairs but he wouldn't have it, even if he was somewhat slower than usual. Getting him undressed was, however, another matter and he had no choice but to accept my help so we could eventually get it done.

And then there was the binding.

"You look like half a mummy," I complained, picking surgical tape free with my fingers and doing my best to ignore his periodic involuntary flinching.

"What? And not like a Christmas gift?"

"I doubt it," I muttered. "I can't imagine it's going to be too pretty underneath."

Damon twitched and put a hand to his bruised face with a resigned sigh. "There is that. Are you ready for it?"

I ignored him.

In actual fact, it didn't appear quite as bad as I'd anticipated, even if it was still definitely far from attractive. At least some of the swelling seemed to have subsided, though the deep purple/blue-black fist-sized bruise remained, surrounded by a mixed palette of bruises of varying shades.

"Gorgeous," I observed dispassionately.

I threw my robe over him and stripped off my own clothes before wrapping a towel around my waist.

"Crying shame," Damon murmured.

"What?"

"Here I am, in your house, naked, and we're about to shower together and there's not a damn thing I can do to enjoy it."

"Incorrigible," I said.

Despite his words, I was still hard-pressed to keep his mind on the simple business of a shower and in the end, I resorted to threats of physical repercussions if he couldn't control himself.

"But I'm injured," he said. "Aren't you supposed to be treating me with tenderness and concern, not threats of violence?"

"I bloody well would if you could stop behaving like a letch and start behaving like a patient," I growled at him, once again dodging his attempt to fondle me. "It's not as if you can even remotely hope to follow through so can't you just stop tormenting me?"

He sighed in resignation, and finally stood still.

I got him out of the shower and dried him off before giving him a pair of pyjama bottoms to wear. Despite the bruises, or perhaps because of them, he looked even more spectacular than ever, his bare torso gleaming, his muscular body as always making my breath catch.

"You're even more spectacular yourself if you but realised it," Damon said, again reading my thoughts .

"Shut up," I muttered.

I opened the jar of salve Grandmother had given me and gingerly applied it to Damon's injuries. Closing his eyes, a twitch appearing along his jawline, he remained silent even though a sweat broke on his brow to trickle down his bruised cheeks. When I was done, I fetched Grandmother and she carefully and expertly re-bound him.

"Goodnight, my sons," she said softly as she left my room.

Damon and I looked at each other and tears glittered in his eyes.

"Shut up," he muttered. "Just shut up and don't say a fucking word!"

I helped him to the bed and propped him against my pillows. "I'll sleep on the floor," I said. "I think you'll probably need the space."

"Like fuck you will," he growled, grimacing as he reached out to make a grab for me. "Get over here."

I sighed. I knew when it was pointless to argue with him and this was one of those times. I slid cautiously into bed alongside him.

Damon's injuries forced a whole new dimension into our relationship. He couldn't be intimate in the manner to which he was accustomed and he couldn't even kiss me, never mind do anything else. But I held him, cautiously, and he rested his head on my arm and was content to rest there quietly. I didn't say anything and neither did he and eventually he fell asleep and a short time later, so did I.

I woke abruptly sometime in the night to his restless movements and his muttering. He was hot and slick with sweat and when I managed to reach over to turn on the bedside light, his face was etched with the lines of some kind of intense inner conflict. He groaned and I lay a hand gently on his cheek, kissing him softly.

"Damon," I whispered. "Damon, are you all right?"

He groaned again, the sound visceral and laden with a pain beyond that of his physical injuries, and one hand clenched into a white-knuckled fist which I took into a hand of my own to hold tightly.

"Damon!"

His eyelids fluttered but he didn't wake and his legs twitched, his muscles rippled and flexed beneath his clammy skin, and his breathing became laboured. I began to get more than a little concerned.

"Damon!" I said, more insistently. "Damon, you're only dreaming. I'm here."

He moaned, his body tensing and straightening, his face a mask of an emotion I couldn't identify, and I held him even more closely.

"Damon," I whispered in his ear. "Damon, listen to me. I'm here, I've got you. You're safe here."

Although he still didn't wake, he finally became still and gradually his tension eased, the fist in my hand opened, and his breathing returned to normal. I kissed his cheek and kept talking, telling him I loved him, that I was with him, that I had no intention of letting him go or of leaving him and, at last, whatever nightmare had claimed him passed and he slept. I left the light on, not wanting to disturb him further by attempting to turn it off, and I too slept.

Chapter Sixteen

Damon had improved by morning and he even made an, admittedly uncharacteristically restrained, attempt to get physical with me.

"Stop it!" I growled at him, slapping his hand away. "And stay here! Grandfather and I are quite capable of handling the store on our own and besides, you'll only end up getting in the way and distracting me."

I fully expected him to argue with me but he didn't, instead lying back against the pile of pillows he'd bunched together and watching me get dressed.

"Are you quite sure you can't kind of, like, ditch and stay with me a while?" he asked, giving me what could only be described as a lecherous smile. "After all, I'm injured."

"Can't, won't, so stop trying," I replied. I tucked in my shirt and pulled on overalls and paused before leaving the room. "I was wondering," I said, "if you had any thoughts about what you might like for your birthday. What can I get you, or do for you?"

Damon's grin grew wider, even though it made him flinch. "Apart from you, on both counts?"

"You already have me so I can hardly give me again, can I?"

Damon's grin slipped and his expression grew serious. "Actually, there is something," he said.

"What's that?"

"Come over here and give me a good morning kiss first."

I sighed but followed his request and went to his side. I dropped to a crouch beside the bed and he took my face in his hands and kissed me, if somewhat delicately because his lips were still split and swollen, and then stroked a hand over the dragon tattoo and the scars beneath.

"I want one of these," he murmured. "One just like yours."

I stood up, my hand going to my dragon as his slipped away and looked down on him with wide eyes.

"This?"

"Yes," he confirmed. "That."

I tilted my head and my eyes narrowed. "You haven't got any tattoos, Damon. Why now? And why this?"

"Isn't it obvious?" Damon asked, staring at me.

I wasn't happy about it and I sighed deeply before nodding at him. "If that's what you really want, Damon," I agreed reluctantly, "but you have to be more than one hundred percent sure. This isn't a stick-on. It's for life."

"I'm counting on it," Damon said.

I discussed Damon's request with Grandfather while we were stocking shelves together.

"Is he quite certain this is what he wants?" Grandfather asked. "He is aware, isn't he, that once he begins, there is no going back?"

I shrugged.

"You know Damon by now, Grandfather. Do you think he's likely to take no for an answer? If we don't do it for him, he'll simply take it upon himself to get it done somewhere else."

Grandfather gave a dry chuckle and nodded. "I suspect you are right, Eike. Leave it with me."

"Thank you, Grandfather."

Damon's birthday was on the following day, the same day as the inter-collegiate swim tournament in which Coach Harmon refused to allow Damon to participate.

"I'm sorry," Coach Harmon had said, "but there's no way you are getting into that pool in your current condition."

"But…" Damon had begun.

Coach Harmon's face had set in a grim, determined scowl and it was more than obvious that any further argument was futile. Damon had hung his head and conceded.

Grandfather was true to his word and by the time we got home after my final swim practice he'd already made arrangements for Damon to get his tattoo, the following day and immediately after the swim tournament. Damon was ecstatic.

"This is absolutely perfect," he said. "First I get to see you ace the tournament and then you get to hold my hand while I get branded for life."

I wasn't as enthusiastic. "Are you really sure about this, Damon?" I asked for probably the tenth time. "I mean, it is, it's for life, forever. And what's your father going to say?"

"I don't give a fuck what my father's going to say," Damon stated acidly, his face instantly setting in a bitter scowl. "I only want to be close to you."

"You don't need a dragon to do that," I pointed out to him.

He turned hard eyes in my direction and I shook my head and smiled at him in resignation.

"If it's what you want," I said, "you know I can deny you nothing."

His eyes instantly softened and he drew me close to hold me, if still somewhat gingerly. "Have I told you lately that I love you?" he murmured in my ear.

"To be honest," I admitted, "I think you might only ever have said it once."

"Is that so?" Damon asked, sounding genuinely surprised. "Then I'm sorry and I'll say it again. I love you. You're the best thing that's ever happened to me."

"That is such a cliché," I told him, "but feel free to say it as often as you like."

"Which part?"

"Both."

He insisted on remaining with me another night, adamant he was not yet ready to return home and, as I'd already said I could deny him nothing and my grandparents certainly indicated no objection, he did.

Spex called directly after dinner.

"Hey, I was wondering if you still wanted to get some study in tonight?"

Shit, yes, I'd forgotten about that.

"Damon's still here," I said.

"Oh," Spex said. "Ok, do you want me to come to yours or would you rather pass?"

I thought about it for a moment.

"Let's not pass," I told him. "If Damon has a problem, he'll just have to get over it. We've got exams pretty damn close now and Damon may find this shit easy but I'm not so sure I will if you don't give me a hand."

Spex laughed. "You have so little faith in yourself, Eike. You really don't need me and truth be known, it's me that needs to study with you, not the other way around.

I snorted. "Right. As if. You coming over now?"

"Yeah," Spex said. "See you in about ten."

"Spex?" Damon asked as I hung up. "What was all that about? What do I have to get over?"

"Eavesdropping?" I asked, easily evading his attempt to grab me and dancing around the table.

His eyes narrowed. "And if I was? Is that why you're playing hard to get?"

"If you must know," I told him, facing him across the length of the table and shifting my weight from foot to foot as I eyed him warily, "Spex is coming over to study with me and the last thing I need is for you to distract me. Can you not maybe contain yourself for just a little while?"

He made an attempt to cut me off between the kitchen table and the bench and caught himself on the corner of the table. He blanched, sucked a sharp breath through his teeth, and swore.

"It serves you right, you know," I said bluntly, catching him around the waist and helping him into a chair. "Do you not have an off switch?"

"Not when you're around," he admitted.

"Then I suggest you stay here and Spex and I will go up and study in my room without you," I said. "Would you like me to make you a cup of tea or something before he gets here?"

"It's not a cup of tea I want," he sighed, running the tip of his tongue suggestively over his lips. "And besides, how can I trust you and Spex up there alone together?"

I shook my head and disengaged myself from him, on the verge of irritation though I knew he was only teasing.

"Hopeless," I muttered.

"I can't help it, and I blame it entirely on you."

"Of course you do," I responded, "and if you weren't already damaged goods, I'd put you resoundingly in your place."

"Promises, promises."

At that moment, Spex walked in and Damon feigned despair with a huge melodramatic sigh as he threw his head onto his folded arms.

"What's up with him?" Spex asked, looking worried.

"Nothing a cold shower wouldn't fix," I grumbled, and I grabbed Spex by the arm and led him upstairs.

Damon took himself up to my room after Spex had left.

"Are you going to help me shower again?" he asked, looking decidedly more lecherous than in need of assistance.

"No," I said, "and I'm sure you can put your own salve on too. I'll do that binding for you afterwards but only if you promise to behave yourself."

"What? Why? Aren't you supposed to be nursing me or something?"

"Because," I said with raised eyebrows, sidestepping him even as I passed him a towel, "this is still my grandparents' house and I absolutely don't trust you, that's why."

"You can be so heartless."

"And you are insatiable."

Damon grinned. "There is that," he agreed.

Damon's phone rang as I was in the middle of re-applying his binding. He picked it up, looked at the caller ID and immediately stiffened. It took several rings before he reluctantly answered it.

"Dad," he said, his voice devoid of emotion.

I couldn't hear what was being said but Damon stared blankly at the wall in front of him and remained completely motionless.

"Yes, sir," he said after a while. "Yes, I understand."

He hung up and tossed the phone onto the bed as if it was diseased and I finished tucking in the ends of the bandage and securing it with tape. I didn't ask. I figured he'd speak if or when he was ready.

"That was my dad," he said after I'd gotten him back to the bed and helped him to get comfortable.

"I gathered that much," I admitted. "And?"

"He has *requested* my presence for dinner tomorrow night," he said. "Rough translation, *demanded*. I show, or else."

"Or else?" I asked, my hand instinctively reaching for the bruises colouring his face.

"Privileges," Damon reassured me. "The truck or the credit card or, at worst, my college allowance. Still not worth the hassle over a lousy dinner."

"Oh."

He sighed deeply and his brow puckered in discomfort, his hand straying to his waist.

"Shit!" he muttered. "That still hurts, goddamn it."

I sat down beside him and took his hand in mine, resting my head on his shoulder.

"When?" I asked him. "What time will he expect you to be there?"

Damon turned to brush his lips across my forehead. "He'll want to make a performance out of it," he said. "It'll be somewhere public and it'll be late enough to make a statement so plenty of time for us to get done what we're doing beforehand."

"You mean the tattoo?" I asked. "You still intend to go through with it?"

"Yes," Damon stated tightly. "Oh hell, yes."

"Damon…" I sat up and turned to cup his face gently in my hands. "Damon, please. You're going to turn up to dinner with your father, on your birthday, with a new tattoo? *My* tattoo?"

"Yes," Damon said, and I could tell there would be no swaying him.

I shut my eyes and sighed in surrender. Damon was hard work but at the same time I could appreciate where he was coming from, even if I couldn't even begin to say I could relate.

"Are you angry with me?" he asked quietly, catching me by surprise.

"Angry? Of course not," I reassured him. "Just worried, that's all. I don't want you hurt any more on my account," I added, placing my hand over the bandages around his waist.

"It's not on your account," he said, his voice ever-so-slightly broken at the edges, "it's on mine and this is a show-down that was already long overdue. Don't worry about me, all right? I've got this."

I wanted to ask how his current condition in any way proved he had anything but he didn't give me opportunity to respond. He put his arms around me and rolled me back into the bed, even though it made him grit his teeth in pain. I made no effort to stop him. It was clear this was what he needed, and who was I to argue?

He was slow and gentle, not only because he was still in a good deal of pain but also, I think, because his intimacy was more about a need for comfort than about passion or lust. Afterwards, he was content to lie in my arms, his own arms clasped over mine.

"Just hold me," he whispered, his voice bearing more than a hint of unshed tears.

"I have no intention of letting go," I reassured him.

We slept, and this time there were no nightmares.

The following day's swim tournament went much as anticipated. Although it was the first time I'd stepped out in public with my scars exposed for all to see, I bore them with pride rather than shame and besides, once I was in the water, there wasn't a soul to whom they were noticeable, never mind of importance.

"Swim for both of us," Damon had said to me when we'd arrived at the pool with my grandparents.

"I will," I'd assured him.

While my grandparents discreetly headed off to go and find seats for them, he kissed me.

"I love you," he reminded me.

"I love you, too," I said.

With Damon's words and his lingering kiss to spur me on, I swam the best I'd ever done in my life and the nearest rival in any race was left so far in my wake I might as well have had the pool to myself. I effortlessly took the Championship trophy and Damon and Coach Harmon were delighted, though no more so than my grandparents. Grandmother had tears in her eyes as I returned to Damon's truck with them.

"Your parents would be so proud of you, Eike," she said. "*We* are so proud of you."

"Thank you, Grandmother," I acknowledged, hugging her gently. "I couldn't have done it without you."

Grandmother asked to be dropped off at home while Grandfather accompanied us to the studio of his friend the tattooist, the same tattooist who had inked my own tattoo.

"You realise," Junsu explained to Damon, "that you have chosen a most sensitive area for a tattoo, especially a first?"

Damon looked at me. "Eike did it," he pointed out, "and his is over his scars."

"So you are ready for this?" Junsu persisted. "Once I begin, there is no going back."

It was obvious Damon was psyching himself up as he took a deep breath and forced a tight smile. "Yes," he said. "Yes, I'm ready. Let's do this."

To his credit, Damon didn't flinch, didn't move, didn't request so much as a single break even though he broke into a sweat on several occasions. I sat as close as I could without impeding Junsu's work but I made no effort to touch him, knowing this would only interfere with his self-control and, undoubtedly, also his pride. Meanwhile, Grandfather waited patiently, only occasionally leaving to take himself outside for a puff or two on his pipe.

Junsu, as expected, did a spectacular job and when he was finished, though the tattoo was raw and fresh, it was barely distinguishable from mine. Damon studied it proudly in the mirror Junsu offered him.

"Perfect," he breathed. "Absolutely perfect. Thank you. From the bottom of my heart, Junsu, thank you."

He offered Junsu a formal, if decidedly stiff, bow which Junsu mirrored and which clearly impressed the tattooist, and then turned to Grandfather and offered him the same courtesy.

"Thank you, Grandfather."

"You are more than welcome, grandson," Grandfather said. "Welcome to the family."

Damon's eyes glazed with tears and he turned away, reaching out a hand to me as he did so. Drawing me close, he leaned into me.

"Thank you," he whispered, his voice catching with emotion. "And I'll show you just how grateful I am the next time I see you."

"You're not coming home tonight, I assume," I said, missing the significance of how easily I'd used the word *home*.

"*Home*," Damon repeated huskily. "No, I won't be home tonight but tomorrow, tomorrow I'll be home."

He kissed me, discreetly, on the cheek and we walked out to the truck. He dropped Grandfather and I at the end of our drive and was gone. It was a very long time before I saw him again.

Should I have known? Could I even remotely have anticipated what happened next? I don't know. Hindsight is 20/20 but, looking back now, I can think of nothing I could've known, nothing I could've done, and nothing I could've changed.

Damon had been gone no more than an hour and I was lying on my bed with study notes when my phone notified me of an incoming text. Damon.

Things definitely not going well. I'm leaving. Can you meet me at the pool in twenty?

Perhaps this is the only detail I should have questioned, Damon's rendezvous request, but even then, it seemed logical to me. Damon had a key to the pool and it would be unattended, quiet, and empty. If he had issues to deal with in relation to having met with his father, what better place to do so? What didn't occur to me was why he'd ask to meet me there rather than come to pick me up himself. Damon needed me and if Damon needed me, I'd be there. I grabbed a jacket and headed downstairs to inform my grandparents I needed to go out for a short time.

"I think maybe things haven't gone too well for Damon at home," I told them. "He wants to meet me at the pool so I'll be back later, ok?"

"He's not swimming, is he?" Grandfather asked with concern. "He should not get the tattoo wet just yet, and he is still injured."

I shrugged. "I don't think he plans to swim, Grandfather. I think he just needs a quiet place to, well, you know."

Grandfather nodded sympathetically. "Bring him home when you are ready," he said. "And be careful biking in the dark, yes?"

"Yes, Grandfather."

I got my bike out of the garage and pedalled unhurriedly towards the campus pool. With twenty minutes I should arrive at about the same time as Damon but when I got there, he hadn't yet arrived. I locked up my bike and headed for the steps into the front of the building.

To be honest, I never stood a chance.

Chapter Seventeen

They were waiting in the shadows and they attacked as I reached the bottom of the steps. The first one took a swing at me with a baseball bat, striking me cleanly behind the knees, and I went down in a sprawling heap on the steps, stunned but instinctively rolling to meet my attackers, and the baseball bat swung again, narrowly missing my head. Then they were on me, four of them, not boys or even college students but fully-grown men, big and strong and pumped up on adrenalin and menace and knowing exactly what they were about. They grabbed at my arms and my legs and punched me to the ground, and one of them dropped to my back with both knees. Skin split and blood began to flow at about the same time as I heard as much as felt my ribs crack and all my breath left me in a single explosive rush.

"Bring him to the truck," one of them ordered, "and let's show this little fuck what happens to queers who mess with what doesn't belong to them."

A hand locked in my hair, an arm was braced around my throat, and rough, powerful hands locked onto each arm as they lifted me upright and half-carried, half-dragged me around the corner of the building to where, through the sweat and blood now running down my face, I saw a big old pickup truck and a second vehicle, a black four by four that looked much like Damon's. I was dragged towards the pickup and slammed into the bonnet and one of them kicked my legs apart.

"So, this is how you queers like it, right?" the same voice that had commanded me brought to the truck grunted coarsely in my ear, his breath rank with cigarettes and whiskey. "Let's see how you like it when the big boys come out to play, huh?"

"Hey, Bull, what're ya doin'?" a second voice challenged. "We're just supposed to be roughin' him up. What the hell?"

"I figure that while we have him, we might as well have some fun," the one called Bull replied, his hand already reaching around to the dome of my jeans and pressing what was unmistakably an erection to my buttocks.

My blood ran like ice through my veins and my heart faltered. He intended to rape me, right here in the parking lot against the hood of this truck.

"You just gonna stand there? Help me get his damn jeans off and I'll let you have seconds."

For a split second, I expected someone to object, for the three co-offenders to be sufficiently horrified by Bull's intentions to actively intervene. But they said nothing and instead the two pair of hands holding my arms increased their grip and an additional pair of hands ripped at my jeans. The outcome seemed inevitable. There were four of them and one of me and it was a situation of do or die. If I was to have even the remotest hope of survival, I had to stop giving into panic and think. Cool air caressed my skin as my jeans were pulled down and off along with my trainers.

It's funny how they say life passes before your eyes as you're about to die. It wasn't my life, as such, but there were certainly some significant memories, none of them helpful.

Xia, *Boys shouldn't be pretty and boys shouldn't like boys. Boys who like boys get into trouble.*

Paul, *You know you want it. You've always wanted it, haven't you?*

Grandfather, *The path you have chosen will have more hurdles than most.*

I was in undeniably the worst predicament I'd ever experienced in my life, and my life itself was at stake. My knees burned and pain shot up the back of my legs, spread and locked wide apart, my jeans absent. I was bent over the bonnet of the truck, my most likely broken ribs grating against the rolled top, the wheel cover pressing into my stomach, and my head turned so one side of my face was pressed against the warm metal. Incongruously, I could hear the ticking of the cooling engine beneath my ear. My arms were also splayed, a solid body holding onto each one, and there was a terrifyingly large presence behind me, one who was already fumbling with his fly. I closed my eyes and did my best to calm my thoughts and my laboured and panicked breathing, and think.

Given the circumstances, difficult. Almost impossible.

Almost, but not completely.

I *fainted*. I relaxed every muscle in my body, becoming a dead weight against the hands and bodies restraining me, and slid limply down the side of the vehicle.

"What the fuck?!" a new voice exclaimed, one attached to my left arm. "What just happened?"

"The little bastard fainted, that's all," voice number one, Bull, said. "C'mon, prop him up already."

"What?" the newest voice asked. "Shit, dude. We ain't fuckin' killed him or somethin', have we?"

"Of course, we haven't. He's just a fuckin' soft cock, that's all. Now for fuck's sake, prop him up!"

And they did exactly what I'd hoped they'd do; they relinquished their restraint of me sufficiently to adjust their position and slide me back up the bonnet of the truck. And in the very instant they loosened their hold, I took the only opportunity I was likely to get and I came up fighting. Taken completely by surprise and therefore completely unprepared, they lost their grip on me. I twisted free and placed a kick directly into Bull's groin, doubling him over and leaving him gasping for breath, and ducked beneath the roundhouse punch aimed at me by the assailant from my left side so that I heard his knuckles break as he connected with the side of the truck instead.

I used every move I'd ever learned, every punch and kick and evasive manoeuvre, and I'm certain I improvised a fair number more. I was fighting for my life and I knew it and I completely forgot I was fighting half naked. But, needless to say, my advantage didn't last long. They were hard men, big and raw and, even if they were far from Hapkido fighters, they were certainly street fighters. I was slammed repeatedly to the ground where I'd roll and spring back to my feet only to be slammed back down again. Punches connected with my face, my ribs, my stomach, my kidneys. A blow from the reappearing baseball bat caught me low in my back and I flew across the pavement, grazing my face, rolling, barely able to breathe before I was once again back on my feet only to catch a blow under my chin. My head was reeling and blood was flowing freely though I could no longer tell from what injuries. Blinking against the fog threatening to overwhelm me, I sank to my knees and vaguely heard what sounded like that first determined voice say, *"That's it! Grab him!"*

And then there were screaming tires and a blaring horn and one of my assailants yelling, "Shit! What the fuck?! Let's blow!"

There were slamming doors, roaring engines, more squealing tires, and they were gone while I remained on my knees, my head hanging to my chest, one arm hanging at an unnatural angle at my side, and a profound buzzing in my ears. I heard someone speaking but I couldn't understand a word and then an arm fell across my shoulders. I swung instinctively back into the defensive and tried to strike with the broken arm, only to collapse in a heap before blacking out.

I woke up in hospital.

As I discovered later, it was Coach Harmon who'd been the hero of the day. He'd apparently left something of importance in his office, come to retrieve it, and seen the vehicles parked behind the pool building. Coming to investigate, thinking it was youngsters come to drink or even to vandalize the building, he'd seen my attackers and driven straight at them, scattering them. He also now sported a black eye courtesy of yours truly as I'd apparently still managed a reasonably good blow with my flailing fist even though my arm was broken in several places.

But it was Spex and my grandparents who were present when I first came to.

"Damon," was the first word past my split and swollen lips.

"Eike!" Grandmother began, but I looked past her, my eyes out of focus and so swollen I could barely open them, seeking Damon's familiar face, his voice, his presence.

"Damon," I repeated, tasting blood.

"We tried to call him," Spex said, "but his phone's disconnected."

The text, the text from Damon which had sent me to the pool to begin with, there was no way that had come from Damon, no way in any part of my imagination he could knowingly have sent me into what had been waiting for me. Where was Damon? I tried to sit up.

"Eike." Grandfather put a restraining hand on my shoulder and I winced and bit my lip, which also hurt a good deal more than I'd care to admit. "Don't worry about Damon right now. I'm sure he's all right and will come as soon as he can."

"What happened?" I asked, my memory blurred and my head pounding.

"You were attacked," Grandfather explained bluntly, his voice strained. "Coach Harmon found you and called an ambulance and the Police. You're at the hospital."

"Will I live?" I asked, trying to smile and failing because my mouth refused to cooperate.

Grandfather turned his head, tears welling in his eyes, and Grandmother tried unsuccessfully to stifle a sob. Spex muttered something about coming back later.

"What?" I pressed. "I'm going to live, right?"

Grandfather regained his composure and managed a nod. "Yes, Eike. You are going to live."

"Well, I guess that's all right then, isn't it?" And I must have lost consciousness again.

When I again came to, my grandparents had gone and it was only Spex sitting by my bedside, though this time with Cara.

"Hey, Eike," he said as I prised open reluctant eyes.

"Grandfather and Grandmother?" I struggled to ask through cracked lips and the metallic taste tainting my mouth.

"Your grandfather took your grandmother home," Spex explained. "She was about to pass out or something 'cos she sure didn't look too well."

Cara elbowed him in the ribs and Spex pursed his lips and looked down.

"Sorry," he mumbled. "I'm sure she'll be ok, it's just, we've been sitting here a while."

I would've nodded if I could've moved my head, but I couldn't. "Thirsty," I croaked instead.

Spex lifted a paper cup from the bedside cabinet with a hospital standard curly paper straw dangling from it. He put the straw to my mouth and I managed to get a couple of sips though it hurt like hell to swallow.

"Damon?" I asked when he'd removed the cup.

Spex reluctantly shook his head. "Nobody's heard from him," he said. "We've got no idea where he is and, to be honest, nobody's brave enough to go up to his place looking for him."

Having personally witnessed his father in action, this much I completely understood, but that just made me even more frightened for him. Where was Damon, and why hadn't he come?

"Thanks for coming," I said. "Or staying?"

Spex shrugged. "I'm sorry I'm not Damon but somebody had to be here when you woke up. I hope you don't mind that Cara came," he added, glancing at her with a self-conscious smile. "She was worried about you too, we all are, and, well, she was keeping me company."

I once again tried for a smile and, once again, failed. "That's ok," I said. "Thank you, thank you for being here." I contemplated sitting up, changed my mind, and closed my eyes. "How long have I been out?" I asked after a while, forcing my eyes back open.

Spex looked at Cara and she gave him a reassuring smile.

"You might as well tell him," she said. "It's not as if it changes anything."

I raised my eyebrows although even that hurt. "Spex? How long?"

"You came in on Wednesday night. It's now pretty much Saturday morning."

"What do you mean by *pretty much*?"

Spex checked his watch. "It's half past four in the morning. You came in at some time around eight-thirty Wednesday."

I did a rough calculation in my head, which resulted in an instant headache. Saturday morning. I'd been out the better part of two and a half days and there'd been no sign of Damon? And... two and a half **days**?!

"Eike, have the doctors talked to you yet?"

"If they have, Spex, I don't remember a thing. I can't even remember getting here." This wasn't entirely true, flashes of memory were beginning to return to me, I just didn't want to accept them yet. Especially the part where I'd had my jeans ripped off. "Spex? Can I talk to you a moment?" I paused and ran my tongue nervously over my split lip before glancing at Cara. "Alone?"

Cara stood up. "It's all right," she said. "I'll leave you guys alone now." She gave Spex a discreet kiss and I heard her say, *Call me*, and then she was gone. I stared at Spex, my cheeks burning.

"Go ahead," he said. "What do you need?"

Heat rose into my face and I was struggling to catch my breath, but I needed to know, was desperate to know, even if at the same time, I didn't. Oh, I so didn't. I swallowed down rising bile and closed my eyes as I lowered my head to ask the question I hardly dared ask. "Did they... did they get me, Spex? Tell me the truth, did they rape me?"

Tears slid down my cheeks at even the thought of it. If I'd been raped...

"No, Eike," Spex said firmly. "No, you were not raped. You fought those dirty bastards off and they did **not** rape you, you hear? They didn't get you."

The relief was so profound it left me breathless. Not raped. Not raped. Not... raped.

But my relief couldn't outweigh my greater fear; where was Damon? Tears flowed anew.

When I'd regained some semblance of control and Spex had taken the liberty of wiping my face with a flannel, carefully, I recalled his question about the doctors.

"Why'd you ask me if the doctors had talked to me yet?" I asked him.

Spex blushed, flustered. "I shouldn't have brought that up," he mumbled. "It's not, well, I probably shouldn't be the one to say anything."

I stared at him. What did that mean, exactly? "Spex?"

And at that moment he was saved by the bell or, in this instance, a nurse.

"Mr. Nylund. You're awake." The nurse looked sharply at Spex and I thought she was about to place her hands on her hips for added effect. "Why didn't you call to say he was awake? There's a call button right there!"

"Uh, yes, uh, sorry about that," Spex said, falling over his words and becoming even more flustered.

"I think perhaps you should go now," the nurse said. "You can come back later when it's actual visiting hours, now that he's awake. And *after* the surgeon has been to visit."

Surgeon? Wait! What? What surgeon?

I looked pleadingly at Spex and he shuffled his feet awkwardly.

"Sorry, buddy. I'll be back later, ok?"

As if I had a choice in the matter. He gathered his things and was gone, leaving me with the nurse.

The surgeon arrived after dawn light had begun to seep around the curtains of my room, well after the nurse had checked my vitals, or whatever it was she'd done, and left, and far too long after Spex had been forced to go home. I sincerely wished the nurse hadn't been so adamant about his departure. Somehow, being alone in a hospital with absolutely not a clue as to what state you're actually in has to be one of the loneliest experiences it is possible to endure.

Then again, how much did I really want to know?

"Mr. Nylund, how are you feeling?"

Why do medical staff always insist on asking such inane questions? How did he think I might be feeling? I ignored the question as such and responded with one of my own.

"Do you think it might be possible to have people stop calling me Mr. Nylund? It makes me feel as if I'm in even bigger trouble than I think I probably already am."

The surgeon, possibly Korean himself by the looks of him, smiled at me. "As you wish, Eike, isn't it?" he asked, referring to his notes.

"Yes, Eike. Thank you, sir."

The surgeon smiled again and drew up a chair to sit by my bed and I wasn't sure this was a good thing. Didn't doctors normally kind of stand, *um* and *ah* a bit, and leave again? He was making himself way too comfortable for a quick update and flying progress check.

"I take it nobody has said anything to you yet?" he asked.

"No," I said, still unable to move my head without serious pain shooting through it and various attached parts. "Not a word."

I didn't bother to add that I'd either been unconscious or, when opportunity had arisen, the only person who might have said anything had been chased from my presence. The surgeon nodded.

"You're not in good shape, Eike, though at least you're not in what I would consider a *critical* condition."

Not *critical*? Was that a good thing? Not *critical* certainly left plenty of scope within the earlier definition of not being in good shape. My jaw twitched. Which hurt.

"Eike," the surgeon continued, "I'm going to be blunt with you but, before I say anything more, I have to ask you if you want a support person present with you. I can always come back later if you prefer."

Holy shit! A support person? What, like the one the nurse had so kindly and considerately ordered home? And blunt? About what? My heart lurched and I wished, not for the first time, that I knew where Damon was. What I wouldn't give for his presence beside me right now, holding my hand, telling me he'd stay by my side, and reassuring me that everything would be all right. I closed my eyes and held onto thoughts of home, of my grandparents, and of my friends, and re-opened my eyes.

"Let's just get this over with," I said. "Go ahead and be blunt. I'm kind of used to blunt and, to be honest, I don't really have much patience with beating around the bush."

The surgeon nodded again and his eyes softened. He looked sad, which could hardly be a good sign.

"They did a number on you, all right," he said, "and they've left you with not inconsiderable injuries."

That much I'd gathered already. Could he not just get to the point?

"You've got extensive damage to both knees," (I figured that was probably the baseball bat coupled with a few unplanned greetings with pavement) "a fractured pelvis," (steel-capped boots and likely the bat had something to do with that, too) "a bruised spine," (two knees to the middle of my back could have been a contributing factor) "a broken cheek bone and fractured jaw," (explained my inability to smile properly though at least I still seemed to be able to speak all right) "a fractured eye socket," (this was becoming a fairly extensive list) "and two broken arms including a broken wrist, a shattered elbow, and multiple bone fractures. You also dislocated your right shoulder, have three fractured ribs, and a number of internal injuries."

Holy ... fucking ... shit! Wow! So, ok, that sounded a bit as if I'd been under a herd of stampeding elephants (probably not too far from the truth) but it was all repairable, wasn't it?

"There's other damage," the surgeon continued, "most of it surface injuries, cuts and abrasions and the like, and some further damage to the scars you already had, but all of those have already been treated and shouldn't cause too much further distress."

I had the distinct feeling that, despite the comprehensive list he'd already given me, he was hedging and there was still something he hadn't yet told me. I stared up at him and waited.

"Eike, all of these injuries are manageable and we're dealing with them, but some are more complicated than others. There will be surgery. There will be rehabilitation. You've been through something like this before, right? You understand it's a process?"

"Yes," I acknowledged. "The last time took me a year."

The surgeon nodded. "Eike, there's no guarantee how successful recovery will be. You need to be prepared for the eventuality you may never be as you once were. Recovery may not be perfect and there may be residual complications."

Not perfect? Residual complications? My mind raced through the possibilities and realisation hit me like a dagger through the heart.

"I may not swim again," I said.

"I would sincerely hope it wouldn't mean you couldn't swim at all, but I have to make you aware your chances of returning to competitive swimming are limited."

"And running? Hapkido? Biking?"

The surgeon sighed sympathetically and shrugged. "I can't give you the answers to that, Eike. I can only ask you to be prepared for the worst possible outcome. That way, anything better is a bonus, right?"

I had nothing I could say to that.

Chapter Eighteen

I spent six weeks in hospital and in that time, I lost track of how many times I went into surgery. Apparently, *not critical* didn't mean there wasn't still a lot of gluing, bolting, and stitching together to do, never mind the fact that things which had previously been missed kept cropping up as complications. I felt like a voodoo doll by the time they finally released me to return home.

In a way, almost permanently either going *into* surgery, coming *out of* surgery, or recovering *from* surgery kept my mind from fixing equally as permanently on my loss of Damon. By all accounts, nobody had heard from him. Ox told me he was no longer at home and that he'd been withdrawn from all his classes, but where he'd gone, nobody either could or would tell me.

Eventually, I had no more tears left to shed and there was nothing but a dark and hollow place deep inside me wherein rested his memory. I was broken far beyond my injuries.

When I finally returned home, it was to discover the spare room had been cleared out and Junsu the tattooist's son, Hyunguk, had moved in. Hyunguk held black-belts in multiple disciplines and he was there as my bodyguard. I went nowhere alone. Wherever I went, I was driven by Hyunguk, accompanied by Hyunguk, or accompanied by a veritable posse of my friends. I took my first-year exams under special dispensation and, miraculously I thought, passed with flying colours, receiving invitations from no less than six out-of-state colleges for transfer, all without benefit of my swim record.

My attackers were never caught and I couldn't help but think of what Damon had told me about his mother, how he believed she'd been murdered and how no one did anything about it. Damon's father and his cronies were untouchable. I think everybody knew, though it was never spoken aloud, that Damon's father had sent them to remind me, very forcibly, that his son was not mine to have or to hold, and I got the message as clearly from Damon's absence as from the results of the attack.

The months passed, and Christmas was rapidly approaching, as was my birthday, though I didn't celebrate the first and didn't much care for the second.

At least I was finally returning to some semblance of my former self. Hyunguk became far more than just my bodyguard, he was also my personal trainer, and, with his steady persistence and encouragement, I worked out daily. We'd begun with walking which gradually progressed to jogging and then to running. Often, I experienced shooting pains and spasms in my legs and back and Hyunguk would expertly work out the knots and tension. Though he was far from Damon, the results were the same, even if only from a solely clinical perspective.

Eventually, we moved on to the gym and finally to the martial arts which had undeniably saved my life. I did not, however, return to the pool which, without Damon, I couldn't face again. As Hyunguk wasn't a swimmer, this wasn't something he took upon himself to encourage me to pursue.

A week before my birthday, Ox brought me a letter.

It was a plain white envelope marked with nothing more than a simple stylized black Korean dragon. My dragon. *Our* dragon. Just as Ox had known immediately it was meant for me, I knew immediately it was from Damon.

"It came in a letter for my mom," Ox said. "I think he probably took a great risk in sending it."

I held the envelope in shaking hands. "Thanks, Ox."

"You're welcome," he said, "and, for what it's worth, I'm sorry.'

He didn't have to elaborate for me to know what he meant. I said nothing and he shuffled his feet in discomfort.

"Look, I know you'll probably say no, but we're all going out tonight, not to Meg's but to the new joint out at Four Corners. Fat Sam's. You know it?"

I nodded.

"Well, look, anyway, if you'd maybe like to come, we'd really like to have you along, you know, we've missed you, too."

I was touched and a little ashamed. I knew I'd been avoiding my friends, *our* friends, for far too long. I looked down at the envelope in my hands and back at Ox. I had no idea what the letter inside might contain but it was distinctly possible I might need my friends in the aftermath.

"You know what?" I said, taking a deep breath and resolutely squaring my shoulders. "I'd really like that. Can you pick me up?"

Ox looked both stunned and very pleased. "Really? Yeah, sure thing. I'll pick you up at seven?"

"Sure," I agreed. "I'll see you then."

Ox hopped back in his mother's old Ford and was gone, leaving me standing alone in the driveway with the envelope in my hands. I turned slowly to return to the house.

I sat on my bed for a long time holding that envelope, unwilling, afraid, to open it. I couldn't imagine what to expect and, after all this time … what could Damon possibly have to say? I'd thought about it, of course. Endlessly. But now it was here…

I put the letter on my desk and got changed from jeans and shirt into track pants and a sleeveless tee. What I needed first was to run or to fight or to do anything **but** think about the letter. Leaving it, I went in search of Hyunguk.

I found him about to begin washing his car but he stopped as I came out the back door.

"What's up?" he asked as I leaned on the bonnet of his immaculate '71 blue Camaro SS.

"I've got a letter from Damon," I said tonelessly.

"You've not read it yet," he guessed, "and you need some time to think about it before you do."

"Yeah," I admitted, grateful he understood me so well.

"Fight or run?" he asked.

I shrugged. "You decide."

"Let's run," he suggested. "I'll get changed."

He was only a few minutes and when he returned, we set off down the road at a comfortable side by side lope.

"You've changed, you know," Hyunguk observed as we ran.

This was true and I knew he wasn't referring only to the physical changes, although there were plenty of those.

I had more scars now, both from the injuries received in the assault itself but also from the various surgeries I'd had subsequently and, as a consequence, I had a multitude of new tattoos, courtesy of the incomparable skills of Junsu. I was leaner, harder, darker, my body no longer that of a swimmer but that of a fighter and, as Hyunguk regularly liked to tell me, I reminded him of the cage fighters he'd once trained with in Thailand. Factoring in that I now kept my hair cropped short, to prevent any risk of its being grabbed at, and that my face was equally as scarred as my body, I definitely no longer looked like a model and *pretty* couldn't even remotely be used to describe me. Amy had recently described me as downright dangerous, terrifying even, and I wished I'd discovered this image a whole lot sooner.

But the changes Hyunguk referred to ran much deeper than those which could be seen on the surface. Smiles were rare and I found myself with increasingly little to say. Conversation for the sake of conversation seemed pointless and I kept my thoughts to myself and my feelings buried in silence within. I don't think I could be described as sullen or moody but I certainly volunteered little. I guess, instead of cowing me as might've been expected, the assault had the completely opposite effect. I walked proud, issuing a silent challenge to people to dare to comment and, as a result, they had nothing to say. The whispering quickly stopped and people moved aside for me and, instead of contempt, it was often fear I caught in their eyes when they were unfortunate enough to meet mine. Truth be known, I think I was waiting for conflict, waiting for somebody, *anybody*, to take me on again because this time, *this time*, there would be no taking me by surprise. The black dragon was no longer inked only into my skin, it was inked into my soul and had become an inseparable part of me.

Hyunguk and I ran for many miles and, in the end, it was he who pulled up first.

"I'm sorry," he said, "but I have to catch my breath. The student has officially surpassed the master."

I made no reply but merely reduced my pace and, gradually, we came to a walk.

"Have you any ideas about what the letter might say?" Hyunguk asked after we'd walked in silence for a while.

"Plenty," I said, betraying no hint of the emotions welling up inside me, "but I don't know that anything he can say can change anything. What's done is done, and we move on, don't we?"

Hyunguk shrugged.

"Perhaps, but you don't really know what his circumstances might have been or what his motivation was, or is."

A part of me knew I was being irrational and completely unfair to Damon, but I was suddenly as angry as I'd previously been afraid. "He left me behind," I stated acidly. "In the end, that's all that counts."

Hyunguk made no reply and for a little while longer we walked in silence.

"Do you know how my father and your grandfather came to be friends?" he asked after we finally made the last turn for home.

"No," I admitted. "Grandfather doesn't talk about his past very often."

"Did you know he lost his brother, Sehun, and his best friend, Minho, in the Gwanju uprising?"

That much I did know and I clearly recalled Grandfather telling me as much the day Damon had been assaulted by his father.

"Yes," I acknowledged. "That much I knew."

Hyunguk extended his stride slightly and rolled his head on his shoulders and it occurred to me he wasn't half as young as his lean physique tended to suggest. "My father was already dating my mother, Hyuna, who was Minho's sister," Hyunguk began, "and they were both there, at the protests. Just before the fighting broke out, Minho and Sehun insisted he take Hyuna home. He didn't want to. He wanted to stay but they made him go, saying it was getting too dangerous and that they'd leave themselves if it got much worse. A short time after he and Hyuna had left them, both Sehun and Minho got caught between the protesters behind them and the soldiers in front and they couldn't get out. Both of them were shot in the streets."

Holy shit.

"It was my father who had to break the news to your grandfather. He was the one who had to admit he'd left them behind and that they'd been killed."

I recalled Grandfather's words from the night that now seemed so long ago.

Sometimes it isn't about leaving or staying, it's about being brave enough to know which is the right choice.

I understood now what he'd meant and my thoughts returned immediately to the letter sitting neglected and unread on my desk. Suddenly, I wanted to go home. Taking a deep breath, I increased my speed and began to jog, forcing Hyunguk to run to catch up.

"Oh, I see how it is," he laughed. "Come on then, let's go!"

We ran home.

Despite my sudden enthusiasm to read Damon's letter, I still took the time to shower and get changed and, as always, my thoughts turned unerringly to Damon as I got under the blessed relief of the hot water.

I still suffered and there wasn't a day that passed where I didn't ache, inside and out. It wasn't only the lingering repercussions of my injuries, which often ached and throbbed and burned, but the dark and empty space inside which never seemed to fill. I pressed my hands against the shower wall and hung my head between my arms, recalling Damon's hands on my back, my shoulders, my body, taking not only the knots out of my muscles but the aches out of my soul. I missed him more profoundly than I could ever admit and missing him made my determination to never be vulnerable again an even more powerful force. I turned off the shower and laid my hand against the dragon in my neck, feeling it breathe, feeling it grip me in its ink-black claws and strengthen me.

Getting out of the shower, I got dressed, purposely selecting clothing I'd purchased since Damon's departure, all snug and black.

I picked up the envelope.

The letter was hand-written on plain white paper, the writing spidery and shaky, as if either written while the writer was in transit or by a heavily trembling hand, and the paper itself was splotched, the ink in many places having run, as if it had been written in the rain.

Tears?

> *My precious Eike, what can I say? How do I cover for*
> *the torment of this time that has passed, time I can never*
> *get back? I tried so many times to get this to you, tried*
> *to call or send you a message but I am watched*
> *constantly and I couldn't take the risk, couldn't put you*
> *and your family, <u>my</u> family, in any greater danger.*

Watched? Damon was being *watched*? And what danger? I'd understood all along that I'd been in danger but, my *family*? My *grandparents*? Maybe Ox and Hyunguk were on the right track after all.

> *I can't tell you enough how much I wanted to be there*
> *for you, how I know you must have wondered where I'd*
> *gone and where I've been. I don't have the words to tell*
> *you how sorry I am, how much*

The words trailed off and there was a huge splotch on the paper. The words continued further down the page, as if he'd had to write around the wet patch.

> *I can't tell you where I am, most days I'm not sure*
> *myself as my father has me transferred regularly but*
> *know only that I think of you constantly and my only*
> *goal, my only remaining reason for living at all, is to*

> *get back to you and to somehow make up for all that*
> *has happened.*

His father was regularly *transferring* him? What was he? A prisoner?

> *I think my father's idea is that if he keeps me busy, if he*
> *keeps me disoriented, I'll simply forget about you and*
> *eventually do as he expects me to do. I pretend but he*
> *has people watching me constantly and I go nowhere*
> *and do nothing, see nobody, talk to nobody that he*
> *doesn't know about. He made it clear, Eike, that if I*
> *contact you, that if I try to see you, what happened to*
> *you <u>before</u> (and he told me about it, Eike) will be*
> *nothing in comparison to what he <u>can</u> do. And I believe*
> *him.*

Jesus Christ!

> *He can't keep this up forever. Sooner or later, he's*
> *going to have to let go. I'm not a child and I'm not*
> *giving up, but please, Eike, don't give up on me, either.*
> *Branded for life, I am still, now and forever, your*
> *dragon.*
> *Damon.*

I put down the letter and found my hands shaking uncontrollably. *Jesus fucking Christ, Damon! Where the hell are you?*

But he'd said he hadn't given up. He was still mine. Wherever he was, he was still mine. Despite the letter, because of the letter, a huge weight lifted from me and the darkness, that deep, black, empty hole that had been there since I'd first woken to find him gone, that had threatened to engulf me as even the loss of my family had not done, retreated just that little bit. I threw myself onto my bed and hugged the letter to my chest. *I won't give up on you, Damon. I'm still here!*

A part of me felt lighter, freed, released. If I could've, I would've gone to the pool but campus was closed and besides, I'd not swum since the long ago tri-collegiate tournament and I doubted Coach Harmon would approve of me hitting the water without company, and the only company I could conceive of wasn't here. Yet.

Another part of me, that part residing in the darkness within, battled against a rising tide of helpless anger. Damon was trapped, and alone. What was I supposed to do now? To whom could I turn for help when the very person I would've turned to was the one who needed me?

With no immediate answers, I spent the remainder of the afternoon helping Hyunguk wash the Camaro and doing some odd jobs for Grandfather.

"You seem different today, Eike," Grandfather observed. "Is it all right for me to ask the reason?"

"I got a letter, Grandfather."

"From Damon?"

"Yes."

Grandfather nodded and smiled but he asked no more, and I was grateful.

I returned to my room after dinner to once again get changed. I'd debated with myself for some time about my earlier decision to accompany my friends before coming to the conclusion that sitting at home dwelling on what I couldn't immediately find answers for wasn't likely to be of much help to me. Perhaps what I needed was to come at the problem sideways and a change of scenery might be just the right catalyst for inspiration. I stood for quite some time studying my wardrobe before getting dressed.

Ox pulled up at almost exactly seven o'clock and I was ready and waiting for him.

"Dude," he observed with raised eyebrows as he got half out of the car and leaned across its roof, "what's with the threads?"

"Game-changer," I said enigmatically. "Are we ready?"

"Yeah," Ox said. "Get in."

He pulled out of the drive and shot a glance across at me, the curiosity etched clearly on his face. "This have anything to do with the letter?" he asked.

"Yes," I admitted. "It does."

Ox nodded. "It suits you but it sure as hell's going to get some attention."

"I'm counting on it," I said, offering no further explanation.

We drove in silence for a bit until I realised we weren't heading in the direction I'd expected. "Where are we going?" I asked. "This isn't the way to Fat Sam's, unless I've maybe got the wrong place in mind?"

"Sorry," Ox said. "I forgot to tell you we're meeting at Icon for pizza first. Is that ok?"

I shrugged. "Sure, but if I'd known, I'd have skipped dinner."

Everybody was waiting for us when we got there: Spex and Cara, Brett and Amy, Ed and his new girlfriend Lanie who I'd met a couple of times previously, and another girl I'd never met before.

"Eike, this is my girlfriend, Toss," Ox said as we joined the group. "Toss, this is Eike."

Toss stood up and offered me a slim but strong hand. "You're nothing like what I expected," she said, tossing a remarkable length of glossy black hair over one shoulder. "Is it rude of me to say you're positively gorgeous?"

"Only if it's rude of me to ask how you ended up with a name like *Toss*," I said in response. "Your parents not like you or something?"

Toss laughed, a warm and genuine laugh that had me instantly liking her. "It's Patricia," she said, "but call me that and…"

"I know, I know," I acknowledged with a conspiratorial grin in Ox's direction, "watch out."

"Something like that," Toss agreed.

I took a seat and Spex reached out a hand to clap me on the shoulder.

"What's with the new look?" he asked.

"Yeah!" Amy chimed in. "Toss is right, you're looking positively gorgeous!"

"Hey!" Brett interjected before I could respond. "Way to go for giving the rest of us an inferiority complex!"

"Just saying, right girls?"

"Yeah," Lanie agreed. "Are you quite sure you're gay?"

"Jesus," Ed said. "What is this, the Eike fan club?"

The girls laughed.

"Could be," Amy agreed.

"Well cut it out already," Ed grumbled. "It's enough to put a guy off his pizza."

"As if," Ox laughed.

Despite having already eaten, I was more than happy to share pizza, though I declined the beer in preference of Coke, and then we were organising who was travelling with whom to head off to Fat Sam's.

Oddly enough, although I was the only one without a partner, I didn't feel in the least out of place. Though there was a significant empty space, after the letter, I felt as if Damon was already as good as at my side and there was a definite energy to my step which had been absent a very long time. I'd figure this out, I knew I would. Somehow, one way or another, I'd get Damon back.

"Dude," Spex observed as I walked to Ed's truck with him, "what's up with you? Jeez, you're like a frog on hot rocks!"

"Just show me to the music," I replied, cutting him off to slide into the back seat beside Cara.

"Hey," Spex objected, forced to sit beside me and leaving me in the middle. "What's with this? You're not making a move on my girl, are you?"

I chuckled, dropping an extremely suggestive kiss on Cara's cheek, and she squealed and hugged me.

"Maybe," I said.

"Fuck off," Spex said.

Cara leaned on my shoulder and sent mischievous grins in Spex's direction the whole drive, which he studiously ignored. We pulled up in the parking lot of Fat Sam's and waited for Ox and his retinue to pull up alongside.

"Ready?" Ox asked, tucking Toss under his arm.

"Hell, yes!" everybody echoed. We headed in a loosely united group towards the front doors.

I spotted it just as we reached the steps, a big old pick-up truck, and it looked disturbingly familiar. I stopped and Ed crashed into my back.

"Dude! What the fuck?!"

"That truck…" I began.

"Bull Redwood's truck? What about it?"

Bull Redwood?

Hey, Bull, what're ya doin'?

A shadow fell across my vision and my hands knotted into fists.

Chapter Nineteen

"Eike!"

Ox had paused, bringing Toss with him, to see what the hold-up was, and I fought down the wave of rage which threatened to engulf me and managed a stiff smile.

"Sorry, it's nothing. I'm coming."

I shot a last glance over my shoulder at the truck, at *Bull's* truck, and followed my friends into Fat Sam's.

Fat Sam's, much like Meg's, is an eclectic mix of cultures which permits it an equally eclectic mix of clientele. It is part bar, part diner, part dance venue; and it was packed!

We walked in and, as my friends and I had in equal part anticipated, apparently my objective had been accomplished. People stared and whispered as I passed.

"You're like a one-man music video," Amy observed, standing on tiptoe to whisper it into my ear. "I'm almost jealous if it weren't that some of the looks make me a little nervous for you."

I laughed. "Don't you go worrying about any of them," I reassured her. "You're going to dance with me, right?"

"Dance with you? Eike, you can dance?"

"I'm half Korean and I was raised on K-Pop, of course I can dance," I informed her, not adding I'd taken dance classes alongside my Hapkido until the fire had stopped everything.

"Oh hell, yes!" Amy squealed. "I'm in!"

"Excellent."

We made our way to probably the only table left available and while Spex and Ox dragged over more seating, Ed, Brett, and I made our way to the bar. Carefully balancing trays, we returned to our table and the whole way my eyes scoured Fat Sam's, seeking a group of four men, one of whom would have to be *Bull*.

"He's not here, you know," Brett said, seeing me searching.

"What? Who?" How could Brett possibly know who I was looking for?

"Damon. He's not here."

I was momentarily caught by surprise before I caught up with what Brett had been thinking, and relaxed. "No," I said. "He's not."

Brett nudged me reassuringly with his shoulder, his hands being full, and gave me a comforting smile.

"It's ok, dude," he said. "You've still got us."

"Thanks," I replied. And I meant it.

We'd only just returned to our table when Amy was on her feet and taking my arm.

"So, Eike," she said. "About that dance?"

I grinned. "So soon? You don't want to settle in and have a few drinks first? You've just eaten pizza."

"What's to settle?" Amy snorted. "Come on, this is one of my favourite songs!"

I had to admit that although the sounds at Fat Sam's were hardly my beloved K-Pop, they had a good beat going with a DJ who was definitely able to do them justice.

"As my lady wishes," I conceded magnanimously, taking her arm and turning her from the table. "Sorry, boys. My attention is demanded elsewhere."

"What the fuck?" Brett groused. "How do you do that?"

"Natural born charisma," I told him.

I walked Amy through the near chaos that was Fat Sam's and onto the equally jammed dance floor.

It's true, I can dance, and if I didn't have natural-born charisma, perhaps I did have natural-born rhythm. It'd been a long time, probably since well before the fire, but dancing works its way into your blood and, just like swimming, you never forget. Besides, I no longer gave a damn who was watching or what they thought. I swung that girl all over the dance floor and, eventually, it was she who begged to stop.

"I need a breather," she gasped, resting her hands on her knees. "And a drink. Come on."

She preceded me back to our table but before I could reclaim my seat, Cara was on her feet along with Toss and Lanie.

"Our turn," Toss said. "We'll share."

"I swear, Eike," Ox grumbled, though his tone lacked any real conviction, "if we didn't all know for a *fact* that you're as queer as fuck, we'd be bloody upset!"

"Too true that," Ed agreed.

"Nothing stopping you joining us, or taking my place for that matter," I observed blandly.

"Yeah, right," the four guys intoned in unison.

I returned to the dance floor with the three girls and, before I knew it, we'd been joined by more. Hilarious!

I should've known, of course, and perhaps, in a way, I'd more than half been hoping for it. When next we returned to our table, there were several unfamiliar and definitely less-than-happy looking guys gathered around it.

"What's with your friend?" one of them asked Ox. "He's moving in on all our girls."

"Seems to me it was more like your girls were moving in on him," Ox pointed out calmly, "but he's here now so why don't you ask him yourselves. Just a word of warning, however," Ox added, his lip twitching with wry humour, "he's not called *the Black Dragon* for nothing, so don't say we didn't warn you."

I was? And I had warnings attached? I myself had had no idea but the revelation pleased me immensely. *Black Dragon?* It beat the hell out of being any variation of *pretty* or *half-breed toy*.

I circumvented the gathered group and graciously returned my three escorts to their seats.

"Is there a problem?" I asked, keeping my expression neutral.

"Too damn right there is," one of the group said. "You're cramping our style, asshole!"

I tipped my head and eyed him speculatively. "You actually have to have style in order for it to be cramped," I observed.

"Fuck you sideways!" the first guy spat. "You want to take this outside, 'cos we'd be more than happy to show you some fucking style!"

I smiled, slowly, rolling my shoulders suggestively, every well-defined muscle rippling beneath my skin. There was a united intake of breath and at the same time Ox, Brett, Ed and, I was surprised to note, even Spex and the girls rose unanimously to their feet. There was an expectant hush and for a moment it was as if everything beyond the immediate perimeter of our table ceased to exist. Nobody spoke and nobody moved and then, looking first at me and then at my friends casually pushing back their chairs, the gathered group seemed suddenly to lose their swag.

"Fuck you," the ringleader repeated, the venom gone from his tone and already backing away. "C'mon, guys," he said to his friends. "He's not worth it."

They turned and walked away, trying to look casual, but we laughed anyway.

"That's right," Ox muttered. "Walk away, pussies."

We took our seats and Ed feigned wiping a sweaty brow. "Shit, that was close," he said. "You sure know how to have an effect on people, Eike."

"It's a gift," I said with a grin. "Could've been fun."

"Fun? **Fun?** What's up with you, dude?" Spex asked, taking a deep breath and sinking back in his chair. "Me? I've never swung a fist in my life!"

Not *entirely* true, if I recalled correctly.

"You probably wouldn't have had to," Ox commented, cracking his knuckles and looking a little disappointed. "We could have taken them all and swept the pavement with them!"

"Well, I, for one, am glad it didn't come to that," Brett admitted. "Are we having another round, or what?"

"Why don't you come and dance with me instead?" Amy asked him.

"What?"

"Well, you wouldn't want us to have to drag Eike up again, would you?" she persisted, theatrically batting her eyelashes at him.

Brett stared wide-eyed at her, and then swung his gaze around the remaining three girls.

"You wouldn't! After what just about happened? You wouldn't dare!"

Amy's eyes narrowed and she glared at him. "Girls?" she queried, not shifting her gaze from Brett.

They rose to their feet in one fluid show of female solidarity and Brett grabbed in desperation at Amy's arm.

"Wait, wait already!" he begged. "Truce! Guys? Don't make me do this on my own."

There was some concerted mutual grumbling but it pretty much appeared there wasn't a choice and in the end they all departed for the dance floor leaving me to sit on my own. I didn't mind. I was grateful for the respite.

She was no mere girl and, in fact, I think I could state fairly authoritatively that it must've been more than a few years since she'd been asked for her ID. She came up beside me and dropped a slender, well-manicured hand to my shoulder, bending down to talk quietly into my ear.

"Not dancing this time, handsome?"

I raised my eyes to look at her and I'd have to say if I wasn't batting for the same team, she'd undoubtedly have got my heart racing. Instead, I simply picked up my iced water and shook my head.

"No, time out," I said.

She dropped onto the chair next to mine and I raised an eyebrow.

"Do I know you?" I asked, knowing with certainty I didn't.

"No," she admitted. "But you could."

"Oh?"

What could she possibly want with me? Didn't she know who and what I was or had I managed to hide it better than I'd anticipated? She reached out a hand to stroke my cheek, her long, blood-red fingernails gently raking across my skin and my scars, and my eyes narrowed in response though I managed not to draw away.

"Is there something I can do for you?" I asked, my voice neutral.

"Oh, I'm sure there is, honey," she murmured, continuing her caress down to my shoulder and along my arm.

My jaw tightened. "I think you've got the wrong impression," I said. "Whatever it is you're after, you're in entirely the wrong place."

"Oh, I don't think so handsome," she replied, her voice smoky with suggestion. "I think you have *exactly* what I want."

This had definitely gone far enough and I stood up and backed away a step so her hand could fall away from me. She pursed lips as red as her nails.

"Now what'd you have to go and do that for?" she asked petulantly. "You know I could definitely show you a good time."

"I sincerely doubt it," I informed her stiffly.

Which was when I sensed the presence behind me.

I'd been distracted by her and so I was caught off-guard. I turned around and a large man with coarse tattoos and a hairy chest showing above a dirty work shirt was standing far too close for comfort.

"What's goin' on here?" he asked, his voice rough. *His breath rank with cigarettes and whiskey.*

I froze, my heart pounding in an erratic tempo behind my ribs, a red haze rising into my vision, heat boiling in my veins. It was him. It was *Bull.*

"This guy botherin' you, Angie?"

He clearly didn't recognize me but he was still far from pleased at *Angie's* presence in my company. My hands clenched involuntarily into fists.

"Just talkin', Bull," Angie said, her speech slipping to match his. "Nothin' wrong with talkin' now, is there?"

Bull made to shove me out of the way so he could reach out and take Angie's arm.

"I think perhaps you'd better back down, mister," I told him, my voice dripping contempt. "Like the lady said, we were talking."

He paused, astonished. I don't imagine he'd been told 'no' too often, in any kind of manner.

"'Scuse me?" he asked. "What'd you jus' say to me?"

I pulled myself to my full and not inconsiderable height, bringing me to at least several inches taller than him, and leaned towards him, ignoring his foul breath, my eyes fixed implacably on his. "Let me put it in plain English so you'll understand. Back … the … fuck … off!"

"D'you have any idea who you're talkin' to, you little fuck-punk?" he snarled, his eyes narrowing to little more than slits and his face turning red.

"Do *you*?" I asked in reply. "*Bull*?"

He scowled. "So, you know me, do ya? Who the fuck are you and do you really wanna be startin' somethin' with me?"

I smiled humourlessly. "Turns out I'm known as the Black Dragon," I informed him, "and yes, I most definitely do. Question really is, do you?"

He bristled and I swear he actually expanded in size, not unlike a rooster puffing out its feathers or a cat its fur.

"Outside," he rasped. "Let me show you exactly what kinda pain you jus' brought upon yerself!"

"I hope you've got your friends with you," I said as he began to turn away.

He paused. "What'd you jus' say, punk?"

"I forgot for a moment there that English isn't your strong suit," I said to him. "I said, I hope you have your friends with you. I'd hate to think of you being outnumbered by one."

I was full on baiting him, and though I really didn't want to be starting a fight indoors, not at Fat Sam's, not with this about to become my friends' next favourite hang-out, I admit I was beyond caring. For a moment I thought he was about to take a swing at me right then and there but he too must have managed to consider the consequences.

"You poxy little fuck," he swore. "I'll see you outside'n you best be ready because, yes, I have my friends with me and we're gonna kick your mother-fuckin' arse straight to the curb!"

"Excellent," I assured him quietly.

He turned and stomped away and as I made to follow, a restraining hand fell on my arm. Angie.

"I sincerely hope you're not doin' this on my account, honey," she said. "But whatever your reason, it ain't worth it."

"Oh, but it so is," I assured her, and I disengaged her hand from my arm and began to make my way to the door.

The boys caught me as my hand fell on the door handle.

"Dude!" Ox exclaimed. "What the fuck are you doing? Do you have any idea who that is?"

"Bull Redwood," I replied matter-of-factly. "And, with any luck, three particular friends of his."

Ox studied me with a concerned frown. "What's all this about, Eike? Why the hell would you want to pick a fight with Bull Redwood and his trio of brain-dead Neanderthals?"

I ran my gaze over my gathered brothers, as I'd suddenly come to view them. "Because," I said calmly, "that bottom-feeding cluster-fuck and his pack of piranhas is the reason I'm covered in even more scars than I began with, and the reason Damon is no longer with me."

The silence in response to this was profound and it took a while before anyone seemed able to find their voice to comment.

"Oh ... my ... god!" Spex managed at last. "That's him? That's the guy who, you know, almost, almost...?"

"Yes," I responded, my voice remaining remarkably level. "He and his hyenas are the ones who beat the living fuck out of me and put me in hospital. They're the reason I don't swim anymore. They're the ones who ruined *everything*."

"Holy shit, Eike," Ed said.

"And? Anybody have anything more to say?" I asked. "Because there's some payback owing."

"On your own?" Ox asked.

"My fight," I stated bluntly. "They started it, but I can promise you I sure as hell mean to finish it."

"Not on your own, you ain't," Ox assured me. "Where you go, we go. Right guys?"

The others looked far from as certain of this as Ox, and I shrugged.

"You owe me nothing but if you want to come along and see the blood fly, be my guests."

And I stepped outside.

They were waiting by the truck, *that* truck, and the rage already building like a tsunami under my skin threatened to overwhelm me. I swallowed hard and forced it down, finding the inner calm which had helped me and undoubtedly saved me the last time I'd faced them, when my very life had been at stake, and the black dragon inked into my skin burned with sympathetic power.

I approached them fearlessly, barely aware of the entourage at my back and oblivious to Fat Sam's entire patronage emptying into the parking lot behind them.

"Recognize me yet," I asked, stopping a short distance from where they were leaning idly against the truck.

They disengaged themselves and Bull eyed me with a patronising smile. "Should we, punk?" he asked. "Seems to me you're nothin' more'n anotha stupid little freak with a death wish."

I tipped my head and gave him a smile. "What? No sweet hello and how do you do?" I said. "Not ready to show the *queer* how the *big boys* play? I have to admit I'm more than a little disappointed. Or do you only like to play when you catch a guy by surprise and have a baseball bat in your hand?"

Bull frowned, the cogs turning slowly in his thick skull. "No," he said. "It isn't. Not the little fuck from the swimming pool car park? Not the pretty boy?"

His friends all turned to look at him, the pennies beginning to drop.

"This is the faggot? This is the little punk King sent us after?"

A gradual murmuring began building behind me. Their voices, loud and distinct especially in the still night air, were carrying and by now half the clientele of Fat Sam's gathered for the pending confrontation were beginning to register what was going on.

"That's right," I said. "Bet you didn't think you'd ever be seeing me again, did you?"

Before they could work out a response, I was moving.

I hit Bull with all the power of a runaway freight train and with the added impetus of all the rage and pain and frustration which had been steadily building since the attack. He made a sound like a kick bag being dropped from a great height and fell to his knees and I drove my own knee into his face for good measure. He went down like a felled tree and I was moving sideways, picking my target, sliding down low and kicking the feet from under the next man in line, rising in the same fluid motion and driving fixed fingers into unprepared eyes.

All hell broke loose.

I don't know whether my friends even got a chance to join in and I suspect it might well have been more risk than they were prepared to take given the chances I might mistakenly have attacked them as easily as those I was actually there to fight. I don't recall exactly in what order things happened, I only know the bloodlust was not unlike the surge that took me when I was swimming. I was a blur of motion, a whirlwind of fury, and those great brainless thugs never stood a chance. They hit each other more often than they struck me and they barely landed so much as a single blow. Even if I'd not consciously been aware of it, I'd been preparing for this moment from the very day I'd woken up in hospital. Every run, every session with Hyunguk, every blow I'd taken and every move I'd practiced was all for this one moment in time and I was unstoppable.

It was only when the last one fell that I finally came to a standstill and stood, shaking, my breath and my heartbeat roaring in my ears.

"Eike!"

I barely registered the voice calling my name.

"Eike, dude, it's over."

Spex. The others were too afraid to come too close, understandably concerned I might take a swing at them as I'd similarly taken a swing at Coach Harmon that night long ago.

I turned slowly to face them.

They were lined up in a roughly straight line and behind them was the gathered throng of the Fat Sam patrons. Literally at my feet were Bull and his three thugs, groaning and moaning and spitting blood to varying degrees.

"Eike, holy shit, dude. It's over. Let's take you home."

I managed a shaky nod and, as they moved to support me, I fainted.

Chapter Twenty

I came to in the back of Ed's truck with Cara one side of me and Spex on the other.

"Eike, are you ok?" Spex asked.

I sat up from where I'd been resting in Cara's lap and groaned, my head thumping. "Yeah," I managed to say. "I'm fine, I think. Head rush is all."

"Dude," Ed said from the driver's seat, "that shit was freaking awesome! What the hell are you, like Jet Li or something?"

"No," I said, rubbing at my eyes. "I was just mad."

"Shit, dude! Remind me to **never** piss you off!"

"Never happen," I reassured him, and then, as I glanced out the windows, "Where are we going, by the way?"

"Ox's," Spex told me. "He said chances were you wouldn't want to go to the hospital and that his mom would check you out."

"He's right," I said, "but there's no need to trouble his mom. Let Hyunguk check me out. I'm fine. Honestly."

"What about Ox, and his mom? They're waiting for us."

"Flick them a text. They'll understand."

Ed reluctantly u-turned the truck.

Fortunately, Hyunguk was home and he and Grandfather came out to escort me to my bedroom, despite my protesting I was perfectly capable of getting upstairs on my own account. With varied and therefore somewhat muddled instalments, Spex, Cara, Ed, and Lanie did their best to fill them in on the evening's events.

"Four?" Grandfather asked, seeking clarification as he and Hyunguk deposited me on my bed, and scowling deeply. "He took on *four*, and they were men, yes, not boys like yourselves?"

Although I bristled a bit at his reference to *boys*, I had to concede I understood what he meant.

"Definitely not guys like us," Spex elaborated, unnecessarily, I thought. "These guys were like WWF wrestlers, scary as…" He stopped himself at the last moment and ducked his head with a blush. "Really scary," he finished lamely.

Hyunguk, unlike Grandfather, seemed suitably impressed, though he tried to keep this to himself. "I'll take care of him, Grandfather," he said. "Leave him to me."

"If I weren't so relieved, I'd have Hyunguk punish you and I'd ground you for a month," Grandfather grumbled. "I think I need a glass of wine and my pipe and as for the rest of you people, you can all go home now. There's been far too much excitement already for one night, especially for this old man!"

"Hey, Eike," Spex grinned as Grandfather began ushering them all down the stairs. "Way to go, dude!"

The door closed and we were left with the kind of silence indicating we were all alone. Hyunguk pulled up my chair to sit facing me.

"Plan or opportunity?" he asked.

"Opportunity," I responded honestly. "They were there, I was there. I don't know, call it the fates aligning or something." I rubbed self-consciously at my dragon and dropped my gaze to the floor. "I wanted to kill them," I admitted quietly.

"But you didn't," Hyunguk said.

"No. But I wanted to."

Hyunguk nodded as if satisfied and rose to his feet, pushing my chair back to my desk.

"Come on then. Get in the shower and then I'll take the aches out for you."

Much as I appreciated his expertise and looked forward to it, it wasn't the same as what I wished for. But I did as I was told.

My friends returned early the next morning, all of them, making a ruckus like a soccer riot and dragging me from much needed sleep. Grandfather had left me home while he and Grandmother went to the store and it was Hyunguk who intercepted them in the driveway beneath my bedroom window.

"We really need to see him, Hyunguk. Please! It's really important."

"Important enough to drag him from his bed after what he went through last night?" Hyunguk queried sternly. "Have you no consideration?"

I could imagine my friends shuffling their feet uncomfortably and I stayed tucked deep within my bed, happy to let them sweat. I thought it was very brave of Spex to pursue the matter further.

"Please, Hyunguk. We won't be long and we promise to let him go back to bed afterwards, swear to god."

There was a pause and I could clearly envision Hyunguk eying Spex with his implacable *dragon-master* stare and Spex quivering in his sneakers.

"There is an old saying," Hyunguk said icily, "*Do not wake the dragon unless you are prepared to face his wrath. Do you really wish to wake and anger the dragon?"

Apparently not as I heard them backing away with various comments to the effect they'd come back later if Hyunguk could only let me know they really needed to see me. My curiosity almost got the better of me and I briefly thought about going downstairs and rescuing them but, then again, I really was damn tired and very comfortable. I promptly fell asleep again and I have no idea what Hyunguk's parting remarks to them might've been.

When I awoke again, sunlight was streaming through the gap between my curtains and directly onto my bed. I rolled over, groaning. Despite Hyunguk's efforts of the previous night, every muscle in my body ached as if I'd done several rounds with a few of Hyunguk's Thai fighters. I half fell out of bed and stumbled across to where my clothes hung on the back of my chair.

Damon's letter was sitting on my desk and I picked it up.

"Damon," I whispered, holding the letter to my face and hoping to catch some reminder, some lingering scent of him.

The letter smelled only of paper and ink and, disappointed, I put it back on my desk. There was a gentle tap on my door.

"Just a moment!"

I threw on clothes and opened my door to find Grandmother standing there. Wow, I really must've slept late if she was already back from the store.

"May I come in?" she asked.

"Of course, Grandmother. Please, sit." I cleared the rest of my clothes from my chair and pulled it over for her to sit before dropping onto the end of my bed.

"How are you feeling today, Eike? Are you all right?"

"Yes, Grandmother. I'm fine and I'm very sorry I worried you and Grandfather. It … it wasn't my intent."

She leaned over and rubbed her hand across my head, there no longer being a great deal of hair to ruffle, and I smiled, overwhelmed by a sudden rush of affection for her.

"I've come to tell you that Hyunguk is leaving us," she said.

Hyunguk was leaving? Now? A lump rose in my throat and I blinked back the sting in my eyes. Hyunguk was never Damon but I didn't know that I could deal with him leaving me. Not yet.

"He is? When? Why?"

"He says you no longer need him," Grandmother explained with a sympathetic smile, "and that you are more than capable of looking after our house yourself from now on. Besides, the better part of the threat is gone now, yes?"

I wasn't so sure this was entirely accurate given Bull and his accompanying thugs only worked under instruction from Damon's father and he undoubtedly had plenty more minions to choose from, but I kept these thoughts to myself.

"Hyunguk honours me, Grandmother."

Grandmother nodded. "He is returning to Korea. He has a lady friend there that he would very much like to go and see."

Really, Hyunguk had a lady friend? A *girlfriend*? Somehow, I guess it had never occurred to me to think of Hyunguk's life beyond our doors, and he'd never said anything. I was going to miss him but of all people, I could perhaps understand best how much he'd sacrificed for me and I was happy for him and grateful to him for all he'd done for me.

Without him…

"Your friends have been looking for you," Grandmother added, interrupting my thoughts. "They have been most persistent."

Had they just. I wondered what was so important.

"I'll give Spex a call as soon as I've changed, Grandmother. I hope they've not troubled you too much."

"Of course not, Eike. They are your friends, not trouble." She stood up and rubbed my head once more. "Come down for something to eat," she said. "You must be very hungry."

Come to think of it … I was starving!

"Thank you, Grandmother. I'll be down shortly."

I called Spex before I went down to eat.

"Ok, so what's up? Grandmother says you've been quite the pest today."

"About time you rose from the dead," Spex replied. "We'd begun to think you'd gone into hibernation."

"Tempting," I muttered. "So, can we get to the point? What's up already?"

"Probably best we come and see you. This isn't exactly the subject for a phone conversation."

"What is this? Mission bloody Impossible? You're being very mysterious".

"You'll understand when we get there," Spex said. "Can we come over now?"

I sighed and rubbed my cheek, which by the feel of it was probably sporting a reasonable bruise. "I admit you've got me damn curious but I'm going to have to go down and eat first. Can it wait, like, half an hour?"

"I guess we could wait another half an hour," Spex conceded, "given we've already been waiting half the damn day."

It wasn't quite a half hour but it was close and fortunately they didn't all decide to traipse into the house but sent Spex to fetch me. I wolfed down the last of my lunch, thanked Grandmother and apologised for rushing away, and followed Spex out to the driveway where the rest of the crew were gathered waiting for me.

"About bloody time you woke up," Ox grumbled. "What are you? A vampire?"

"Dragon, apparently," I observed with a shrug. "What's all that about, by the way? How long have I been the *Black Dragon* and not known about it? Or should I not ask right now?" I looked around and shook my head. "Seriously, what's all the fuss about? Honestly, anyone would think you'd all won the lottery or something."

They exchanged conspiratorial smirks and I raised my eyebrows.

"No way," I said. "You haven't, have you? Won the lottery?"

"No, dude," Brett said, with a grin that stretched pretty much across the breadth of his face. "But you have."

"I don't follow… I don't play the lottery."

"But you've won big all the same," Ed said.

My jaw tightened and a tic began under one eye.

"All right, enough already. Could somebody please explain what the fuck is going on?"

Instead of darkening the mood, they laughed.

"Have you checked Twitter today?" Amy asked. "Been online at all?"

"Well, of course not!" I scowled. "I've only been up an hour if you'll recall. Point, people. I know you must have one."

"It's all over the net," Cara squealed. "It's gone viral!"

"What has?" I asked, edging towards explosive irritation that they all clearly knew something I didn't.

"Eike," Spex said, vigorously motioning the others to silence. "Last night - it got filmed by tonnes of people and it's been posted online. You're trending on Twitter! It's insane. Bull and his cretins were arrested, at the hospital no less, and there's a warrant out for Mr. King's arrest, and there's going to be a huge investigation and…"

"Whoa! What the fuck?"

"The Police will be looking for you," Ox continued. "The big shots from upstate, not the locals. They want to re-open the investigation and it looks like it's gonna be real big, on account of the videos. Eike, they're gonna nail the prick."

"I think I need to sit down," I said, feeling light-headed. "Can we go inside now?"

We trooped inside and Grandmother and Grandfather had to come and hear the story. They fetched Hyunguk from his packing and got my laptop from my room and set it up on the kitchen table. Spex quickly pulled up the videos they'd been talking about.

"I'm surprised they haven't been taken down already, to be honest," Toss volunteered from behind Ox's shoulder. "They're all evidence now."

"They will," Ed said, "but I imagine they'll just keep going back up."

Nearly all the videos (and there were a few!) clearly caught Bull and his ignorant companions admitting their part in my original assault and that it had been Damon's father who'd put them up to it. They also, with varying success, caught my very one-sided fight with them. Hyunguk whistled appreciatively through his teeth while Grandmother put her hand first over her mouth and then over her eyes, and Grandfather quietly patted me on the shoulder. I felt sick.

"I don't feel so good," I said. "I think I need to go and lie down."

They found me at the store the next day, two very serious and official looking men in severe charcoal suits, exactly as Ox had predicted.

Grandfather hadn't wanted me to go, unsuccessfully trying to insist I stay home to further recover, but I wouldn't hear of it.

"I'm fine," I'd said, "and I'd rather be at the store with you than lying in bed with far too much time to think about what comes next. Besides, I don't want Grandmother doing my job for me."

Reluctantly, Grandfather had conceded so that was where the Federal investigators from upstate found me, though they had to spend a considerable amount of time convincing Grandfather with badges, paperwork, and several phone calls first. Grandfather doesn't much trust the authorities, undoubtedly a hang-over from his past. He eventually called me in from the storeroom and offered us the use of his tiny office.

"Mr. Nylund? I'm Chief Investigator Kirkland and this is my associate, Mr. Richards. Is it all right if we take a few minutes of your time?"

As if I really had a choice but, obviously, I didn't say that. "It's Eike," I said, shaking the proffered hand, cool and firm, and then taking that offered by Mr. Richards. "Um, take a seat?"

Chief Investigator Kirkland took it upon himself to sit on the corner of Grandfather's desk while Mr. Richards apparently preferred to remain standing by the door, perhaps to prevent unwanted eavesdroppers. I took Grandfather's chair behind the desk.

"I take it you've heard your, uh, *altercation* of last night has gone rather public?" CI Kirkland asked.

I coloured and bit my lip. "Yes, sir."

"Quite impressive, by the way," the CI admitted.

"Are you here to arrest me, sir?" I asked, already prepared for the worst.

The CI chuckled. "Arrest you? No, son, we're not. By all accounts, you were challenged first and, though I guess, technically, you took the initiative, there'd not be a jury in the *country* who wouldn't say it was pre-emptive self-defence."

I looked down to hide a sigh of relief.

"We would, however, like you to come in at some point and give a full statement," CI Kirkland continued, "not only in relation to last night but also reconfirming the details of the previous assault."

I stiffened. "I already gave a full statement, back when it happened," I said. "Nothing's changed between then and now and I'm not about to retract or change anything."

The two detectives exchanged cryptic glances.

"The thing is, Eike," the CI informed me quietly, "your statement doesn't appear to be on record anymore. The files are missing."

My mouth fell open as I stared at him. "I'm sorry, sir... What?"

"That's why we're here," the CI continued. "There's a full investigation under way and this is only a small part of it but, like I said, your previous statement in relation to your assault can't be found, along with the statement from the witness, Mr. Harmon, or your accompanying medical reports. In fact," CI Kirkland admitted, his eyes darkening, "there isn't any evidence there was ever an investigation *at all*."

Unbelievable. And then again, was it? Damon's father's shadow certainly had a long reach. It was no wonder Damon had remained absent.

"There's another thing," Mr. Richards said. "What can you tell us about an assault at the Winchester Royal Grand, a few days before your own assault?"

Memories of Damon and I in the Penthouse Suite flashed through my mind and I felt sucker-punched. Damon. His father. Damon falling to his knees, the wind knocked out of him. Running a hand across the cold sweat breaking on my brow, I winced as I discovered a few more bruises in the process.

"Mr. King..."

I stalled and looked helplessly at Mr. Richards. How to tell these men what had happened and, more significantly, why?

"It's all right, Eike," the CI reassured me. "We're already aware of your relationship with Damon King and we're not here to judge, we're merely here for the facts, as best as you can remember them."

How could I ever forget? They were burned more indelibly into my memory than my scars were burned into my skin. I tightened my jaw and sat straighter.

"Mr. King attacked his own son," I said. "Knocked him clean off his feet with a left right cross-hook and finished the job with a body blow. Damon never even went to the hospital and nobody did anything," I concluded tightly.

"We managed to find some untampered-with video footage which confirms as much," Mr. Richards admitted with a nod. "Have you got any personal witnesses who can confirm the injuries young Mr. King might have sustained? Did he seek any private medical assistance at all?"

"Yes," I replied. "On both counts. We took him to a friend of ours whose mother is a nurse. Apparently, she's taken care of him on multiple occasions when this sort of thing happens."

"There's a prolonged history then?" Mr. Richards asked.

"So it seems, sir. Years apparently."

Mr. Richards and CI Kirkland again exchanged glances and I had the distinct impression a whole lot of something extremely unpleasant was about to hit the proverbial fan.

"Have you any idea where young Mr. King, Damon, is now?" CI Kirkland asked me. "We'd quite like to talk with him."

Oh, dear lord, so would I. I bowed my head and fought back both tears and the accompanying tightness in my throat. Not now! "No, sir,

I haven't a clue. His father took him away somewhere and told him that if he tried to contact me then…"

My breath caught and I momentarily lost my capacity for speech. It was as if I was betraying Damon's confidence in some inexplicable manner, by referring to the contents of his very personal letter to me but, I had no choice.

"Eike? Then what?"

"My family would be in danger," I said, my voice raw with emotion and my hands involuntarily tightening at my sides. "And what happened to me would be nothing in comparison to what *he*, Mr. King, could do."

"How do you know this?" Mr. Richards asked. "Has Damon been in touch?"

"He managed to get a letter to me, though he couldn't say where he was because, as far as I can tell, he doesn't know himself."

There was empathy in the investigators' expressions and the CI reached out a hand to place it on my shoulder.

"Eike. We're going to need to see that letter."

I knew they were going to ask but anticipating it didn't prepare me for the effect it had. I might as well have been body-slammed and my stomach churned as bile rose in my throat. I studied the tattoo of a scorpion adorning my forearm while I struggled for control.

"If I let you read the letter," I asked CI Kirkland, lifting my gaze to look at him directly, "can you make me a promise?"

"I can't make you any promises, Eike, but whatever it is, I assure you I'll do my best to accommodate you. What is it?"

"Promise me you'll find Damon and bring him home."

"Eike, we'll do our best."

Chapter Twenty-One

Hyunguk was waiting for me when I got home, leaning casually on the bonnet of the Camaro.

"Hey, Eike."

"Hyunguk. Ready to go already?"

Hyunguk nodded and disengaged himself from the car. He dangled the keys. "Want to drive?"

I started in surprise.

"Me? Really? You're going to let me drive the Camaro?" I stopped and frowned.

"Wait, does this mean you're going to make me run home?" I asked suspiciously.

Hyunguk grinned. "Happy birthday, Eike," he said, and tossed me the keys.

I caught them more out of reflex than preparation and stared at him. "Happy birthday?"

Hyunguk's grin grew wider. "Your grandparents and I have come to an arrangement. I'm going back to Korea so I won't be needing her anymore and I can't think of anyone I'd rather leave her with. She's all yours."

Mine? Hyunguk's precious Camaro was mine? *Holy shit!* "Hyunguk, I ... I don't know what to say. Thank you, thank you so much!"

"Well, don't just stand there waiting for the sun to set," Hyunguk said, striding around the sleek blue bonnet and reaching for the passenger door. "Come drive me. It'll make a nice change to not be the chauffeur for once."

I didn't need asking twice.

I drove Hyunguk to Junsu's house and reluctantly helped him take his minimal luggage from the boot.

"I'm going to miss you," I told him.

He embraced me fondly before grasping my shoulders and looking directly into my eyes. "Stay strong," he said. "Never let the dragon sleep."

"Will you keep in touch?" I asked.

Hyunguk smiled as he released me. "You won't get rid of me that easily. What is it you always say? Harder to shake than…?"

"Fleas off a junk-yard dog," I finished for him.

"That's the one. I'll be back to visit from time to time and in the meantime, you could always try writing. Might be good for you to practice that rusty Korean of yours."

I raised my eyebrows. "Seriously?"

"Seriously."

"Couldn't I just e-mail you?"

"You can do that in Korean, too." He paused as he was about to pick up his bags. "Have you given any consideration to those transfer offers?" he asked. "You know some of those colleges offer far more than Seven Oaks, right?"

I shook my head.

"Waiting for Damon?" he guessed.

I shrugged. "I live in hope."

Hyunguk smiled reassuringly at me. "He'll be back. Best of luck, ok?"

"Thanks, Hyunguk. For everything."

"It was an honour," Hyunguk said, and he picked up his bags and walked into Junsu's house without looking back.

I called Spex as soon as I returned home.

"Hey, how you doin'?" he asked.

"Ox was right," I told him. "I had visitors this morning. A couple of pretty serious looking feds from upstate."

"For real? What did they say?"

"They want me to go in and make some statements, you know, about what happened at Fat Sam's but..." I paused.

"But?" Spex prompted.

"But also about what happened before," I continued. "Not only to me but about Damon, you know, when his father beat him up."

"Seriously?" Spex sounded astonished. "Didn't you already make a statement about last time? And since when has anyone tried to do anything about Damon getting beaten by his father?"

Not that Spex could see it, but I shrugged. "Somebody's trying now," I said. "Turns out all the previous files relating to my case don't exist. As in they're either missing or they were never filed to begin with."

"What?!" Spex exclaimed. "You're shitting me!"

"Spex, there was never an investigation. It pretty much got cut off before it began and they're starting completely from scratch."

"Holy shit!" Spex whispered. "This could really get messy."

"Yeah," I agreed. "I think it might."

"You all right?" Spex asked after a bit.

"I guess so."

"When do you think you might go and make that statement? Want me to come with? We could go today, I'll be free shortly. I'm just finishing up."

Spex worked for his parents at the bakery full-time most of his holidays and part-time through the semester. I briefly considered his offer before sighing in resignation.

"Maybe best. You know, get it the hell over and done with."

"Good plan," Spex agreed. "You want to see if Hyunguk can maybe drop by and pick me up in, say, twenty?"

"Sure," I said, smiling to myself. "I'll see you in twenty."

Chief Inspector Kirkland had given me his card and told me to call when I was coming in. So I did.

I half hoped he might not be free, suddenly not feeling anywhere near as sure of myself as I'd led Spex to believe. But he picked up almost immediately.

"Kirkland."

"Sir? It's Eike Nylund."

"Eike? I have to admit I'm surprised to hear from you so soon. Thinking of coming in?"

"Yes, sir. Best to get it over and done with and all that. That is, if it suits?"

"You mean today?" the CI asked. "Absolutely. When?"

"Maybe forty minutes?" I suggested.

There was a pause and the sound of rustling papers and then he became muffled as if perhaps he'd cupped his hand over the phone to speak with someone. He returned.

"Forty minutes is fine, Eike. Just come through to the main desk and ask for me and I'll send Richards to fetch you."

"Is it all right if I bring a friend?" I asked.

"Not a problem," CI Kirkland assured me. "We'll see you soon, then."

I stripped off my overalls and stood and stared at my wardrobe, just as I had the night of Fat Sam's. If I was going to do this, I figured I'd best put on my game face. This called for battle dress, especially if I was going to hand over Damon's precious letter. *Never let the dragon sleep.* I put my hand to my dragon tattoo and it throbbed beneath my palm. _Never let the dragon sleep_. With grim determination, I got changed and picked up Damon's letter.

Spex was waiting on the corner outside Quincy's as I pulled smoothly to the curb in _my_ new Camaro. I leaned over and wound down the window, grinning at the surprise on Spex's face.

"Where's Hyunguk?" he asked as he slid in. "How do you get to be driving his car? Dude, I didn't think he'd ever let _anyone_ touch this baby!"

My grin grew wider as I slipped the Camaro into gear. _"My_ baby," I informed him. "My birthday present."

"No fucking way!" Spex exclaimed, astonished. "Yours? Dude, way to go!"

"Yeah," I agreed.

He looked at me a little more closely. "Dressed for success or for battle?" he asked.

I looked down. "Bit of both, I imagine."

Damon's letter was in the glove box and even though it was hidden from view, the presence of Damon it contained seemed to fill the car, making my heart race and my palms sweat.

"You ok?" Spex asked. "You've gone a bit pale. Green, actually."

"The feds asked me to bring in Damon's letter."

"Shit."

"One way of putting it."

"You ok with that?"

"Not even, but what has to be done, has to be done, and if it brings me even one step closer to bringing Damon home…" My voice tapered off and my hands clenched on the steering wheel, my jaw tightening as I glared at the road as if it was somehow to blame.

"You're one tough bastard, you know that?" Spex observed.

I certainly didn't feel very tough at that moment but I smiled gratefully at Spex, appreciating his vote of confidence. "Thanks, Spex."

Pulling up on the opposite side of the road to the Police station, the only place I could immediately spot a parking space, we got out of the car. The road was busy and there was plenty of traffic to dodge. We waited for a gap, sprinted across and, as we hit the opposite curb, I saw him.

He was standing at the top of the steps to the Police building, just outside the doors and accompanied by two uniformed officers, and I recognised him instantly. Coming to an abrupt halt, my heart began to race, my breath dragged like acid through my lungs, and my vision blurred. I felt weak, shaky, as if I might not be able to stand. Spex put a hand on my elbow.

"Hey, Eike? You ok, buddy? Why'd you stop? Second thoughts?"

I couldn't speak, could only indicate up the steps with one trembling arm.

"What?" Spex asked, and then, seeing what I'd seen, "Oh, oh holy shit."

He hadn't changed a bit, not in all the time since I'd seen him last and he was still as gloriously spectacular as the very first time I'd ever laid eyes on him. Damon. The letter burned in my hand and the dragon tightened its grip around my throat.

He hadn't seen me, that much was obvious. I stared at him. I couldn't move.

Spex leaned over to whisper in my ear. "What do you want to do?"

I didn't know. My legs didn't want to move and I couldn't for the life of me imagine what I could possibly say to him. Besides, the cops. I closed my eyes and struggled for breath. I'd been waiting for this for so long, had wanted nothing more than to look into his eyes, touch him, be with him, and now he was here, only a couple of dozen concrete steps from where I stood. My legs finally began to move of their own volition, as if Damon were a magnet drawing me to him.

Spex followed a step behind.

Coming closer, I could see he was thinner, his face gaunt. There were dark shadows under his eyes, accentuating their bright and familiar Caribbean blue. He *had* changed. He looked exhausted and worn, like a cancer patient in remission, and my heart lurched.

Damon.

He still hadn't noticed me, deep in conversation with one of the accompanying police officers, and I was almost directly in front of him before his eyes turned to me at last. For what seemed an interminable time, he failed to recognise me, his face blank, and then I saw recognition register in his eyes. He stopped speaking, his mouth falling open and his eyes widening, and then he was pushing past the officers and launching himself across the remaining distance separating us.

"Eike!"

I couldn't help myself, couldn't have stopped myself if I'd wanted to, and I most definitely didn't want to. Oblivious to everybody and everything around us, completely oblivious to where we were or that there were people *everywhere*, I threw myself towards him, meeting him in a body-crunching embrace. He immediately locked his head over my shoulder and clasped his arms around me so tightly he almost cut the breath from me.

"Eike!" he breathed into my neck. "Oh, sweet Jesus, I've missed you!"

We stood that way for what seemed forever, though not nearly as forever as we would've liked, before we gradually disengaged ourselves.

"I didn't recognise you," he whispered. "What happened to you? Where did you go?"

I turned my head and laid my lips to his cheek. "This is what happens when the dragon wakes," I told him. "I've gone nearly crazy without you."

He managed a strangled laugh. "Not nearly as crazy as I've been without you," he said. "What are you doing here? I was going to come and see you, I swear. Just as soon as they let me go."

I pulled back and held him by his far too bony shoulders as I looked into his face, his precious and achingly familiar face.

"Let you go?"

Damon gave me a strained smile. "No, I'm not under arrest or anything. Statements. The shit has hit the…"

"Proverbial fan," I finished for him. "I'm here for the same reason."

I held up his letter which was still clasped in my hand.

"At least I won't have to share this now," I said. "Or I shouldn't think so."

Damon's eyes appeared even more blue above the shadows as his cheeks brightened with colour.

"You got it," he whispered. "I didn't know. I could only hope."

"Yes, I got it," I reassured him, once again brushing my lips across his cheek. "*Forever my dragon.*"

His hand rose self-consciously to the dragon in his neck, the one perfectly matching mine.

"It kept me close," he said. "I swear it was joined to you. Always."

I smiled at him. "They have power," I conceded, touching my own dragon before laying my hand over his. "Branded for life.'

"Branded for life," he echoed softly.

We were interrupted by one of the officers discreetly clearing his throat.

"I hate to intrude, gentlemen, but we're expected inside. Would you mind very much accompanying us now?"

We minded very much but there wasn't a lot we could do about it and so, taking Damon's hand in mine and with an apologetic smile at Spex who had been standing self-consciously waiting for us, we proceeded to follow the two officers into the station. Spex jogged up alongside me.

"If you give me the keys, I'll just wait in the car," he said.

Gratefully, I handed him the keys. "No joy-riding," I told him.

"Trust you to spoil all the fun," he snorted.

They separated us, Mr. Richards going with Damon, and CI Kirkland accompanying me, and the next seemingly never-ending hours were spent going backwards and forwards over the events of the past. The CI continuously brought me back to previous comments and observations to ensure they matched later events and recollections and he questioned everything. Eventually, however, he was satisfied.

"I'm sorry I had to put you through that," he said as he got me to sign off the last piece of paperwork, "but it was a necessity."

"I understand," I said, exhausted beyond belief and only wanting to get back to wherever Damon was now. "Thank you, by the way."

CI Kirkland looked at me. "What for?" he asked.

"For finding Damon. You were a whole lot quicker than I anticipated, too."

The CI smiled. "Much as I'd like to take credit for that, I didn't know he was here until he walked in with you. He came in of his own accord."

"He did? Then where's he been?"

CI Kirkland shook his head. "I imagine you'll have to ask him yourself."

"So, can I go now?" I asked, already getting to my feet.

"Yes," the CI said, "but if you could just not leave town for the time being." He saw my face and was quick to reassure me. "Only in case we have any further questions, that's all." He paused. "I'm half of the inclination to offer you protection," he added, his features tight with concern.

"Protection, sir?"

"You've already experienced the length of King's arm once. Would you accept protection?"

I stood and flexed my arms, tattoos rippling like live things across my skin. "I think I'll be all right, sir. But thank you."

"As I thought. Good luck, Eike."

"Thank you again, sir."

I met Damon in the lobby and the strain evident in his face and, in fact, his whole posture, indicated he was equally as exhausted as I was, if not even more so. He brightened considerably, however, when he saw me.

"Eike!"

"Ready to go home?" I asked, taking his hand in mine and briefly touching my lips to his while refusing to acknowledge the stares and whispers this generated around us.

"Home? Oh, Eike, you have no idea how much I've wanted to go home with you and how long I've waited."

"Oh, I think perhaps I have some idea," I argued, and I led him out of the station.

Damon was as surprised by the Camaro as Spex had been.

"A lot has changed," he observed quietly as he got in.

"Yes," I agreed. "Birthday present, but the best birthday present I could ever have hoped for is sitting right beside me."

Damon smiled and Spex shuffled uncomfortably in the back seat.

"Don't mind me," he muttered self-consciously.

"I wasn't," I assured him.

We didn't talk about much on the way home however, and we dropped him off at his house.

"Don't be too alarmed if you don't see us for a couple of days," I informed Spex. "We've got a lot of catching up to do so if you could maybe tell the rest of the guys the same thing? You know, we'll get in touch with them so if they could maybe not get in touch with us...?"

"Way too much information," Spex grumbled, getting out of the car. "I'll see you guys when I do."

"I guess you will," I agreed, and I took Damon home.

My grandparents were understandably delighted to see Damon, and Grandmother cried.

"Welcome home," she said as she hugged Damon, and I wasn't surprised when he cried too.

"I've missed you, Grandmother," he said as she tousled his hair affectionately. "And you, Grandfather. It's good to be home."

"It is very good to have you back," Grandfather told him.

I took Damon up to my room so he could shower and change after he told me he'd driven the whole previous night in order to make it back from wherever he'd been.

"I found out yesterday," he said, "and as soon as I knew he was going to be very busy for a very long time, I figured it was better to get out sooner rather than later, in case somebody suddenly decided I might be more of a liability than an asset. I climbed out a bathroom window and took one of the staff cars. I don't think they had a clue and I imagine that by the time they *did* figure it out, it wasn't worth chasing me."

"Jesus, Damon. You really *were* a prisoner!"

"In a manner of speaking, I guess," Damon conceded. "I'd have come sooner but, you know, the risks…"

"I understand," I said.

And I did.

Sometimes it isn't about leaving or staying, it's about being brave enough to know which is the right choice.

There was a knock on the door as we were about to get undressed for the shower and I opened the door.

"Grandfather."

Grandfather smiled at me. "I'm sorry to disturb you," he said apologetically.

"It's ok," I said. "We were just about to have a shower…" I stumbled over my words, realising what I'd said, and blushed.

"It's all right, Eike. I've just come to let you know I called Junsu. Grandmother and I are going to stay with him for a few days, to give you some space."

Overcome with gratitude and affection, I bowed deeply and gave him a hug, something my grandfather rarely accepts from me. He surprised me by hugging me tightly in return.

"I have faith in you, Eike," he said. "Call us at Junsu's when you are ready for us to return."

"Thank you, Grandfather. Thank you for everything."

Damon and I sat on my bed and held hands and waited and after a short while we heard my grandparents' car pull out of the drive and we were alone.

Chapter Twenty-Two

"We may have to invest in a bigger bed," Damon observed as he rose slowly to his feet, drawing me with him, "because I fully intend to never leave you again."

Looking from him to my bed and back again, I grinned at him. "Oh, I don't know," I said. "I'm kind of fond of it and besides, it'll keep you closer."

"There is that, I suppose," Damon agreed, pulling me into his arms and resting his head on my shoulder. "I missed you so much, Eike. Are you still *mine*?"

"It's only what you see on the outside that's changed, Damon. My heart remains the same."

"Then can I catch up on what I've missed?" he asked, running his hands down my back and resting them at my hips as if asking permission.

"Since when did you ever bother to ask?" I teased.

He sighed softly and pulled my shirt free, lifting it over my head and pausing while my arms were caught to press his mouth to mine. Reasserting ownership, checking to see if my words were true. I didn't deny him. Reassured, he dropped my shirt to the floor and drew back, his face immediately creasing in astonishment.

"Jesus, Eike!"

I looked down, my lips twitching. "Only what's on the outside has changed," I reminded him.

"No shit it has. What the hell?" He dropped onto the edge of the bed and stared at me. "Turn around," he instructed. "Slowly."

I did as he'd asked.

"Fuck!"

"Does it bother you?"

"Yes. No. I don't know. Jesus, if it wasn't so disturbing, I'd say you were sexy as fuck."

"What, and I wasn't before?"

"Yes, yes of course you damn well were but ... I don't know, Eike. I had no idea. I just, I guess I couldn't have…"

I shrugged, smiling sympathetically. It must've been a shock to him, especially without the benefit of the gradual introduction to the changes he would've seen if he'd been present while they'd been happening. Though if he'd *been* present, chances were they wouldn't have happened to begin with. He traced the line of a jagged scar beneath a vibrant tattoo with one finger.

"Eike."

My body was a canvas of Korean art: intertwined dragons and tigers and symbols in bold blacks and bright colours. They covered the better part of my torso, back and front, wrapped my arms to the wrists and crossed the backs of my scarred hands, and he'd discover soon enough they didn't stop at my waist.

I was also so much leaner and harder than the last time Damon had seen me. I was no longer the collegiate swimmer, no longer the *pretty boy* hiding my identity from the world. I was a fighter and every inch of me screamed power and rebellion. Not an ounce of surplus body weight remained and where I wasn't inked, my skin was darkened by frequent exposure to the elements as Hyunguk and I had trained outdoors more often than not.

Damon scanned me slowly from the top of my head, with the intricate patterns shaved into the sides below my close-cropped hair, to my booted feet, and his expression was inscrutable. I waited patiently, unconcerned. It was only skin and I had every confidence Damon's feelings for me would remain unchanged. Eventually, having resolved some silent inner debate, he placed his hands on my hips and drew me closer, softly and yet possessively laying his lips to the hard, flat planes of my stomach.

"You are now and forever my Eike," he stated calmly, "and I have the feeling trouble is something you're more than capable of dealing with."

"It turns out I've somehow been given the title *Black Dragon*," I told him. "I wouldn't have earned it without you."

Damon lowered his head and looked away.

"I suspect for all the wrong reasons," he murmured, his voice laden with what sounded suspiciously like shame.

I tilted his chin to look into his eyes.

"Branded for life," I said softly. "Has what you went through been any the less because of me?"

He stared at me and gradually the light returned to his eyes. "You're still a drug I can't do without," he said.

"I think that shower is in order, don't you?"

His lips twitched suggestively and his eyes sparked. I laughed.

"You haven't changed," I told him.

"We'll see," he said.

He *had* changed, subtly and yet unmistakably, and fury burned in me anew as I traced the evidence of his absence on his body.

In a way, I'd expected our reunion might have been rougher and more desperate, especially in the more intimate setting of the shower in which, it could be said, our relationship had first begun. But rediscovery turned out to be far more gentle and reserved, as if we were both a little fearful of what we might find. Damon wanted to explore every inch of my new skin, every individual turn and design of my intricately patterned outer self and I, for my part, was more than willing to allow him to do so while simultaneously rediscovering him. Which was how I discovered he had scars of his own.

They weren't initially visible, though the changes in his body were. He was leaner too, though not in the same way as me. Suffering long periods of incarceration and inactivity had made him smaller, somehow. His body was pale and soft and when I ran my hands over him, I felt bumps and knots beneath the surface I knew with certainty hadn't been there before.

"What are these?" I asked, already knowing. "What happened to you?"

He placed a hand over mine and kissed my neck, saying nothing.

"One day," I whispered tightly, "I'll fucking kill him! If it's the last thing I do, I'll watch him burn!"

He put his mouth to mine, claiming me in a smouldering kiss that could do nothing but silence me, and when he finally withdrew said merely, "It isn't worth it. Let it go."

"When was the last time you slept?" I asked as he followed me back to bed.

"Does it matter?" he replied. "I've no intention of sleeping now."

"You may not look the same but you sure as hell sound the same," I observed, fending him off as I tried to finish towelling off.

"You're wasting time talking," he said. And he took the towel.

Though I could clearly have resisted if I'd wanted to, I allowed him to push me onto my back on the bed and hold me down with his hands to my shoulders.

"I've waited a long time to look at your face," he said, his voice husky. "Especially like this."

I raised an eyebrow. "Oh?"

He lowered himself against me, pushing his shoulders up under my knees and rising slowly closer and deeper as he once more claimed my mouth with his. I closed my eyes and allowed him to lose himself in me though he was far gentler than I anticipated and I could only imagine what it must have cost him in terms of self-control.

"Still holding back, Damon?" I asked when he moved his mouth from mine long enough for me to speak.

"Are you really ready for me to do otherwise?" he asked, his body suddenly still.

"What do you think? Do you really think I can't handle anything you might have to offer?"

"You're still dangerous."

"Still? I'm more dangerous than ever," I responded softly. "So stop treating me as if I'm the fragile one. Unstoppable, and unbreakable. Let go."

And he let out a sigh of relief, and did.

Finally wearing himself out, Damon gave into sleep and I with him, enfolded in each other's arms. There were no nightmares and he didn't wake through the night, though I'd expected he would. I woke before he did and, carefully extricating myself from his embrace, I took myself to the shower. Although I was alone and to some extent wishing I wasn't, I was content to know he was at least not far away. And besides, perhaps for the best. Given the freedom I'd encouraged from him, he'd been rough. I was feeling it.

I got dressed, tucked the comforter more closely around him and kissed him, and went downstairs.

It was odd, the house being empty not only of Hyunguk but also of my grandparents, but not uncomfortable. I could do this, share a house with Damon. I could easily envision us together forever and although I didn't dare to look too far ahead, I wanted to hold onto this thought as a natural progression of where we ought to be going.

Of course, as Grandfather had once pointed out, our road was destined to have more hurdles than most and this much had certainly already been proven but if it only took me wherever Damon was going, I'd be content. I started on breakfast, though it was by now nearer to lunchtime.

He came down as I was about to put the food on the table and wrapped his arms around me, laying his head on my shoulder. How much had I missed this embrace? How often had I stood here in his absence wishing he were present for him to do this just one more time? I sighed in satisfaction and he whispered in my ear.

"You weren't there when I woke. You scared me."

"I'm sorry," I said, laying my arms over his. "I didn't want to wake you."

He bit my ear and nuzzled my neck. "Next time?" he murmured. "Wake me."

"You're so bloody demanding," I told him. "Especially when you haven't been fed. You'll regret having asked me come tomorrow."

"Highly unlikely." His hands drifted determinedly south.

"And still incorrigible," I noted wryly. "Get off. I've made us brunch."

"Couldn't I have you instead?"

"Though it might be very tempting, I happen to be starving and besides, I cooked which, I might point out, is highly unlikely to be happening too often so best you enjoy it while you can."

"And you are still hard!" he grumbled, pulling away.

"And who's bloody fault is that?" I asked, making a show of rearranging my clothing. "Now sit!"

He did.

He offered to help with the washing up after we'd eaten but I suggested he shower and dress instead.

"Aren't you coming with me?" he asked.

"You can't see I've been there, done that already?"

"Yes, but not with me. The house is empty. Come shower with me."

As always, he was nothing if not persistent and, in the end, it was easier to simply concede.

"So bloody demanding," I told him, not for the first time. "Fine. I'll be up in five so go and get some clean towels or something."

It was a long shower but I had to admit I didn't really object half as much as I'd made out.

He didn't want to get dressed either but the line had to be drawn somewhere and this time I was determined to have my own way.

"We have things we need to discuss," I told him firmly. "Now you can either get your arse dressed and downstairs or I'm going to go and find Spex and spend my afternoon with him."

"You wouldn't! Not on my first day home!"

"Try me," I challenged him.

He sighed deeply in resignation. "You would, wouldn't you."

"Yes," I replied bluntly. "I would."

"Then I guess I'll raid your wardrobe and see you downstairs."

It was just as well he'd also lost a considerable amount of weight or he'd have struggled to find something to fit. Our separation had definitely had its effects on both of us.

Damon found me in the parlour with Grandmother's tea service and tears pooled in his eyes as he picked up the cup I'd poured him.

"I missed this almost as much as I missed you," he said, his voice catching. "Wherever we go, promise we'll have one of these."

Wherever *we* go? Done.

"About that," I said.

"About what?" he asked. "The tea set?"

"No, dumb arse. The *wherever we go*."

"Oh."

"What's the situation?" I asked bluntly. "What are we, *where* are we right now? And what do you see happening next?"

"Well," he said, sipping his tea and lifting his eyes to look suggestively over the rim of the cup, "I see us as two hot young men who haven't seen each other in far too long sitting in this parlour drinking tea, and then I see me tossing you onto that sofa over there and…"

I scowled at him.

"You know perfectly well that's not what I meant," I said, my voice low. "Could you just for one moment get your mind out of your crotch?"

He grinned at me, completely unapologetic. "Can't blame me for trying."

My eyes hardened.

"Sorry," he murmured.

He leaned back in Grandfather's armchair where he'd chosen to make himself comfortable.

"Are you committed to staying at Seven Oaks?" he asked. "Have you ever considered maybe applying for transfer?"

"Well actually," I admitted, "I've already had several offers from other colleges but…" I shrugged. "I was waiting for you."

He smiled, his eyes sparkling. "You had faith."

"Yes," I agreed. "I had faith."

"All of my father's assets have been frozen," he said. "At least until the investigation is over, and that could take months, if not years.

They're doing a full audit, of everything." He paused and stared into the bottom of his cup. "This has become far bigger than what happened to us and I think they were really just looking for an excuse, any excuse, to start something on him. We just happened to be a convenient catalyst for what was coming anyway."

"Where does that leave you?" I asked.

He shrugged as he put down the cup. "I have some personal assets," he said. "Property and funds my mother left in trust for me so I'm ok. And it isn't as if I'm incapable of looking after myself. I mean, fuck, I've been doing it long enough already."

I fidgeted with my own teacup. "And us?" I asked. "What do you see happening with us?"

"Us?" he asked, sounding confused. "We are you and me. Where you go, I go. As far as I'm concerned, Eike, that's all there is."

I lifted my gaze to him and studied him carefully. "You know it's not going to be that easy, don't you?"

Damon threw back his head and laughed. "You can honestly ask me that?" he demanded. "After all we've already been through? Eike, we've been through the bowels of hell and only come out stronger. In my humble opinion? Bring it the fuck on!"

"I guess there is that, isn't there? But you have no idea how happy I am to hear you say it."

Damon winked at me. "Come over here and I'll show you just how happy I can make you."

"Promises, promises," I laughed at him.

But I got up and dropped into his lap anyway.

We didn't leave the house for two straight days but, eventually, life had to go on. Grandfather and Grandmother returned from Junsu's, and I called Spex.

"About time we all got together," I said. "Want to get everybody together for a visit to Fat Sam's?"

"Seriously?" Spex said. "I thought you two had done a runner on us and we'd get a postcard from Jamaica or something."

"You know what? That never occurred to us. Thanks for the suggestion, Spex. Jamaica. Inspired."

"Hey wait! You wouldn't, would you?"

"I wish people would stop challenging me," I muttered. "No, we're not going to Jamaica, tempting though that might be. Just get everybody together, will you? And we'll meet you tonight at eight. It's my birthday tomorrow."

"No shit? I'd forgotten."

"Gee thanks, Spex."

There was an embarrassed silence on the end of the line.

"Kidding, Spex. Kidding. Tonight at eight. Fat Sam's. Ok?"

"Yeah, yeah sure, dude. See you then."

For my grandparents' sake, Damon managed to restrain himself through the day and I was grateful.

"Thank you," I said as we went upstairs after dinner to get ready for our night out.

"Whatever for?" he asked.

"For behaving yourself."

"Yes, well, I have every intention of showing absolutely **no** restraint once we get out of this house," he informed me bluntly.

"I'm counting on it," I told him. "You've not been to Fat Sam's before. I think you'll like it. It's an interesting place."

I opened the door to my bedroom and he immediately dragged me inside and spun me to the wall, blocking me with his body and plastering his mouth to my neck.

"I could always try being quiet," he said, his hands already sliding down my body to pull at my shirt.

"Get off!" I told him. "Always with you. What is it with you?"

"I can't help myself. Can you blame me?"

"Perhaps not but if you don't control yourself, I swear I'll get you a collar and muzzle!"

"You are such a bloody spoil sport," he said, still nuzzling at my neck though he'd at least ceased fondling me.

"Get in the shower and get dressed," I ordered him. "We have places to be, people to see, and things to do."

"Oh, agreed," he murmured. "We **so** have things to do. Are you having a shower with me?"

"Get ... off!"

He sighed deeply and sat on the bed. "Where are my clothes from the other day?" he asked. "You know, from when I got here."

"You're not seriously thinking of wearing them, are you?" I asked, horrified. "They're filthy!"

He raised a bemused eyebrow at me. "My wallet?" he said. "You know, my licence, my cards, random semi-important stuff?"

"Oh. Right. Sorry. Over there in the corner with the rest of the dirty laundry I haven't gotten around to yet, owing to the perpetual distractions," I said with a wry smile.

He grinned. "There were those, weren't there?" he admitted.

We took the Camaro to Fat Sam's and we definitely turned heads getting out of the car, not least because Damon had lost none of his insistence on making his claim on me clear for all to see. I no longer cared and, if anything, I found the whole experience to be singularly exhilarating. I mean, who was going to dare mess with us? Seriously? Especially in light of what had happened the last time I'd been at Fat

Sam's. We walked hand in hand, shoulder to shoulder, and strode into Fat Sam's as if we owned the place.

As was now common for Fat Sam's, especially given Meg's had been temporarily closed as part of the investigation into Damon's father, the place was packed, the music thumping, and our friends easy to find. Chairs were quickly found for us and Damon pulled me so close I might as well have been in his lap.

"I think," he said, "that the time for discretion is well past."

I couldn't have agreed more.

"So, this is the infamous Damon," Toss observed with a grin. "I can see now what all the fuss was about. Jesus, you two make a hell of a pair!"

Damon looked at Toss and then at me with raised eyebrows. "She's pretty straight up, isn't she?" he observed mildly.

"Damon, meet Toss. Be prepared because this is guaranteed to be just the beginning."

"Really?" Damon laughed. "Awesome. Let's keep her, shall we?" He kissed me and Ed groaned.

"And so it begins," he grumbled.

"Hey, Eike," Amy interjected, "does this mean you won't dance with us anymore?"

"Dance?" Damon asked. "Eike, you dance?"

"He doesn't just dance," Amy informed him. "He's a damn *legend* out on that dance floor!"

"Is that right? Well, that's just something I'm going to have to see," Damon said with enthusiasm. "Don't let me hold you back, girls. Take him!"

"What happened to never let me go?" I muttered in his ear. "You're throwing me to the wolves already?"

Damon grinned wickedly even as Cara was leaping to her feet.

"Really?" she squealed, as she had a habit of doing. "Do you hear that, girls? We still get to borrow Eike!"

"Now look what you've gone and done, you prick," Ox muttered. "We'll never get any peace now. And you've only been back five bloody minutes!"

The girls hauled me to my feet and I shot a mock look of despair at Damon as they dragged me towards the dance floor.

When we returned, Damon put up his hands to stop us before we could retake our seats.

"Ladies, absolutely spectacular," he told them. "And as for you," he said, looking at me, "you are simply breath-taking." He got up from his seat. "Makes this almost an anti-climax," he added, dropping to one knee in front of me.

"What?" I mouthed, staring at him. "What the fuck, Damon?"

With a huge grin and a dramatic flourish, Damon produced a velvet bag from a back pocket and fished inside it, withdrawing two perfectly crafted, interlocking sterling silver dragon rings. He carefully separated them, put one on his own finger, and extended the other to me on the palm of his hand.

"Eike Nylund," he said. "Would you please do me the honour of never parting company with me ever again?"

Epilogue

One year later

There are any number of clichés that come to mind to describe moving on: 'Anything that doesn't kill you can only make you stronger', 'Adversity builds strength', 'Steel forged in fire', and so on and so forth. It would be wrong to suggest we don't still have our fair share of hurdles to cross or that our relationship doesn't from time to time suffer conflict, but Damon and I are strong and there will be no parting in this lifetime, nor even in death.

Always bonded.

We switched colleges, having chosen the only college to which we were both accepted for transfer, and we share a small apartment Damon was able to purchase with funds released from his mother's estate. I (briefly and ineffectively) argued the point but Damon's reasoning was that if we owned it, nobody could comment on how we chose to live in it. I had to concede he made a valid point.

Obviously, Damon no longer has access to either his credit card nor his father's once seemingly endless resources, these having been frozen in relation to the investigations into his father's affairs, but we get by. We both work part-time at a local night club as bouncers, where we are known, affectionately, as the Twin Dragons, and Damon continues swimming though I have officially retired. (Which is not to say we don't still often go swimming 'for fun').

As for Damon's father, we try not to allow him too much space in our thoughts. Already convicted on several counts of tax evasion, bribery, fraud, and a litany of other financial crimes, he is awaiting trial on various counts of assault in relation to Damon, conspiring to inflict harm not only in relation to me but, following investigation, in relation to a number of others as well, and possibly even murder. Obviously, he remains in custody and, though there is undoubtedly always the risk he might reach us, we think he probably has far more important things to concern himself with right now. Besides, Damon and I remain ever watchful, Hyunguk's words having become our motto and our watch call: 'Don't let the dragon/s sleep.'

As for Xia, his voice no longer echoes in my memories and I believe his spirit is at last at rest.

We visit my grandparents often, on every possible weekend or break, and Damon says he will always consider it his first home, which pleases my grandparents as much as it does me. When the rest of our friends are around, we still hang out at Fat Sam's together, where I, at least, seem to be about as close to famous as it's possible to be in a place like Oakridge.

We've also received two wedding invitations for the coming year: one for Spex and Cara, who clearly don't believe in waiting, and another for Hyunguk, in Korea. I have surprised myself by actually writing to Hyunguk fairly regularly with the added bonus that my Korean is definitely much improved, which will be helpful when we make our trip.

We still have the Camaro, which is just as well given Damon lost the truck to the asset freeze, and I don't think I'd willingly part from her any more than I'd part from Damon. Ok, Damon might possibly hold a somewhat more secure place in my heart (I write as he threatens grievous physical repercussions while he reads over my shoulder!)

Who knows what tomorrow may bring but in this moment Damon and I walk forward, always together, and try not to spend too much time looking into the past. We are happy and that's really all anybody can ever ask for.

Branded (and bonded) for life.

BV - #0002 - 270919 - C0 - 197/132/12 - PB - 9781912964024